You
For That

You Wrong
For That

Toschia

URBAN BOOKS LLC
www.urbanbooks.net

Urban Books LLC
10 Brennan Place
Deer Park, NY 11729

ISBN 1-893196-74-7

First Printing November 2006
Printed in the United States of America

10   9   8   7   6   5   4   3   2   1

*This is a work of fiction. Any references or similarities to actual
events, real people, living, or dead, or to real locales are intended
to give the novel a sense of reality. Any similarity in other names,
characters, places, and incidents is entirely coincidental.*

Submit Wholesale Orders to:
Kensington Publishing Corp.
C/O Penguin Group (USA) Inc.
Attention: Order Processing
405 Murray Hill Parkway
East Rutherford, NJ 07073-2316
Phone: 1-800-526-0275
Fax: 1-800-227-9604

Acknowledgments

Wow! There are so many people I have to acknowledge. First and Foremost, thank you, God, for all Your many blessings. To my family . . . there are so many of us, but a big shout out to: Donnie, Shad, Jay, Tisha, Lex, Kamilah, and Bernie. Thank you all for indulging me and making me laugh. My family, all of you are the love of my life. I love you, Mommie! Aunt JoAnne, Vera, Mary, Linda, Carolyn, I love you. Y'all are the wind beneath my wings. A big kiss to you, Alex! To the rest of the family, I love you all. To my 5011 cherun, sorors, kids, my li'l cousins an 'em. Trey baby, Indigo, Ahmari, my princess. AJ in Arizona, Sion. *Para mi familia y mis amigos en Espanol . . . Gracias!* Prudencia, Hector, Chichi, Rivera, Tico, Debra, Maria, Frances, love you! Vidette, I miss you, girl. R.I.P. Richardo, Tyler, Inza and Annie Mae. Will see you again one day. To my new friend, Shellie. Thanks so much for your advice about the "donor." I love you, girl.

To my silly-ass friends, sorors, sisters that stayed up all night with me on the phone, laughing uncontrollably, I love you all so much! There are two special people that were there from day one . . . Velencia and Angela H. I owe you so much! Thanks for being available all times of day and night. V and Alex, thanks for the SBParade . . . and Angie H, girl, you know how to decipher some text. To Adele, thanks for your effort. To my website designer, Dorrie, thanks

6 ACKNOWLEDGMENTS

a bunch. To all of my family in Greekdom, your support has proven to be so invaluable. First and foremost to my sorors, the awesomely arrogant women of Alpha Kappa Alpha, INNNNNNCorporated, a big ol' skee-wee to you all. There are so many that have shown support. We are truly the bomb diggity! Soror Nicole, my best friend 4 life, Jenny Purple, all my LS's. Heather in Chicago . . . hey, girl. Soror Katrina, Lisa, Monique, Shemeka, Amanda, I'm done with you and the Blockbuster Card. Soror Jamie . . . and thanks Soror Jennifer in SC. The other writers of AKA . . . A big shout out to Soror TJ Butler, Soror Felicia Madlock, Soror ReShonda Tate Billingsley, Soror Monica P. Carter, Soror Monique Bostick, Soror LA Banks, Soror Tonya Marie Evans, and to all my fellow AKA authors on tour. A special thanks to Soror Yasmin of APOO and to Soror Sharon Hudson for your book. To my author friends, Sheila Goss, Kendra Norman-Bellamy, thanks for your support. To my friend Eric Gaither, you are awesome! Thank you to the Sorors of San Antonio for all your support. To the wonderful sorors of the IVY Bookclub, thanks a bunch. To my older sorors, thanks for your support, even if you don't always agree with my content. Especially a big ol' skee-wee to Soror Sandra Sapenter! To my friend Chris in Austin, I love you, sis. To the other Greek family members . . . Mr. Nupe, Nupe . . . JR 007, you are the biggest promoter on the planet . . . I love ya, big bro! To all the other bro's of KAY, thanks, especially to author Victor McGlothin . . . for answering my stupid questions Kunta. To the dapper, debonair nupe 4 life, Miles Barry Caggin III of Hampton University, you are a riot! To all my Central Texas Greeks, thanks for your support . . . To the other Kappas that I forgot . . . Ralphie, you are so sweet.

Roosevelt, love ya! Mr. Alphie Clark, my old boss in Chicago . . . thanks for all your insight. To my FRAT, the men of APHI'06! I love you all! Shawn, Riggs, BJ, Lemar . . . smooches. To the Sigma Bro's . . . Shalun, what would I do without you? Arrion, you are AWE-SOME. And Latham, a big hug to you, and, "Yes, I've had my woooooood today!" To the Mr. G! of Phi Beta Sigma, you know you dead wrong on so many levels . . . And the Dawgz, we gon' keep the Q's quiet!! Shh!!! Shh! Let's keep it a secret (ROFLMBAO) A big shout out to the Greeks at West Point, Duke, Northwestern, SC State, University of Kentucky, University of Texas at San Antonio . . . Ms. Cheryl of Zeta Phi Beta . . . you are my cheerleader. Rhonda Lawson of Zeta Phi Beta. Author Ms. DST Ja' Adams. A big thanks to the Crew of HBU associates and Alpha Skee! Mr. Tony Austin, #1 Sigma, and my sorors Amanda Bell, and Mrskonskeeted08. Trina . . . love ya like a play cousin! Brian Jones, keep on groovin' with Groove Phi Groove. To all the book clubs, especially my own. The women of all 14 chapters of the Circle of Friends Book Club, thanks for your true sisterhood. A special thanks to our founder, Jennifer Copeland, and to our own very talented PR person, Ms. Shunda Leigh of Booking Matters Magazine. You are my hero, girl! Thanks to the Black papparazzi, Jamill Leigh. Rofl. To my Chapter XIII, thanks for your support. To the book-stores that welcomed me with open arms, thank you. A special thanks to the staff of Under One Roof bookstore for all your initial help. Babatunde and Miss Johnnie, thanks so much . . . Thanks Adele and to Dave from Resloc Printing. To all the bookstores in Texas, but especially to the wonderful, beautiful spirit of Joyce Hunt of Mitchie's Fine Black Arts and Mr. & Mrs. Pettis of Jokae's African-American Bookstore. A special thanks to Michelle of the Afro-American BookStop in New Orleans. Thanks to the city of San Antonio, to Angelique, Adeeva Publicity and the ReadinColor Family . . . thank you. You crazy 4 real! You could publicize a dog being born and make it look good with your psycho behind. LOL to the other online clubs out there. Thank you to Tee and RawSistaz, Grits, The REAL Reviewers, and the rest that I forgot, I'm sorry. To Dawn of the Mahogany Book Club. You were my very first reader and reviewer. Thanks. To the sweet reader named Indira from Boston. Fans like you are the reason we do what we do as authors. The San Antonion Readers and Writer's Conference committee . . . thanks to you all. Kathy, Addie, Gladys, Elaine, Author Alisa McVea. And my new surrogate parents Professor/Author Frederick and Venetta Williams. To the following authors from the Texas clique . . . Evelyn Palfrey, Maureen Smith, Martha Inglehart, David Coleman (of TN, we adopted you). Katherine Jones, Gregory Simpson of ATL. To all of my past teachers, professors, Dr. JT French, Dr. Gibson, Attorney Kennedy, Judge Watson, thanks so much. To Mr. Larry Dean Johnson, R.I.P. You influenced my life in so many ways. To all teachers out there, keep on doing what you're doing. Don't give up. To the Dell family . . . Thanks for indulging me. Especially Chrys Hamilton and Moncheire Bedford and John Lilley, Mark Dorsey. I love you guys. Clare and David, I miss you. To Eric Marion, thanks for everything. You were my first web designer, graphic designer, you did the first book cover. (We really didn't do this on Dell time) Ha, Ha. To SFC Anderson, the original model on the self-published cover. Where you at, Kunta? To the new designer, Keith, thanks a bunch. Ladies, this is a hottie. To my associates at the National Hispanic Bar Association, Sigma Tau Delta Honors English Society, The Southern Poverty Law Institute, keep on fighting for justice. To my past classmates . . . Takisha, Alisa, Vidette, Professor Terrance Hayes, Monica, Dana, DD Lawrence, where are you? FH . . . all I can say is "Wow."

To my Urban Books family. I look forward to a wonderful and prosperous relationship with you. So many wonderful authors to work with and Jihad, you a hot-ass mess! Thank you for everything . . . Thanks to Robilyn, Maria and Roy. To my editor, Martha, thanks a bunch! Thanks for your insight and talent. To my agent, Marc, of The Agency Group, thank you so much! Besides my family, two very special people come to mind as I complete this novel . . . author Mary Morrison . . . I love you, and thank you so much for all your support. To Mr. Carl Weber . . . thanks a bunch for this opportunity (with yo' crazy ass). Keep Drama Alive! And last but not least, thanks to all of the readers, radio, TV stations and media avenues out there!

Remember, the revolution has always been perpetuated by the few, not the masses, and by America's youth. Remember to get involved and Rock The Vote. Don't forget. If you do what you've always done, you get what you've always gotten.

(P.S. I know I'm wrong for all these acknowledgments, but you are more wrong for reading them.) Please accept my humblest apologies, to anyone that I might have forgotten.

Toschia '08

CHAPTER 1

First of all, I don't know what was this guy's problem. After all, I did his black ass a favor. I'm beautiful, intelligent and Ivy-league educated. Dear Jesus, son of Mary and JoJo, how did I end up in this three-ring circus? To think, all this madness over one man. I tell you, this was so much drama, somebody could have made a movie about all of this shit. If I'd only heeded the words my great-grandmother had spoken to me when I was a teenager. Grandma Ann always said, "God tries to warn us. Warning goeth before destruction." I think that's how the scripture goes. Yes, I can hear her now. "What y'all young people call intuition is really God's way of talking to you. Always follow your first mind, chile." And my first mind told me not to go to work on that windy morning in March. Then I wouldn't have met the likes of Davis Hickman.

The divorce from my ex-husband Marcus was enough drama for one lifetime, or at least so I thought. We'd known each other all of our lives, lost touch for several years, then reconnected at a holiday gathering. He was my older brother Toussaint's best friend, but I'd never really hung out with Marcus. I'd see him around the few times I went to visit my brother at medical school, but never really thought much about him. Then years later when I saw him again, I was like, *Whoa*! He was fine. He was tall and light-skinned, with beautiful gray eyes and a six-pack that made me want to sop him up like a biscuit.

Then he was also brilliant. On our first date, we talked about Czar Nicholas and the Bolshevik Revolution in Russia. I was so impressed that he also believed the theory about Princess Anastasia escaping from Russia alive. That was the night I fell in love with him.

We married two years later. Our families were both from the islands—mine from Cuba and Haiti, his from Belize. Since our parents expected us both to date and marry other Caribbeans, our families were thrilled about us being together. He was a physician, and I had just completed my doctorate in international relations and marketing. We were a match made in heaven as far as they were concerned—two young, successful people with the "right" backgrounds.

Most of the guys I dated before Marcus were American. I'd never really had an allegiance to men from the islands, but Marcus was different. I thought he was the love of my life and that we would be together forever.

I'd heard through the grapevine he was a man-whore, but I convinced myself he'd never cheat on me. In the beginning it was easy to maintain that belief, but it didn't take long for Marcus to show his true colors.

Looking back, there were so many clues I'd been too naïve to pick up on. I would find numbers in his pocket, but he would always have a believable explanation, and I was just dumb enough to buy it every time. In fact, he was even trying to run game only days before our wedding. When we went into the tuxedo shop to finalize the arrangements, my cell phone rang. I looked down at the caller ID and saw it was my boss, so I stepped outside to take the call. On my way back in, I saw the salesgirl hand Marcus a small slip of paper. He took it, his hand lingering a little too long on hers, then he winked at her. When I questioned him about it later, he claimed he was merely getting her number for my brother. I was all too willing to believe whatever this man told me. After all, even if I was starting to have my doubts, how do you call off a wedding days before the date?

My parents were so happy, not to mention the fact that they had already spent well over a hundred grand on the arrangements. I was a good girl back then and never disappointed my parents, and this would be no exception. So I turned a blind eye to his behavior and prayed he would change.

He didn't. Marcus cheated on me with his receptionist after only two and a half years of marriage. The way that whole scenario went down was just straight ghetto.

I belonged to a local book club called the Sisters of Bonding Book Club. Being in a book club, reading all types of books every month with a group of diverse women, you sometimes found out things about people, whether you wanted to or not. One of the members, Crystal, was going through a rough time. She had been fired from her job at the telephone company, her boyfriend had just been locked up for boosting merchandise, and to top it off, she'd just had a miscarriage.

Some of the other book club members looked down on her because she didn't have a college degree and sounded so ignorant when she spoke, but I took her under my wing. That girl would just talk about all her personal problems in front of this group of women, and I don't know, it just made me feel sorry for her pitiful ass. I should have listened to my friend Cheryl from the start.

Cheryl hated Crystal. She kept saying there was something sneaky about her. One meeting, a casual discussion of a sex scene from Mary Morrison's novel, *Soulmates Dissipate,* somehow led to Crystal revealing the fact that her boyfriend was locked up and had been denied bail. It seemed Crystal had to have a man at all costs, and couldn't handle the thought of not having one while hers was serving time. A handyman, a drug-dealing man, an old man . . . any kind of man would do, and she proudly announced this out loud at the book club meeting.

Cheryl whispered under her breath, "Her ghetto ass look like she'll suck any man's dick—even somebody else's man."

I nudged her and told her to be quiet. Hindsight is 20/20, but I wish now that I'd seen what kind of a person Crystal was from the start. I might have saved myself a lot of heartache.

Marcus needed a new receptionist, so I told him about Crystal and her problems and begged him to give her a job. He protested at first, claiming she was too ghetto to work in his medical office (he was stuck up like that) but I persuaded him to give her a try. Well, he gave her a try all right. And to think I'd actually sort of felt sorry for Crystal.

One day, a few months after she started working for Marcus, she invited me out to lunch as a token of appreciation for getting her the job. I was actually proud of her. Crystal grew up in foster care and seemed to be doing well, considering her background. She had enrolled in the local community college and had also started to shed some of her extra weight. She was one of those big girls who had a whole lot of self-esteem, so with a few pounds gone, she just thought she was the shit. I admired her confidence.

I began to hang out with her from time to time. Hanging out with Crystal, listening to her escapades with men gave me ideas and helped me get my freak on at home. Marcus always said I wasn't freaky enough. He would want to do shit like jack off and cum in a saucer then want me to purr like a kitten and lick it up. He also had this anal sex fetish. He constantly tried to ram his finger or dick up my ass; I constantly said no. That shit was fucking nasty. There were some things I was unwilling to do, and most of the things Marcus desired were just totally off-limits. But Crystal helped me out with ideas on how to try to please my husband. She wasn't a friend per se, but she was a cool person to hang out with.

Crystal lived life with no worries. If I complained about my stockbroker, she would say, "Girl, I don't worry 'bout none of that shit. I don't even have a bank account because I spend my check soon as I cash it."

She called one night about 2:00 in the morning, said she was bored, and asked me to go to Super Wal-Mart with her. I was bored, too, and had the following day off work, not to mention the fact that Marcus wasn't even home yet. He was constantly using the excuse that he had an emergency at the hospital. Of course, looking back, I wonder how many times that was truly the case.

So, I took Crystal up on her offer to go shopping at 2:00 A.M. I had so much fun. We laughed at the silliest things, and the night stockers were a trip. We could not go from one end of the store to the other without some dude stocking toilet paper or peanut butter trying to pick us up.

Crystal knew all the night stockers by name. There was one, Malvin Smithfield, who approached us as soon as we turned the corner to the toy aisle. He looked at Crystal. "Hey, girl. What's up? " He glanced at my sorority T-shirt and threw up his fraternity sign.

"Hello, Greek." I smiled.

"Hey, pretty girl." He looked at the side of my shirt. "Fall '94? Me too."

I checked him out. He was kinda cute, and I had a thing for guys with glasses. *It wouldn't hurt to flirt a little.*

Crystal interjected, "Malvin, get out of my girl's face." She turned to me. "Rhea, Malvin ain't shit. He ain't nothing but a baby daddy. He got my girl pregnant and he ain't even seen his two-month-old daughter. Then he got a few more kids that he half sees."

Malvin ignored her and licked his lips at me. "Where have I seen you before? Did you go to the Q party a while back at the E Club?"

I looked at him again. Despite Crystal's warnings, I didn't see any harm in talking to him. "Yes, I did. Hey, you're the rose man, aren't you?"

He smiled. "Yes. I do odd jobs here and there. I'm trying to open a comic book store and I'm coming out with an authentic line of oils called the M line."

Crystal laughed. "The M line, all right. M is for motherfucker. Why in the hell would anybody buy some shit with your name on it? Who the fuck are you? You ain't no Puff Daddy. Rhea, this boy cleans up the trash in the bathroom at the strip club. Like I said, he ain't shit . . . but he does clean it up, though."

"Actually, Rhea—wow, that's a pretty name—my frat brother's dad has this concierge service where he cleans up at the club, and I'm one of the restroom managers."

Did he say restroom manager? I tried not to laugh.

He kept staring at me, waiting for a reply, I suppose. When I didn't say anything, he turned to Crystal. "Yo, why you gotta be dogging me out? Nakia was cramping my style. She told me she was going to give the baby up for adoption."

Crystal went off. "Nigga, please. Nakia called you about the baby being born and you had your new bitch answer. And that bitch told Nakia you wasn't interested in hearing about your own child, like she was selling some Avon or something. Now you up here checking out my girl. Come on, Rhea. Let's go." She grabbed my hand and pulled me away.

"Crystal, what's wrong?" I asked as we walked back into the main aisle. "Malvin seemed like a nice guy,"

"Rhea, you are too naïve. That boy worked at the Youth Center but got fired for fucking all the young girls and their mothers. That's why he works stupid-ass odd jobs for a week or two. Then he uses women for money, and had my girl paying his bills. Girl, my poor friend Nakia was in the hospital trying to Western Union him some money because he claimed he wanted to go to the Star Trek convention in Vegas. Come to find out, he took the money and went with his other baby mama for the weekend."

She finished with, "Girl, he a weedhead. Didn't you see his black lips?"

I thought for a moment. "Yes, I noticed they were big."

"Rhea, that boy is a true nigga. He dogged my girl out so bad she had a heart attack. Then the baby got sick and he refused to come to the hospital. As if that wasn't bad enough, he refused to give the other baby mama an insurance card, and that child is a diabetic."

Crystal was on a roll now. "I can't stand his Fred Flinstone-looking ass. Malvin called Nakia sixteen times the night the baby was born and cussed her out on her voicemail. He called her baby a bastard and told her he would never see the baby because she should have given it up for adoption. Then he left her one final message saying he was on his way to fuck his new woman, and to have a good life with the little bastard baby."

"What? That nice guy did that?"

"Nice my ass. It got so bad that the hospital security had to call the local police. And you should see that baby, too. She is so pretty."

"Wow. Poor Nakia. The same day she gave birth? He seemed like a decent guy too. He's a disgrace to his fraternity."

"Rhea, you need to open your eyes. Not everyone is a nice, decent person, you know."

Oh, how true that was. I wish I had read between the lines and gotten rid of her right then and there. But no, I found her ghetto antics entertaining.

"Malvin is a disgrace to black men," she continued. "His broke ass claims he's a Muslim, always peddling oils and incense." Crystal was talking loud enough for half of the night crew to hear.

The other stockers began laughing.

"Girl, stop. I'm laughing so hard my head hurts."

"Rhea, you need to get out of the rich side of town more often."

We left Wal-Mart a few minutes later, empty-handed. We were both wide-awake, so I followed her to IHOP. I called my house to see if Marcus was home yet. He wasn't. I called his cell and got no answer there either. Crystal saw the look on my face and kept talking to distract me.

She confided in me, over pancakes, that she had met the man of her dreams, but there was one slight problem—he was married. She claimed his wife was a controlling, sheltered, rich bitch. She said she gave him an ultimatum to leave his wife. He refused, and that's why she left his ass in bed and called me at 2:00 in the morning.

I was a married woman, so I really didn't know what to say. I definitely didn't agree with what she was doing, but I enjoyed hanging out with her, and I didn't want to ruin our friendship. I just nodded my head as she told her story, all the while feeling sorry for the woman whose husband she was fucking.

Crystal checked her watch and said, "Rhea, I hope I didn't get you into any trouble at home with Marcus. He's such a good boss. I'm sorry I called you so late. I don't have a lot of people I can talk to . . . at least about serious issues."

"Oh no, that's fine. I'm having so much fun. Thanks for inviting me. Marcus is working late anyway."

She gave me a strange smile, and we both finished our pancakes in silence, lost in our own thoughts.

At the following month's book club meeting, I pulled Crystal aside and told her as sisterly as I could to leave that married man alone. He would probably never leave his wife, and she was too good to be some man's mistress. Obviously, I discovered later that she didn't take my advice.

Damn, I hated Marcus, the suave, charismatic neurologist who had everyone else believing he was God's gift to women. He made me sick. When I finally got proof of his affair with Crystal, he had the gall to try to blame me for everything that went wrong in our marriage. One night while we were in a heated debate about his infidelity, he tried to flip it back on me. I became silent. His yellow ass must have gotten scared because he tried to clear that shit up quickly.

He said, "I mean, baby, you're so fine. You have the tightest little chocolate body in the world. You don't know how much pressure it is to have a wife so fine. Men are always staring at you, and I constantly ask myself, 'How did I get so lucky?' I thought you'd eventually leave me. That's why I cheated on you. I've been so insecure. You know what I mean, baby? You see, Rhea, indirectly it's your beauty that made me cheat on you."

I didn't say shit. I couldn't believe this Casper-looking motherfucker was trying to play me.

He continued talking nervously. "You were just too good to be true. I swear, Rhea, if you give me another chance, baby, I promise I'll make it up to you."

This boy was a physician and was talking like a fucking crackhead. I served his ignorant ass with divorce papers the following week.

My mother was livid. She couldn't understand why I was making such a big deal. She wanted to know how I could even contemplate the "D word."

"Honey, all men cheat," she told me, "but he has a budding career, lots of money, and comes from a good family. What more could a woman ask for?"

"Mom, he betrayed me," I said, totally in disbelief that she'd act so nonchalantly about his infidelity.

"But he loves you, darling. Surely he's not going to be with that low-budget girl. I bet no one in her family even owns any property."

" 'Property'?" *What the hell does that have to do with anything?*

My mother really had issues. Both she and Marcus were in for a surprise if they thought I wouldn't follow through with the divorce. Even if I wanted him back, my pride wouldn't allow it. Especially since he'd had unprotected sex with that street urchin.

High-yellow bastard.

After I stewed in my own anger for a while, I had to ask myself a question. Why was I so upset with Marcus? Maybe I had to take some of the blame for our failure. After all, I did marry him, even though I knew before I walked down the aisle that something wasn't right.

My wedding day was a complete nightmare. I felt like I was going to a funeral—my funeral. And the reception felt like I was at the burial ground. My experience was not just your typical wedding day jitters. It was sheer torture. I felt like my soul was slowly corroding from within. Still, I decided I was going to try really hard to be happy on my wedding day.

As the limo arrived at the church, I lined up behind my bridesmaids to walk into the church. I almost excused myself to go to the restroom never to return.

Pretending to be happy was harder than I thought it was going to be. As the bridal processional was played by the harpist, I trudged down the aisle imagining I was having a bad dream and would awake suddenly.

Marcus actually looked happy. His eyes blared into my soul as I was walked toward him. For a few seconds, I looked at him thinking I was the luckiest woman in the world. Not only was he rich and gorgeous, but I was the envy of every woman in Atlanta.

It didn't take long, though, for the reality of the mistake I was about to make to hit me again. As my bridesmaids settled into their places, Marcus' eyes left me and wandered to them. Actually, his eyes went to their cleavage, which was so conveniently on display in the bridesmaids' dresses he had helped me pick out.

Somehow, my feet managed to carry me to the altar to stand next to Marcus, who went back to pretending he only had eyes for me. After a while, I vaguely heard the part of the ceremony when the priest asked if anyone could show just cause why this man and woman should not be joined together. I mentally detached myself from my surroundings, allowing my mind to wander.

I desperately wanted to raise my hands and say, "I do!" like I used to do in the fourth grade.

Sister Mary Alice would always say, "Now, who knows the answer to this question?" She knew I *had* to be the one to answer. My fourth grade reputation depended on me, Rheonique Ramirez Baptiste LaDay, answering the question correctly and articulately.

I'd raise my hand ferociously, yelling, "Ooh, ooh, me, me. I do! I do!"

That evil bitch knew how much I wanted to answer, but just to spite me, she'd choose someone else then smile as if to say, "We'll see. Next time I may choose you."

I stared at the priest. He was probably spiting me on purpose too.

Father Ellison had to have known I wanted to object to the wedding ceremony. He had to be purposely ignoring my mental cries for help. He proceeded on to the next step in the ceremony without so much as a glance in my direction. And to make matters worse, he had the audacity to smile. I wanted to kill him.

Don't smile at me like that! You're killing me and you know it!

I'll scratch your fucking eyes out! You probably molested little boys, you freak!

I swear to God, I might have been born Catholic, but as soon as this wedding's over, I'm joining a Holiness Church!

I willed my hands to move, but they seemed glued to my sides. I wanted to throw my arms up and yell, "Stop!" but nothing was happening. I tried reassuring myself not to worry. My brain would tell my hands to move eventually. After all, it was a proven scientific fact that the brain controlled all bodily functions. A few seconds passed by. I wondered why my brain still wouldn't make my hands move. I looked down only to discover them intertwined with Marcus' hands, like dead weight. I was stuck with him.

My mind screamed to the priest silently. *I do! I have a reason. My reason is because I'm not ready yet, and he's the wrong man! Mommy, Daddy, save me.* I wanted to scream out loud, but my vocal cords were stifled. I couldn't make a sound.

I prayed that a deranged, escaped convict would run into the church and shoot me. Hell, maybe the Rapture would come. I heard the preacher at my great-grandma's church say that after all the prophecies had been fulfilled, the Rapture would take place. Hadn't they all been fulfilled? Let's see . . . The Bible says that in the last days there would be wars and rumors of wars, and men would be laying with men. They both had taken place, so where was Jesus? *Jesus, please come back now.* What was He waiting on? It was a damn shame. Even Jesus was on C.P. time.

I simply needed a distraction. Maybe somebody would trip Marcus before he said, "I do," like JJ tripped Keith on the TV show *Good Times.* Anything. I wanted to die quickly.

My life flashed before me. All the school plays, the late-night study sessions in college, the sorority galas. It took me five years to complete a dissertation and for what? To be somebody's wife? I didn't go to school to receive a Mrs. degree.

Fucking Marcus didn't even want me to work. Sadly, I'd probably end up pregnant in a month by a man I was beginning to secretly loathe.

I held my breath, thinking I could make myself pass out and put an end to this ceremony. Everyone around me was smiling. As I looked out of the corner of my eye, I spotted my mother with a look on her face that said, "It's almost over. Soon you'll be the wife of a prestigious doctor."

These people actually thought I was happy. Couldn't anybody see I was gasping for my life, for all of us? For all of the women who felt as if they weren't complete until they had a man's name. I swear I wish there was a way we could all legally use our first names only. No ties to a man whatsoever. Women are either tied by our fathers' names or our husbands'. We needed emancipation!

I took a deep breath, scanning the crowd in hopes of finding an ally who could relate to my plight. I looked over at my sorority sisters. *Surely they would understand.* No such luck. Missy, Trina, Cheryl, and even my cousin Michelle wore expressions of complete jealousy.

My mind was screaming, *I'll trade with any of you! Somebody switch with me!* No one was listening. Finally, I gave up and put on a happy face—my mask, I called it. I'd gotten used to putting on such masks, thanks to my mother and her bourgeois friends. Talk about fakeness. The only thing worse than fake-ass rich black Americans were fake-ass Blacks from the islands who didn't think they were black.

"We wear the masks that shades and hides." The poem by Paul Lawrence Dunbar kept playing over and over in my head.

Save me, somebody! Mommy, Daddy, please help me. This is my last call for help before the mask totally engulfs me.

The inner depths of my soul were crying out for help. As we were finally pronounced husband and wife, I wanted to die. I used to watch Court TV, where convicted murderers said they wished they could be sentenced to immediate death as opposed to rotting in a cell for the rest of their lives. At least death was instant. Marriage, at least to Marcus, was probably going to be everlasting torture. I succumbed, and as Marcus puckered his soft, pink lips then lifted my veil to kiss me, I forced myself to stifle the gag forming inside my esophagus.

I did try to make the best of the honeymoon, because for better or worse, I was now Mrs. Marcus English.

Although I have rich chocolate skin, I applied a bronzer to make myself look even more exotic. My girls had hooked me up with some lingerie that was

freak nasty. As Marcus went to shower the first night
of our marriage, I changed into the skimpy red teddy
with a matching thong. I looked at myself in the mirror. I was not vain, but I was beautiful. I still ran five
miles a day, a routine spilled over from my college
soccer days. I was curvy in all the right places, and
men went crazy over my Afro-Latina curves, my curly
hair and almond eyes.

When Marcus came out of the bathroom and saw
me, his dick got so hard, he came just playing with
my breasts. He apologized because he couldn't get it
back up. I ended up masturbating on my wedding
night. I mean, he had been lousy in bed ever since
we started dating, but since he was such a "good
catch," I figured I'd manage as long as I had my vibrator.

Marcus' penis was only four inches long, and he
always had an orgasm within six minutes. The man
could not even perform oral sex correctly. It took me
weeks to find a flexible Band-Aid to put on my clit
after the honeymoon. That nigger must have thought
it was a chicken liver or something, the way he kept
gnawing on it. When I asked him to suck slowly, bless
his heart, he would start to blow air on my lips as if
that shit excited me. I never wanted to hurt his pride
by telling him he didn't satisfy me sexually, but after
a while a woman can only take so much. Once I was
pretty certain he was cheating on me, I let him know
how I really felt about his sexual performance.

I lay there patiently, while he was blowing air on
my lips, and thought about how my mom would blow
my food and tap the spoon against the edge of her
tongue to make sure it wasn't hot before putting it in
my mouth, when I was a little girl. I began to laugh
uncontrollably. Marcus became irate. "You're so damn

silly, Rhea. Why are you laughing while we're having sex?" He rolled over, pouting.

"Marcus, your ass couldn't get it up. That's why you're turning over. You cheating dog! Don't think I don't know why you constantly want to go down on me. You ain't going to blame me for that shit by saying I'm fucking up the mood by laughing. Whoever you're cheating with is only fucking you for the money or prestige, not because you're good in bed."

I could actually deal with the fact my husband was lousy in bed, but to think I was stupid enough to believe the lies too . . . I was almost positive he was cheating, and it would only be a matter of time before I got some proof. He made me sick with his white-looking ass. He was just a big red dog. His mammy should have named that muthafucka Clifford. Yes, Clifford the big red dog. Hell no, I couldn't forgive his cheating ass, especially since he slept with Crystal, of all people.

I was so pissed at Marcus. How could he cheat on me with Crystal? I tried to be a good wife, I really did. I remembered our last argument just like it was yesterday.

"Rhea, maybe if you pretended to need me, weren't so damn independent, I wouldn't have run to another woman."

"So, Marcus, what you're saying is you cheated on me because I was independent?"

"No, Rhea. I'm saying that, as a man, sometimes I want to feel like I'm in control."

"What are you talking about? You come and go as you please."

"That's not what I'm talking about. You have a big mouth and you have to be right about everything."

"Maybe if you did what you were supposed to do I

wouldn't fuss. Hell yes, if I have to ask you to take the trash out five damn times I'm going to raise hell."

"That's the shit I'm talking about, Rhea. You are not my mother, and you are not going to be talking to me like I'm a fucking child. You get pissed when I don't jump when you say, Jump.'"

"Jump? Marcus, it takes you ten hours to do simple shit like fold laundry, and then you get pissed when I do it myself."

"Damn it, that's why we pay a housekeeper. I'm not going to pamper your ass and put up with your little tantrums."

"Marcus, go to hell!"

"Like I said, Rhea, maybe if you shut the fuck up sometimes I wouldn't have cheated on your ass."

"Fuck you, Marcus! If you want a li'l uneducated bitch to kiss your ass and make you feel good, fine. As a matter of fact—how 'bout *get the fuck out!*"

That was the last argument I had with him before he moved out.

Fortunately he didn't get down and dirty with the divorce. My parents paid the downpayment as a wedding gift, so I kept the house. He took the boat, his Bentley, and we split the two summer homes.

In some ways I was glad to have him out of my life, but I was still left wounded. Part of me wondered about his words to me during our last fight. Was I really too independent? Was it my mouth that got me in trouble when it came to men? Maybe next time around I'd try to be more docile. Or maybe there wouldn't be a next time, and I would just be alone forever.

CHAPTER 2

It had been almost two years since the divorce was finalized, and even though I'd made the right decision to divorce Marcus, the pain was still there. You just can't go through a divorce without some sort of mental repercussions, and I was emotionally drained. Marcus had taken something out of me. A part of my soul was gone, not to mention my self-esteem. Why did he have to sleep with someone I knew? I practically put the two of them together.

One of the most embarrassing parts of the whole thing was that everyone in the book club found out that it was Crystal who had wrecked my marriage. I couldn't even count the number of times I heard "I told you that bitch was no good" from the members of the club. And of course, they just loved to remind me that I had actually thrown the girl a baby shower before I knew who the father of her child was!

When Crystal announced at a book club meeting that she was pregnant, I was so happy for her. I planned a baby shower at the country club. At the time, I was feeling pretty generous, because I actually thought my marriage was taking a turn for the better. Marcus and I had started going to marriage counseling. He promised to become more attentive to my needs, and I promised not to be so argumentative. Things were going well, and then one night I got a phone call that Crystal was going into labor.

The nurse on the phone told me which hospital Crystal was at, and that she had requested that someone call my house. I was touched. Poor Crystal had no family and wanted me there to comfort her during the delivery. Little did I know that the phone call wasn't really meant for me.

I rushed off the phone and told Marcus where I was going. To my surprise, he offered to come along, saying, "I don't want you driving alone so late at night."

I started to tell him, "no, I would be fine by myself," but remembered my promise during counseling.

We hopped in the car and rushed to the hospital. We got in the delivery room just minutes before Samantha was born. I held Crystal's hand and Marcus held mine. When the baby came, the doctor looked at Marcus. "Dad, you want to cut the cord?"

I interjected, "Oh, he's not the father. This is my husband. We're just friends of the mother."

Marcus motioned for the doctor to cut the cord. Suddenly Crystal began crying. Marcus turned to me and said, "Rhea, I need to speak to you out in the hallway."

That was the day I thought my life ended. Whatever doesn't kill you makes you stronger, and now two years later, I had just about buried my sorrows in every brand of Boone's Farm cheap-ass wine that was ever created. I knew every brand, and each year they were patented. Strawberry Hill 1973, Sun-Peak Peach 1989, and the latest flavor on the Boone's circuit, Hard Rock Lemonade. There were some things from college I just couldn't let go.

When I wasn't drowning my sorrows, I was visiting my shrink, Dr. Jones. It took countless sessions at $120 an hour before I was able to come to the conclusion that Marcus had never been the love of my life. I had chosen him to please my family by marrying a man they found worthy. Well, with Dr. Jones' expensive help, I decided that I was going to choose my relationships on my own terms, to make myself happy. My stuck-up mother would just have to deal with it.

Dr. Jones also listened patiently as I talked about a strange recurring dream that started not long after the divorce. In the dream, I would see a witchdoctor with white paint on her face, standing over me with a big butcher knife, the sound of a screaming baby in the background. I didn't want to believe that the baby was Crystal's child. Even as pissed as I was about everything, I didn't want to think I was capable of wishing harm to that baby.

Dr. Jones reassured me I wasn't a psycho, and I shouldn't worry. He said the witchdoctor might represent my mother and her Haitian roots. Maybe the baby had something to do with my own childhood and my strained relationship with my mother. Whatever it was, he told me I was just under a lot of stress from the divorce and the dreams would probably stop in time.

To try to take my mind off everything, I spent lots of time at work. I was a marketing executive for the nation's largest energy company, Sebastian Energy.

Because of the current corporate scandals that were taking place nationwide, the company was quickly acquiring territories throughout the country, so I was extremely busy. As director of the marketing department in Atlanta, I had led my team to increase customers within the minority community at an astronomical rate, in part due to our hip commercials.

When I wasn't overworking myself for Sebastian Energy, I also enjoyed teaching English literature at the adult education center. Although my degree was in marketing, reading was my hobby, and I loved sharing my love for books with others. I taught a lot of the single moms who were taking classes to obtain their GEDs in hopes of one day going to college. I was dedicated to helping these women better their lives. Maybe if they could get degrees and take care of themselves, they wouldn't feel the need to have a man take care of them—or someone else's man, like Crystal did. As for me, I didn't think I would ever need or want another man in my life after how Marcus had hurt me. Then came the fateful day that I met Davis Hickman.

It started out just like most other days, with me running late for work. When I finally got there, I took my time walking inside the building. I showed my ID to the security guard and went downstairs to get some herbal tea. The cashier touched my hand a little too long and winked as he gave me my change. He was a li'l cutie, but I vowed never to deal with a light-skinned brother ever again in life.

That little encounter got me pissed all over again, thinking about Marcus as I left the café and walked toward the elevator. A couple of stiffs in suits walked by and smiled. Then my mind wandered to the unfairness of men in corporate America. I worked my ass off in the marketing department, but they were the ones getting all the promotions and raises. My mind went from Marcus to my job then back to Marcus. This put me in such a horrendous mood, I just knew it was going to be a bad day.

The elevator opened, and I was treated to the beaming stare of Stan, the head of marketing for the entire company. I couldn't stand his arrogant ass, and I hated it every time he visited from Denver. Yes, Stan's presence had just confirmed that it was going to be a very bad day.

He looked down at his watch. "Hey, Rhea. You're just the lady I wanted to see."

I tried to remain professional. "Is that right, Stan? You couldn't have been waiting long. I pulled into the parking lot right after you did." I stepped onto the elevator and hit the button for the fourth floor.

My hair was still a little wet from my shower that morning, so I'd pinned it up.

Stan smiled. "Your hair looks great like that."

"Thanks." *I hate this dumb-ass white boy.*

A janitor stepped into the elevator at the second level; then it went back down to the ground floor rather than up to the fourth. I rolled my eyes and tapped my foot impatiently. I couldn't wait to get out of this confined space.

"Wanna take the stairs?" Stan asked with a creepy smile. It had been rumored for years that Stan loved black women and allegedly paid for black prostitues every chance he got.

"No thanks," I answered. *There is no way I'm going to get stuck in a deserted stairwell with your perverted ass,* I thought as I gave him a fake smile.

Unfortunately, Stan decided to stay on the elevator with me, probably so he could continue to stare at my breasts. It didn't seem to matter to him that they were completely covered up. God forbid I ever wore anything provacative to work. He'd probably blow a wad.

We finally arrived at the fourth floor, and Stan followed me to my office. I had no doubt his eyes were on my ass the entire time. He spent almost forty-five minutes in my office, constantly coming up with bullshit excuses not to leave. Every time I thought we were ready to wrap up our little meeting, he would ask another question about my marketing strategies for the Atlanta divison. He could have gotten all the information he needed in a half-page memo, but then he wouldn't have been able to practice his X-ray vision on my chest.

When I finally pried Stan's attention away from my body and got him to leave, I shut my office door and put my head down on my desk.

Miguel, the office homosexual, burst through it without knocking only seconds later. "Hey, boss," he said in his trademark girlish voice. "Can you do a teleconference call with the Denver office? I just don't have time to do it, with me moving out there and all. Stan just told me my flight leaves at seven tonight."

I loved Miguel, but he was getting on my last nerve. He was always coming into my office, trying to pawn his work off on me. I would miss him, but part of me was glad he was moving to the Denver offices.

I didn't answer his request about the conference call. I just dropped my head back down on my desk.

He walked over and touched my forehead. "Girl, you need to get over whatever has got you down. You're losing so much weight, you look like a two-dollar crackhead."

"Thanks, Miguel. I always enjoy your compliments, so motivational and moving. You are truly an asset to the gay pride movement," I replied sarcastically.

"I'm serious, girl. Stop acting like a damn fool. Men come a dime a dozen."

This was truly a farce. I had to have been down in the darkest pit of life, kind of like Jonah in the whale. I was getting advice on men from a 45-year-old homosexual who wore women's lingerie under his suit.

Miguel opened up his compact mirror and began putting corn silk powder on his face. "Girl, you gonna have to come see me in Denver. I heard us queers are so open out there, not like this Bible belt here in Atlanta." He looked at his watch. "Oh, let me go, girl. I cannot be late for my appointment. I have to get my bikini line waxed." He tied his walker's bag around his waist. That was his way of telling me he was taking the day off. He didn't even bother to ask me again if I would do the call to Denver for him. He just knew I would.

I shook my head. "Get out of here, Miguel! And shut my door—no, lock it on the way out."

When I finally got myself together, I had a productive day. I did the teleconference call with the associates in Denver then actually got a lot of work accomplished. By the end of the day, I was so motivated I decided to stay late.

My computer had been acting a little funny, so I began installing a new anti-virus software. As I was working at the computer, my telephone rang.

Who's calling me at 7:00 on a Friday night? I guess I'm not the only one out there with no life.

I put aside my thoughts of self-pity and answered the phone in my best professional voice. "Sebastian Energy. This is Rheonique. How can I help you?"

"Hello, Rheonique. I take it by your name that you are either Black or Hispanic, but your voice sounds like you're Caucasian.

"Who is this?" I laughed, thinking it was one of my friends.

"Well, are you?" he asked again.

Damn, whoever this was had a sexy voice.

"Actually, I'm Haitian and Cuban. Yes, I'm black." I smiled, still trying to guess who it was.

"Haitian. Oh, a voodoo girl. I see I better not piss you off," he said with a laugh. "Seriously, though, this is Davis Hickman from the Denver office."

"Who?" My smiled quickly turned into a disgusted frown. *How unprofessional. And who the hell is he? He must be crazy to call a complete stranger and start off a conversation like that.*

"Miguel said you were testy," he answered. "Well, anyway, like I said, I'm Davis Hickman from the Denver office. I've been working with Miguel on a few projects. He said you would be taking care of the Atlanta stats from the briefing in Berlin."

"You almost got your feelings hurt, Davis. Besides, how do you know you didn't offend me?"

"Well, if I offended you, then why were you smiling?"

I laughed. How did he know I had smiled? "Are you sure you're not the psychic from Haiti?"

"Oh, see, you do have a sense of humor," he teased, then went on to entertain me with jokes and flirtatious comments for a few more minutes.

This guy was a piece of work, another Dave Chapelle. Everything that came out of his mouth was funny. After a while, though, I found myself enjoying the conversation a little too much. This didn't fit into my post-divorce plan to stay away from men forever.

"Get off of my phone, Mr. Hickman, you are a mess," I told him, hoping to bring things back to a more professional level.

"Come on, girl, I ain't a mess. You know you like talking to me," he said, still flirting.

"Mr. Hickman," I answered, "you don't really want to know what I think of you."

"Maybe I do. What do you think of me, Ms. Baptiste-LaDay?"

"Are you sure you want to know the answer to that question?"

"Um, yes."

"Okay, I think you're one of those people that thinks because we're only a handful of blacks at Sebastian Energy that we should feel some type of kinship or bond. You know, that same feeling you have when you're on a crowded elevator and there are just two black people on it—you and the guy with the torn plastic Michael Jackson jacket and the dried Jheri curl. Then he gives you this look as if to say, 'We're connected. We're representatives of mother Africa.'"

He laughed. "You got jokes and a creative imagination. I like that."

Davis wasn't offended at all by my comments. In fact, I got the impression he liked the challenge of trying to win me over. He continued to babble on about himself, telling me he was very attractive, and how every woman of every nationality wanted him. When I didn't act impressed, he finally got the message.

"We need to work on getting the stats information by the end of the month for Stan," he said, suddenly sounding professional.

"Oh, okay. I'll get with Miguel, Mr. Hickman."

He whispered really low in the telephone. "You can call me Davis E. Hickman, and the *E* stands for Edwinn with two *N*'s."

I actually liked this guy. He seemed nice, and he was so funny. But my drama with Marcus made me leery and distrustful of all men. The second Marcus popped into my head, I began trying to think of a way to poison him and get away with it. Maybe I could invite him over for dinner and fry him some chicken with d-Con rat poisoning in the fry batter. Nah, that might be traceable if an autopsy was performed, but I wondered if it was worth a try. I decided that before I risked going to jail, I would need to do some more research.

"Is your computer on?" Davis interrupted my thoughts. He had jolted me out of my fantasy of watching Marcus die slowly like a rabid dog. Maybe if Marcus died I'd be able to move on and let another man into my life.

"Why?"

"Check your email." Davis's tone was still professional, but I was starting to entertain the idea of getting to know this man better.

"How do you know my last name?" I was sitting back in my chair, smiling like a silly little girl, twirling a strand of hair around my finger.

"You work with Miguel, don't you? And besides, how many Rheoniques do you think are listed in the company directory, girl? I typed in your first name, and your last name popped up."

We both laughed.

"I'm installing a new antivirus program, so I won't be able to check my email right now."

"Okay. So, how's the weather is Hotlanta?"

"Hot." I laughed again. This brother had no game.

I almost felt sorry for his silly ass, but there was something so warm about his voice. I was glad I'd decided to work late.

After a little more small talk, I started to feel tired. It had been a long day. I stretched my arms and yawned. "Well, Davis Edwinn with two *N*'s Hickman, thanks for this lively conversation, and I'll be sure to check my email later."

"Wow, cut a brother off," he joked.

"Oh no, I'm sorry. I've enjoyed this conversation, but I've got to run. I'll be in touch."

"Oh, okay. Bye."

Since I couldn't do anything on my computer while the program finished installing, I decided to go downstairs to the gym to work out. Maybe it would wake me up a little so I could come back up and finish my last little bit of work. I grabbed my gym bag and headed toward the stairs. I saw the "toy cop" security guard, Rashawn, making his rounds. I prayed he wouldn't see me.

Rashawn was a super-nice guy, but he always made up an excuse to come over to talk, and talk he did. His five-minute conversations turned into forty-minute sermons on life. Most people ignored him, but I always tried to be friendly. Rashawn was actually kind of pitiful. He worked Friday, Saturday and Sunday nights as a security guard at Sebastian. Every week he told me the same story about the good ole days when he was "somebody," when he did security for all the big stars like Hammer, Vanilla Ice and the Jets. His claim to fame was a part as an extra on the set of *CB4*.

I just wasn't in the mood to hear these stories for the hundredth time. I thought that maybe if I hurried I could make it to the stairway undetected. Crap.

Our eyes locked. He began sauntering over. As Rashawn went on one of his tirades, my thong kept creeping up my butt. I prayed he would shut up soon. I finally cut him off and told him I had to run.

I glanced down at my watch. It was 8:15. Indulging Rashawn and his delusions of grandeur had cost me precious workout time, not to mention the fact that it ruined my brief fantasy of ever dealing with a man again. I went to the gym anyway, and the first thing I did was put on my granny panties before changing into my workout clothes.

After a few minutes on the treadmill, I got lazy and left. I went by the vending machine, got some pretzels and a Coke, then went back to my office, giving myself a pep talk that I was going to get some work done.

The antivirus software had finally finished installing, which was a miracle, since I think my computer happened to be the world's slowest. Sometimes I wondered how Sebastian stayed in business when they gave their employees such ancient technology to work with.

My instant messenger alert flashed on. The message read: DAVIS HICKMAN HAS ADDED YOU TO HIS SEBASTIAN ENERGY BUDDY LIST.

Davis was still at work and was still trying to get under my skin. Shit. I tried to log off quickly, but I was too late. He sent me a message.

DHBLUE14: Hi, beautiful.
RLADAY: Leave me alone. You are a mess.
DHBLUE14: *Muy caliente* and feisty too. So, what's a beautiful young lady doing at work on a Friday night?
RLADAY: First of all, how do you know I'm beautiful? I could be bald-headed, five hundred pounds and cross-eyed.

DHBLUE14: Well, you're Haitian and Cuban. Oh, believe me, you're fine. Besides, Miguel has already given me the low-down on you.

RLADAY: Yeah, I bet he has.

He probably sucked your dick too. I laughed out loud.

DHBLUE14: Yes indeed, y'all chocolate girls are fine.

RLADAY: Is that so?

DHBLUE14: Yes, it is. What do you know about voodoo, Rhea?

RLADAY: I know if you don't get off my damn computer, I'm going to put your name in a jar. Then I'll have my grandma put some herbs in it, and your black ass will turn into a frog before sunrise.

DHBLUE14: Dang, you're mean, girl.

RLADAY: Look, I'm not trying to be rude, Davis, but I have work to do. Besides, why do men always try to find out what a woman looks like?"

DHBLUE14: I don't know. I guess we have it like that.

RLADAY: I've really got to go. Messing around with your crazy ass, I won't get any work done.

DHBLUE14: Messing around, I like that. Okay, good night. So, Rheonique, I'll hit you up on Monday, my little chocolate buttercup

RLADAY: Have a good weekend. Chocolate buttercup, eh? Davis, are you really working?

DHBLUE14: Hell no, just waiting out the traffic. How about you?

RLADAY: Honestly, I had good intentions of working late, but I'm getting lazy.

DHBLUE14: Well, if I was in Atlanta, I'd take you out to dinner tonight.

RLADAY: Gotta go. Bye.

I logged off quickly before he could respond. I did not want to go there with him, talking about going out to dinner. This was the closest I had come to even thinking about another man since my divorce, and it was scaring me. Davis had sparked something in me with his jokes, his compliments, and his flirting. I didn't want to think about what might have happened if I met someone like this and he actually lived in Atlanta. I grabbed my briefcase and left the office, headed home to my empty house.

CHAPTER 3

During the drive home, thoughts of Davis and our conversation kept entering my mind. He brought a strange giddiness out of me. After going home and trying to relax, I couldn't rest, so I called Cheryl, hoping she would be at home on a Friday night.

"Hello," Cheryl answered.

"Hey, Cheryl. What's up, girlie? I'm surprised you're still home."

"I know, right. I was just getting ready to call you. Do you want to go to the *Q* party tonight?"

"Cheryl, I'm too old for that shit." I chuckled. "First of all, we are not in college anymore, and besides it just breaks my heart to see thirty-five-year-old men trying to step. Where is this party at? I hope not on anybody's college campus."

"No, Rhea, it's at the *E* club. The graduate chapter is sponsoring it. You know they're gonna have them fat-ass, ugly girls that never went to college or them ghetto groupies chasing them." She laughed. "It is kind of pitiful, these ol'-ass men trying get their groove back."

"Tell you what, Cheryl—Why don't I rent a movie and come by your place?" I didn't want to go to the frat party, but I also didn't want to stay at home.

"Cool."

"Let me take a shower. I'm just getting home from work."

"Girl, all you do is work."

"I know. That's why I need to laugh. I'm going to rent *Dolomite*; I'll be right over."

"Rhea, you stupid. *Dolomite*? You might as well get *The Mack* while you at it then."

"Okay, I will."

"I'll leave the key under the mat. I have to make a quick stop."

"A quick stop." I snickered under my breath.

"Yeah, girl. Jerrod claims he's staying in tonight to study for the bar."

"Oh, okay."

Yeah, right. He ain't studying for the bar. His ass is at the bar, I thought as I hung up the phone.

Jerrod was the youngest alcoholic I knew. He didn't drink regular alcohol, he drank old people shit, like Pabst Blue Ribbon and Wild Irish Rose. The last thing I wanted was to get into an altercation with Cheryl about her drunken-ass boyfriend.

Before I got in the shower, I checked my messages. I only had one, but I couldn't believe who it was from.

"Hello, Rhea. This is Davis Hickman from Denver. I hope you don't mind, but I got your home number from Miguel. I just wanted you to know I enjoyed chatting with you tonight, and I was thinking, since Miguel is transferring here, I was wondering if you would like to work with me on the Berlin account. I'd like to work with you, and it's a great opportunity. But if you want to give it to one of your employees, that would be okay too. If you do choose to accept and do a good job, I may fly to Atlanta and buy you a Happy Meal or something. Think it over and give me a call at home. I'm single, so you can call any time of the night." He left his home number on the message, which ended with him saying, "You can thank me later because I don't give my home number out to just anyone. Like I said earlier, if you choose to accept, I'll definitely make it worth your while. Sorry to leave such a long message."

If I choose to accept, I thought after I listened to the message a second time. *What is this,* Mission Impossible?

I started thinking about Davis's voice. He had the sexiest, deepest, most articulate voice I'd ever heard. This was now the third time he'd contacted me today, and each time I became a little more intrigued. It also didn't hurt that he was offering me a place on a project that would get me to the next level in the company. The offer sounded awesome. I thought about calling him back right away but didn't want to seem too eager. I would definitely be calling him the next day.

I hurried to shower and get dressed to go to Cheryl's house. I stopped by Blockbuster Video, flirted with the sales guy for a few minutes, then gave him a fake telephone number. He gave me the movies for free, and I arrived at Cheryl's with *Petey Wheatstraw, the Devil's Son-in-Law, The Mack,* and *Pimps up, Ho's Down.*

We both fell asleep on the floor watching TV.

* * *

Saturday morning I woke up to a throbbing pain on the left side of my neck. Just the excuse I needed to indulge myself for the day. Cheryl and I had a quick breakfast before she got ready for our sorority meeting. She said she'd call me later with the particulars, since I couldn't attend.

I ran home and showered then dropped my three Shih Tzus, Polonius, Laertes and Rosencrantz (all named for Shakespearean characters) off at the pet spa. Instead of my usual Pilates workout, I went to the day spa for a facial, pedicure and a hot stone massage.

Several hours later, I began the twenty-minute drive to the other side of town, to do my volunteer hours at Big Sisters.

My little sister, Tasha, was thirteen and totally out of control. She had gotten into trouble for putting sardines into the heating system at her middle school. As a result, she was forced to join the Big Sister program. We actually got along pretty well, so I didn't mind giving up my afternoon to be with her.

I was almost at her house in downtown Atlanta, when her mother called to tell me that Tasha went to visit her father for the weekend.

Heifer, you could've called me earlier. I do have a life.

Who was I kidding? I had no life. My life consisted of three damn dogs. One was gay, the second one was a diabetic, and the third one liked the theme music to *Jeopardy*. They would take turns pissing on the carpet if I didn't leave the TV on the Game Show Network. Hell, I didn't even know what was hip anymore. I wore suits all the time, hadn't put on a pair of jeans in years and listened to *Car Talk* on National Public Radio. I needed something exciting in my life.

For some reason, thoughts of Davis Hickman kept entering my mind.

I turned around at the next exit and headed back toward *my* side of town. I made a quick run by the bookstore to pick up the book of the month for the book club. We met once a month at the local black bookstore called All Things Here. The book club actually started out as a good thing, but the constant bickering and arguing over whose opinion was greater was becoming too much. We had so many different types of women who were members, I just didn't know what to expect from one meeting to the next. I swear, some of the arguments that went on about a book, you would think somebody was about to get murdered. Cheryl kept saying, "We ought to change the name from the Sisters of Bonding Book Club to the Simple Bitch Book Club."

Even with all its drama, though, the book club for me was an escape from everyday life. The book club sisters along with my sorors had my back with all the Marcus/Crystal drama. You know that Crystal was never allowed to show her ghetto ass in that store again after the book club members found out what she had done. After their loyalty, I couldn't quit the club, no matter how much bickering went on, which was why I was at the store to pick up this month's selection.

All Things Here was the mecca of black happenings. Anything was liable to happen there. I'd seen weddings and funerals take place at the store. Somebody even gave birth in the back, right between the Buffalo Soldier and the Mason pictures that were on clearance sale.

Whenever I wasn't feeling black enough, or just needed to catch up on my roots, All Things Here was the place to be. It was a place where black people had our own little resort. Someplace where we could call the shots. If someone needed a plumber, they didn't go to the Yellow Pages, they went to the bookstore. All the local happenings and events came through All Things Here. And of course, all the drama and craziness you could handle happened inside that store. Some of the shit that went on up in there made me wonder how many of those people had to go to those slow classes in the afternoon.

I walked into the store and saw Craig. He was one of the youth pastors at my church. He'd asked me out once or twice. I'd always declined because I had this suspicion he was bisexual. He spoke, and his girlfriend Lanai grabbed his arm. She was in my book club and constantly kept shit started with her messy ass. I wanted to scream at her, "Nobody wants that ugly motherfucker but you and his boyfriend."

This girl was a trip, and I kind of thought Craig liked drama, because he'd purposely start a conversation with me just to piss her off. I don't think Lanai was real swift either. One time we were discussing Toni Morrison at our meeting, and her simple ass said, "Oh, I love him. *The Sopranos* is my favorite show."

While Lanai was rolling her eyes at me and holding on to her man like an old woman clutching her purse, another book club member, Ms. Teese, came in to buy her book. She was such a nice lady, but she was over forty-five and walked around with practically no clothes on. She would always wear Daisy Dukes and cropped shirts. God forbid a male author came to town. Then she really showed her natural black ass, literally.

Ms. Teese was one of those poor women who started fucking at twelve, had a baby by thirteen, and barely finished junior high. Now that she was a grandma, she was out there trying to "live her life." I felt so bad for her. I mean, the woman had five grandchildren, and her biggest concern was hoping the tag that she stuck inside the arm of her new dress didn't get sweaty so she could return the dress to Dillard's after she wore it out to the club. The poor woman was so desperate, she would leave the book club meetings early because she had to get her seat up front at the strip club. I smiled at her politely and tried to avoid a conversation with her.

Craig was still trying to talk to me, too, at least until Tina Mack came in.

Tina was one of the deacon's daughters. She was a beautiful girl, with rich brown skin and a sweet smile. I actually felt sorry for her. She had to pretend to be such a good girl because her dad was a deacon. With a body like hers and the way she carried herself when her father wasn't around to see, I knew that if she got the chance to go off to college, she was going to become a full-fledged ho.

I'd heard rumors about her antics in the back of the church with Craig. I almost stayed around to see how the two of them panned out in public together in front of his girlfriend. She gave Craig a flirtatious stare, and Lanai grabbed his arm tighter. I smiled at Craig. *Just another stupid-ass cheating man.*

"Hey, Miss Rhea," Tina said.

"Hey, sweetie. You are the cutest little thing." I gave her a big hug.

"Thank you."

"What are you doing here? Looking for some books?"

"Oh, no. I'm looking for some CDs by Peatey Popper and Five Cents."

It took the store owner, Abutu, a few minutes to figure out that the poor child was talking about Petey Pablo and the Rapper, 50 Cent.

Craig and his pathetic girlfriend began walking out. "See you ladies tomorrow at church." He waved goodbye. Lanai turned around and rolled her eyes at both me and Tina.

Now, that was a simple bitch! I'd run into so many of them lately, I'd been contemplating starting a Simple Bitch Parade. Maybe I would print out some applications and take votes on who the Simple Bitch of the Year should be.

I was going to hang around and shoot the breeze with Abutu, but I purchased my book and got my black ass out of the store real quick after somebody from my church pulled out a knife on this other lady who'd made a comment about Pastor Lee and his infidelity. That was just too much.

I went home and relaxed in my Jacuzzi. I lit candles and enjoyed a glass full of Boone's Farm, realizing my ghetto ass was really not any better than some of them clucking chickenheads that hung in the bookstore. Here I was, sitting in a Jacuzzi in a half-million dollar home, drinking cheap-ass wine out of a Waterford crystal wineglass. As I closed my eyes and sunk down in the bubbles, thoughts of Davis Hickman came to mind again. Should I call him? What did he look like? I was so intrigued by him.

Carpe Diem. Seize the day. I reached for the phone.

Was I on crack or what? I couldn't believe I was calling him! I sat there with the phone in my hand long enough to convince myself that I was only calling to talk to him about the job offer he'd made. I dialed his number. The telephone rang, but I got no answer. It was a Saturday night, I reminded myself. Maybe he was out on a date.

Just as I was about to hang up, he answered. "Hello."

I was suddenly nervous. "Hello, may I please speak to Davis?"

"What took you so long?" he responded casually.

"Hi," I said cautiously. "This is Rhea from Atlanta."

"I know."

"How did you know?" I was surprised. Did he remember my voice?

"Miss Cleo's my aunt." We both laughed.

The laughter quickly subsided into an awkward silence.

I had to admit to myself that the phone call had nothing to do with the Berlin account. There was something so intriguing about Davis. I wanted to find out why he had gotten under my skin so quickly. Basically, I had called because I wanted to hear his sexy voice. But I couldn't tell him that, of course.

After a few seconds of silence, Davis spoke.

"No seriously, Rhea. I can call you Rhea, can't I? Rheonique sounds too formal." He didn't bother to wait for my answer. "Really, I knew it was you 'cause I've got a playa-hater box, formally known as the caller ID. So, what's up with you, pretty lady?"

I blushed. *Why am I behaving like a sixteen-year-old?* I got compliments every day about my looks. What was the problem? Maybe it was just the way Davis said *pretty lady* that made me want to run around like a wild hyena in heat.

Okay, Rhea, get it together.

"What do you mean, what's up with me?" *Is he asking me out? Maybe he'll fly to Atlanta to visit.*

"Do you think you can handle it?" he asked.

"Excuse me?"

"Handle the Berlin account?" He laughed.

"Oh," I said, embarrassed. *Girl, get your mind out of the gutter.*

He laughed again as if he knew exactly what I was thinking. I was speechless.

"Your man won't get upset with you putting in all the extra hours, will he?" Suddenly his tone changed before I could answer his question. "Well, Rhea, I'll give you a call on Monday around nine your time."

"Oh, okay. Talk to you Monday," I said reluctantly.

"Bye, Rhea." Something about the way he said my name made me so eager to talk to him again. I was already looking forward to Monday.

I got out of the tub and dried off. As I rubbed myself down with lotion, I began to imagine Davis rubbing his hands all over my body. It had been way too long since I'd been with a man, and something about Davis Edwinn Hickman excited the hell out of me.

CHAPTER 4

I woke up the next day with thoughts of Davis on my mind. Cheryl and I normally carpooled to church, and it was her turn to drive. By 10:30, she still wasn't at my house, and we were already thirty minutes late. I called her to see what was up.

"Girl, I'm busy," she said, out of breath.

I could tell that she and Jerrod were getting their groove on, so I told her to call me later and dashed out of the house.

The people at my church were so amusing. I had followed through on my silent threats to the priest from my wedding and left the Catholic church. I gravitated toward the Greater Mount Zion Holiness Church and now attended every Sunday. My spiritual relationship had been a source of solace with the pain of my divorce. My church had some of the typical issues like too many building funds and Pastor Lee being accused of fathering half of the youth choir, but nonetheless, I felt such a strong sense a love amongst the congregation that I looked forward to going to church every week.

I walked in right before the sermon started. By this time, I was almost an hour late and made the biggest mistake that one can make in the black church. I tried to walk through the double doors while the deacon was praying.

Sister Corrine was at the door. Unlike some of the more loving members of the church, she was sometimes mean and hateful for no reason. She cussed people out and yelled at them constantly. I, like everyone else, normally ignored her because she was old.

I smiled at her, and she immediately gave me the evil eye. She whispered harshly, "Can't you see they praying?"

I wanted to say, "Can't you see you spitting?" but the Bible does say respect your elders, so I just grinned at her and gritted my teeth.

"You late, so you just gonna have to wait." She looked up at the clock then muttered under her breath. "What the hell you coming for now anyway? The service is halfway over."

After the prayer was completed, she opened the door then pulled my dress. "Go on in." She rolled her eyes. I must not have been moving fast enough because she nudged my arm and gave me a slight push.

I swear to God, Sister Corrine, you may be old, and I know you have problems with your foot because of your sugar, but I will knock you down, you big, fat bitch, if you touch me one more time.

Damn devil. She was hateful for no reason. She and Sister Lula had gotten into a fistfight one time over whose house the preacher enjoyed eating at more. That was the talk of the church for weeks. Sister Corrine and Sister Lula were down on the ground, duking it out like two damn dogs. Sister Corrine had Sister Lula pinned down, her fist raised back, ready to knock Sister Lula the fuck out when Pastor Lee ran out of the sanctuary. He yelled to Sister Corrine. "Just pray, sister! Violence isn't the answer."

Sister Corrine hesitated for a minute. "Lawd Jesus, I'm praying you better strike my hand now with arthritis. I'm counting to ten. If you don't strike me down, I'm gonna fuck this bitch up."

Sister Lula was saved by two deacons who grabbed Sister Corrine from behind, though not without a struggle.

I walked by Sister Corrine into the sanctuary, laughing at all the old people I knew. They were a trip. I was escorted right up on the first row, I guess, as some form of punishment for showing up late.

I was tired and almost fell asleep at one point during the service, but then Pastor Lee announced the call for prayer. Normally I wouldn't move from my seat during services, but something in my spirit made me feel excited and sad at the same time.

I went up to the altar. As I lifted my hands in prayer, Pastor Lee prayed for me. I began weeping and asking God to show me what my purpose on this earth was. I prayed for peace of mind and wisdom in everyday life. I promised God that if I ever got another chance at love and happiness, I would not be overly aggressive and would allow my man to be the man. Marcus had told me that it was my independence that made him cheat, and this had truly wounded me. Something about being here at the altar now made me feel a small glimmer of hope. Maybe someday God would give me the strength to love again.

When I returned to my seat, I felt emotionally drained. Some time before the recognition of visitors, I fell asleep. I was jolted awake, when I heard the organist playing "Jesus, You're the Center of My Joy."

Suddenly, a loud voice bellowed from the deacon's pew. "Church, we've got one more offering. Pastor's appreciation dinner offering. We're asking all saints to pledge twenty-five, and we ain't letting out till we get twenty-five hundred."

Oh, shit. Deacon Eugene was making his way over to the offering table. You would think that the choir would get a little softer when someone was speaking. Oh no, not at my church. It might have been okay if the choir was good, but that definitely wasn't the case. There was always that one soprano that had to sing in falsetto while the other sopranos were singing normally. And the drummer was slow, in rhythm and in learning. He was always playing extra loud in people's ears when they walked by. Didn't he know that shit was not impressive? Those choir members and their director needed to go straight to hell with a pair of gasoline drawers on, just for mutilating the Songs of Zion.

"Come on, church." Deacon Eugene had lost his voice trying to yell over that loud-ass choir. He continued on in the name of Jesus. "'Scuse me, saints. I got a frog in my throat. Pray my strength in the Lord." His voice was raspy like sandpaper. It gave me the heebie-jeebies, like someone was scratching on a chalkboard.

"We need this money." Deacon Eugene Cleophus Brown had to have been a fundraiser in his other life. He was the sole reason why Pastor—or Passa, as Deacon Brown called him—drove a new BMW every six months. Although Deacon Brown lived in the projects and didn't have a vehicle of his own, he was happy as long as his Passa, Bishop, Apostle, or what-

ever the hell they called him this week had the best
of the best.

"I'll start off with the first twenty-five dollars." He
dug in his pants pocket, pulled out a wad of bills and
waved them in the air. He quickly put the money
back inside his pants then reached inside his left
shirt pocket and produced a fifty-dollar bill. Then he
exclaimed proudly, "You know what, saints? The Lawd
just laid it on my heart to pledge another twenty-five
dollars."

*Yeah, right. Jesus just appeared to you and said, "Keep
on letting Passa pimp you."*

"Who else is gonna heed the call of the Lawd and
show our great Passa how much we love him?"

That was just about all the begging that I could
handle. It was time for me to go.

Hopefully, they were not measuring the love the
parishioners had for Pastor Lee based on offerings,
because they must've thought I hated his black ass. I
crumpled up a five-dollar bill, hoping no one would
notice how small my donation was, then headed toward the back of the church.

On my way, I passed Brother Don doing his weekly
shout. He pretended to hit the floor and continued
his holified act until his cell phone rang. He answered
it and said, "What's up, dawg. I'm getting my praise
on. Call me back in an hour," then calmly put his
phone back in his pocket and went to shouting again.

I just shook my head and kept going. I was grateful
for the people of this church who kept me enter-
tained every Sunday, and I thanked God for shining
on my wounded soul that morning, but I needed to
go home and take a nap. I only had one problem. I
wondered if I could find a way to creep past Sister
Corrine, who was still strongholding the front door.

CHAPTER 5

After church, I went straight home and fell asleep. I was in a daze, half-asleep, when I heard someone at the door.

"Rhea, open the damn door."

I got up, looked at the security monitor in the hallway and saw Michelle. She was one of my best friends and happened to be my first cousin as well. Her dad was my mom's brother. Michelle's mother was Dominican, and I think it was the Dominican/Haitian blood mix that caused her to act insane. She lived in Chicago and was an attorney for one of the largest corporations in the country, so I didn't get to see her as often as I would have liked. Even though it was the middle of the night, I was so happy to see her. I ran downstairs and opened the door.

"Girl, why don't you ever ring the bell?

"'Cause I know you got them video cameras. I just wanted to mess with you." She smiled with sparkling white teeth.

"Michelle, what are you doing in Atlanta?" I shivered as I shut the front door. It was a little chilly in the nighttime air.

"Looking for a baby daddy." She plopped down on the sofa.

"You're real silly." I laughed.

Michelle was truly a character. I'd always admired her. She was smart, savvy, and didn't take any shit off of a man. Michelle and most of my friends represented the modern black woman. My mom's generation tended to put women into either a lady or a wild woman status. I totally disagreed with that mode of thinking. A true sistah could be classy, go to the opera, read the classics, and be highly educated, but at the same time could drop it like it's hot in the club, drink Boone's, and get ghetto if the need arose. Michelle definitely fit that description.

Michelle would always say, "Don't let the cute li'l sorority colors and the degrees fool you. I can kick ass and go off just like Fuquanda an 'em from the projects. I don't like to go there, but if you open the door, I'll go gladly."

My biggest concern for Michelle was about her relationships with men. She liked to use them. In fact, the license plate on her custom-made Bentley read **UZEM 1ST**.

Michelle had done some of the most psychotic things that I'd ever seen when it came to men. "You need to get some fucking backbone and lose your conscience, Rhea," she would say to me when I disagreed with her behavior. "If men are good to me, fine. If not, I will fuck 'em up." And that she did.

She had gotten so much abortion money from alleged pregnancies that I stopped counting at twelve. The guys she fooled around with were so stupid. They never demanded a pregnancy test and never went to the doctor with her. She'd even lied once and said that she was six months pregnant, when her stomach was flat as a board.

Michelle knew it was easiest to play this trick on guys who were married. They had the most to lose, so they wouldn't question her. Basically, she preyed on men who had no choice but to comply with her every wish.

God forbid one of them was stupid enough to get caught up in a lie. Then it was really on. This is what Professor Larry Dinkins, J.D., LLM Admiralty and maritime law professor at Columbia University did. She had this particular rendevous during her second year of law school. Michelle actually liked this guy, and for a while thought he might be the one. He'd told her he was divorced, but it turned out he was married.

Michelle started to put two and two together after he'd never take her to his house. One night after sex, she took his wallet and got all of the pertinent information that she needed. She showed up at his house one day and introduced herself to his wife, claiming she was house shopping and wanted to see what the neighborhood was like. The wife invited her in, and after they chatted for a while, Michelle began to cry. She told the wife that she was pregnant by a much older married man who'd lied to her and physically abused her.

Mrs. Dinkins tried to comfort her, assuring her there were some good men left in the world, and her husband Larry was one of them. Mrs. Dinkins told Michelle to drop by any time. As she stood up to show her to the door, Michelle pretended to faint. Mrs. Dinkins made her lay down on the couch, which was exactly what Michelle wanted.

The professor came home to find his wife putting a wet towel on his mistress' forehead.

Michelle sat up and introduced herself as Barb then retold the story of the mean, older man who'd lied and gotten her pregnant. She began to sob uncontrollably then asked Larry, "What kind of man would do that?"

Professor Dinkins was speechless.

I think Michelle got a cool twenty grand from that affair, especially since Larry's father-in-law was the dean of the law school. She treated me to a trip to Monaco with some of that money. Even though I didn't always agree with the way she treated men, I had no problem helping her spend her earnings. After Monaco, we explored the Swiss Alps with the rest of the loot.

Larry was by no means the only man who got burned by Michelle's scams. I had a feeling she would end up like J.R. on *Dallas*. If she ever got shot, it would take the police ten years to track down all of the possible suspects.

Her scams weren't just limited to men either. Michelle was really something else. Even though her parents were rich as hell and could give her anything she wanted, she still loved shopping at cheesy stores. Her favorite store was Wally World, not only because of the one-stop shopping, but because they would take anything back, even if it wasn't purchased there. She'd go to Wally World just about every month during her college years, when she was constantly thinking that she was pregnant. She would buy the most expensive pregnancy test they had in the store then go back to school and pee on the stick. Every time, she got the same response. It always came back negative. Michelle would then glue the box back together with arts and craft glue and take it back to the store for a full refund.

That girl was the biggest scam artist on the planet. When we were undergrads, she would often piss her parents off, and they would stop sending her money. Michelle devised something she called Plan B to get her money another way. The details of Plan B weren't always the same, but they always consisted of something illegal.

One time, Plan B involved a con at the post office. She walked in, mailed off a letter then came back and pretended someone had broken into her car. She called the local police and filed a report of theft. Once that was done, we got in her car and headed out of town on a shopping spree. We went only to stores that didn't have security cameras. I had no earthly clue how Michelle knew which stores did or didn't have cameras, but the girl was prepared. We maxed out all of her credit cards, knowing she'd never have to pay the bills since the police report would prove her cards had been stolen. She signed all the slips with her left hand in small, curvy handwriting to purposely alter her signature, and we walked away with brand-new wardrobes, free of charge.

I shook my head as I looked at my cousin and reminisced about the many crazy things she'd done over the years. It's a thin line between sanity and insanity, and Michelle was teetering dangerously at the edge. But I still loved her.

"What you up to, Rhea?" She smiled at me.

"Trying to sleep, Michelle." I glanced at the clock. It was 2:00 A.M. I must have been really tired, because the last thing that I remembered was sitting down on my bed after I came home from church.

"Michelle, why didn't you call first?" I fell back on the couch, exhausted.

"Shut up, Rhea, and stop fronting. You never have company, so I didn't see the need to call."

I rolled my eyes at her. "You really should have called."

"You can roll your eyes all you want. You need some dick. That might help your funky attitude." Michelle had this way of hurting my feelings then changing the subject as if nothing ever happened. She walked over and began to stare at the same photos on the wall that I'd had for years.

"Michelle, why are you so insistent upon looking at the same photos every time you come here?"

"Trying to see if your ugly ass gets any cuter." She laughed.

"I'm going to have to put some blessed oil on your forehead. You are bringing all kinds of spirits and demons in my house."

"Anyway . . ." She came over and gave me a big hug. "Rhea, you look great. Been working out still?"

"Not really." I fluffed my T-shirt. "Just working. I forget to eat half the time."

"You need a vacation. I'm on my way to the Bahamas for a week. I've already booked your flight, so you have to go with me."

"Michelle, you didn't have to pay for me. How much was it? I'll write you a check." I began to look around the living room for my purse.

"Oh no, Rhea, my treat. Besides, I owe you."

"Owe me? For what?" We hadn't borrowed money from one another since college.

"Um, you know Great-Grandmother Catherine was supposed to come and stay with me this summer?" She stopped. She was infamous for her dramatic pauses. "I sort of made plans and volunteered you as the designated babysitter."

"What!" *This girl had some nerve!*

"Come on, Rhea. It won't be that bad."

I loved my great-grandmother, but she was a full-blooded Haitian voodoo priestess. She spooked everyone in our family. Our Great-Grandma Ann was my grandmother's mom, and she was just a good old-fashioned Geechee from Beaufort, South Carolina. Grandfather's mother was Great-Grandma Catherine, and I didn't want to spend any time alone with her. She gave me the creeps. I would have to talk to my mother and make sure I didn't get stuck with that responsibility.

"Michelle, you know I don't like that voodoo shit. I wish that you would've told me you were going to volunteer my services. What if I had something to do?"

She began to laugh until tears rolled down her face.

"Shut the hell up, Rhea. You don't do shit. That's your problem. Maybe Grandma Catherine can conjure up a fucking man for you."

"Girl, I'm so stressed I'm not going to even argue with you this time. What time does our flight leave?" I asked, heading down the hall toward my room to look for a suitcase.

"In six hours. Come on, I'll help you pack."

"Dang, that's pushing it. Let me call into work and make up a lie real quick."

I shushed her to be quiet as I left a message for my secretary. I asked her to transfer all calls to my cell phone and to only send me pertinent emails. I'd log into the company's network from my laptop.

Next, I called Stan and left him a message that my great-grandfather had died and that I had to go back to the Caribbean. After all, he really was dead. He died when I was two years old. I believed in too much superstition to lie on a person that was still alive. Finally, I called the director at the adult education center to let him know that I was not going to be able to teach my class that week.

I changed into my low-cut pink-and-green sundress with the matching hat and luggage. We went to IHOP for breakfast, and from there went on to the airport. I almost felt guilty about work, but that quickly subsided. I was never sick or even took personal days. Sebastian Energy could survive without me for one week. I was going to have some well-deserved and overdue fun.

CHAPTER 6

The flight was non-stop to the Bahamas. The thought of five days in Grand Cayman was going to be a welcoming and refreshing change of pace. We rented a candy apple red Mustang convertible and two bicycles. Michelle had chosen the Green Turtle Cayman Island as our vacation spot. She'd leased a secluded villa on Coral Bluff, overlooking the sea, about fifteen minutes away from town.

I was so exhausted from the flight that I was content for the first few days to just lounge by the pool and catch up on some reading, while Michelle hopped around the island on her quest for a baby daddy. On Friday night, I decided to finally accompany her out on the town. We ended up going to the Sugar Shack Karaoke lounge. There was a mixed crowd of black, white, native, American, gay and straight people.

We walked in, and a group of executive types elbowed each other as we walked by. Michelle strolled to the bar, while I found a table and ordered a cup of ice from the waiter who approached me as soon as I sat down. I checked out a few guys, but none seemed to appeal to me. I thought about Davis Edwinn (with two *N*'s) Hickman. He'd been entering my mind quite often since our conversation the week before. Even on vacation, I couldn't escape thoughts of him. I still wanted to know what he looked like, if he had a face to match that sexy voice.

Out of the corner of my eye I saw Michelle dropping it like it was hot on the dance floor. It was amazing how she still partied at twenty-eight the same way she did when we were eighteen.

"What's up, wordy?"

I turned around. Lo and behold, there was this blond Justin Timberlake-looking guy with two gold front teeth, licking his lips at me.

"It's pronounced *war*dy," I corrected him.

He shrugged his shoulders. "Whatever, but I bet I can pronounce *fine*. And I must say, damn, you a fine li'l chocolate thing. Where you from?"

I gave him a fake smile. "Oh, a little island on the south side of hell. It's called *kiss my ass* canyon."

"You got jokes. Well, I'm from Stamps, Arkansas you know, not too far from Hope, the town where Bill Clinton is from."

Yeah, Hope, all right. Too bad there ain't no hope for your ignorant ass. I stood up to go to the restroom.

He looked me up and down then licked his crusty lips again. "Damn, baby. You look so tropical."

'Tropical'? Tropical *is used to describe food, a wine . . . I think the word you're looking for is* exotic, *Simple Simon.* I was actually pretty proud of myself for only thinking these things and not speaking them out loud. Normally, I would have let a loser like this have it. But since Marcus had told me my big mouth was my biggest problem, I was determined to turn over a new leaf. That was the promise I'd made when Pastor Lee was praying over me, and I was determined to keep it. This fool was making that hard to do, though. *If he keeps talking much longer, I just might have to open my mouth.*

Just then the DJ saved my life by calling me up to sing Karaoke. I sang "It's Raining Men" by the Weather Girls. Every gay man in the house jumped to his feet. Mister "You look so tropical" disappeared into the crowd.

After my performance, I sat down at my table, and Michelle joined me for a while. A few Long Island Ice Teas later, I became dizzy. I stood up to go to the rest-room, and some guy grabbed my chair and sat down to talk to Michelle. I tried not to laugh. He was all of four feet nine inches tall and had on a black outfit that looked like a skort with a long-ass cloak. I kept racking my brain, trying to remember where I'd seen such a strange outfit.

"Michelle, I'm ready to go," I whispered in her ear after returning from the restroom. She seemed to be involved in a deep conversation, but after I repeated myself a few times, she finally agreed she was ready to go too. She told me to go outside and hail a cab while she said good night to the midget in black.

When Michelle came outside, she climbed in the cab, but she wasn't alone. That little fool climbed right in with her.

"Michelle, where's he going?" I asked.

"With us," she said through clenched teeth, then gave the cab driver instructions to take us back to our villa. She explained to me that the short guy was a rapper, and he was on the island to film his latest video. He started talking, before I could tell her I'd never heard of a midget rapper before.

"Y'all the two finest cousins I ever seen. I'm ready to party." He winked at me.

"Oh, hell no! It ain't that kind of party, Morpheus."

"See, I know you're smart." He smiled. "You know I had this outfit made to look just like Morpheus from *The Matrix*. People say I look just like Laurence Fishburne, only I'm a little shorter."

"Oh yeah, I see the resemblance." I tried not to laugh, still trying to keep my promise.

"So, I'd like to party with both of you ladies tonight."

"Whatever. I don't get down like that," I replied.

The taxi driver laughed out loud. Michelle was *out there,* and I knew she'd had one too many beers, but family or not, I would fuck this bitch up.

When we got back to the cottage, I quickly locked myself inside my room, thanking God that I had my own bathroom. There was no telling what them drunk fools would have tried if I used the bathroom in the hallway. I showered, flipped through the local newspaper and went to bed.

I was awakened some time later by the loud sex sounds coming out of the next room. I could tell Michelle was faking her orgasm, just like she used to do when we were in college. She would always brag about how she would have to make herself cum with a vibrator after the guys left.

"Oh, baby, whose is it?" I heard MC Loser Lot say.

"Oh, I don't know. It can be yours if the price is right."

I just laughed and turned on the radio. I couldn't understand how she could just meet a person and have sex with him the same night. She was my cousin, but she was nasty. Michelle had absolutely no morals, and I'd be even more surprised if she still had a uterus. Poor boy. Michelle would probably pretend to be pregnant by him in a month then take the abortion money and go shopping.

I searched the radio dial. I found an old tune, "The Balance Wheel," by Calypso Rose. It was a song about politics and freedom that my mom used to dance to when I was a little girl. Although I was on vacation, I felt a little melancholy, so I called my parents.

Mom answered. "Hello."

"Hi, Mommy." I sighed.

"Rheonique, is everything okay? It's four in the morning."

"I'm fine. Guess what? I just heard Calypso Rose on the radio and thought about you."

Dad picked up another phone in the house. He was probably on the computer like he always was early in the morning. "Rhea, what's wrong, princess?"

I began to cry. "I don't know. I just get sad sometimes. I'm sorry to wake you guys. I just wanted to hear your voices."

"Rhea, did something happen? Are you and Michelle okay?" Mom was starting to sound panicky.

"No, Mommy. I'm just a little down. We're both fine. I'll let you go now."

My father sighed. "Baby, sometimes life gets you down, but you know when life gives you lemons . . ."

All three of us said together, "You make lemonade."

"Dad, you're awesome," I told him.

My mother cleared her throat like she was waiting for me to say the same thing to her, but I changed the subject.

"Uh, before I let you go, I wanted to tell you that I

met a guy. Well, I didn't really meet him, but he works at Sebastian in Denver. I've only talked to him a few times on the phone, and we instant messaged each other once."

Why was I telling them about Davis?

"Rhea?" Mom sounded perplexed. "You woke us up to tell us that?"

"No, ma'am. Just to tell you I love you."

"Well, we love you too, but unless you're pregnant or someone is dead, please don't call us at four in the morning and tell us about a guy that works in another state that you instant messaged one time, okay?" I couldn't tell if she was joking or if my call had really annoyed her.

"Sorry. I'll let you go back to bed."

"Call us back if you need to. We love you, Rheonique," Dad said.

"Love you guys too." I hung up.

My family was the most important thing in the world to me. I had a rich family history that I was extremely proud of, and my father was the love of my life. Although my mother and I didn't see eye to eye on most things, I did love her, just in a different sort of way.

My father, an only child, came to America as a result of *Operación Pedro Pan*. My grandparents, Hector and Maria Ramirez, sent their teenage son along with thousands of other young Cubans to the United States in search of a better life. Daddy would often break down in tears, when talking about the ordeal that is described as the largest child refugee movement in the recorded history of the western hemisphere. Dad lived with his aunt and uncle in the Washington Heights area of New York City then was accepted into Stanford, where he shared a dorm room with Pierre Baptiste LaDay, my mother's brother. He later married Pierre's sister, my mother.

My dad was the founder and CEO of LaDay Cosmetics, the largest cosmetics company for women of color, with offices in Sydney, Paris, and throughout the Caribbean and United States. He was the savviest buisnessman I knew.

My mother, Veronique Baptiste LaDay, was the only child born to Anna Coxe and Michel Baptiste LaDay. My grandmother, originally from Beaufort, South Carolina, was the illegitimate child of a local white minister. She had two brothers, also fathered by the minister, who were light enough that they ended up passing for white. Their father sent them to Cornell University, and they both assimilated into white society. Neither one of my great-uncles ever married, fearing their offspring could possibly result in a display of their black genes.

My grandmother, who wasn't passable because her skin, was sent to Fisk University to study education. Mulattos and octoroons considered themselves a different race of people back then. "We only had each other," she'd say. Bruised, resentful and ashamed of the treatment she'd received in Beaufort because of her fair complexion, she loathed the South Carolina low country with all of its Gullah traditions and tales of "Dr. Buzzard," the famous root doctor.

After graduating from Fisk in Nashville, she returned to Beaufort to try to live amongst her black relatives but received the same rejection and had the same feelings of despondency that she'd lived with most of her life. So, my grandmother left once again, determined never to return.

She decided not to use her teaching degree immediately and went to study vocal pedagogy at the prestigious Juilliard School of Music, where she met my grandfather, Michael Baptiste LaDay. He was a visiting professor from Port-au-Prince, Haiti, and a widower with fourteen children. My grandfather was instantly intrigued by the young, graceful Anna Coxe. She was equally intrigued, and happy that his skin was black as coal. She said she always prayed her children would not come out fair. He married her within six months, and three years later they produced a firecracker named Veronique.

They raised the children in Haiti, and every one of them grew up to be accomplished and well-educated. My uncles all had respectable, well-paying jobs, but those were just a cover for the illegal activities they participated in. I never was told exactly what they were involved in, but I knew my uncles were feared in many circles, and their influence spread far and wide.

My mother, of course, had nothing to do with the seedier side of life. She traveled to the United States to attend medical school. When my father met my mother, they fell in love instantly. His calm, gentle personality was the exact opposite of hers, which could be too rigid and too abrasive. All my life, she had displayed strong opinions about people and their stations in life. In fact, she was so concerned with a person's station in life that she insisted that my brother Toussaint and I carry the Baptiste-LaDay name instead of my father's. That was why Ramirez was my middle name, not my last. My father was so docile and loved her so much that he went along with it.

Sometimes I felt like I had to work hard not to

judge people like my mother did, because children often pick up personality traits from the people who raise them. Luckily I had my father's gentle nature as a guiding force in my life too.

I fell asleep thinking about my parents, my grand-parents, and my rich family history.

I woke up early on Saturday morning to the bright Caribbean sun, feeling refreshed. After calling my parents again to assure them I was okay and hadn't gone "coo coo for Cocoa Puffs," I contemplated going for an early-morning swim or a quick jog on the beach. I ended up doing both then crept back inside the villa quietly, praying Michelle would not wake up. The last thing I needed to hear about was how she pussy-whipped her newfound prey. I hadn't had any in so long, and although it really didn't bother me that I wasn't having sex, the last thing I wanted to hear about was Michelle's escapades.

After taking a quick shower, I changed into a sundress, gathered my straw hat and trudged the three miles back up the hill to the market to do some shopping and explore the island. By noon, the sun was shining brightly, so I settled down under a tree with some fresh fruit and a pastry. I walked back to the villa and slept for the rest of the afternoon.

Late that night I woke up when Michelle came back into the villa. She told me she had spent her day trying to get rid of the rapper. He took her shopping and spent tons of money on her, but she knew she wasn't letting him hit it again that night. He took her to the club, and when it was time to go, he, of course, expected to get in the cab with her and come back to the villa for round two. She made up some story on the spot about how she had received the Holy Ghost that day and she was not ever going to fornicate again. She did tell him, though, that she would stay in touch. I guess that was just in case his video ever actually hit the airwaves and he became somebody. She threw men away faster than most people changed underwear.

We had a few more days left before our flight back to Atlanta. While Michelle continued her quest for her perfect baby daddy, I was content to sip Bellinis by the pool and read anything that I could get my hands on. Though I didn't envy Michelle's lifestyle, with a different man in her bed almost every night, there were times when I felt like it would be nice to have someone in my life again. And every time I started thinking that way, my mind would drift back to Davis Hickman.

CHAPTER 7

After my vacation, I came back home, and my life finally seemed to be all right. Getting away helped me put things in perspective, and I realized I would be okay. Ironically, Marcus started calling a few times a week, begging me to get back with him. He apologized profusely for fucking up our marriage. I told him I wasn't interested in hearing his apologies, that I had finally moved on with my life. Of course, since he was the one who had accused me of having such a big mouth, I was as nice as I could possibly be over the phone. I fucked with his head in more subtle ways.

I would conveniently show up at places where I knew his frat brothers hung out, making sure I was always looking good. I'd show a little cleavage, but not enough to be considered a full-fledged skank. I wanted word to get back to him about what a good thing he had lost. He usually had a report within fifteen minutes.

About a month after my trip to the Bahamas, I

went to the theatre to see the play *Les Miserables,* with the youngest and most handsome Arab doctor on staff at the hospital where Marcus worked. I knew many of the physicians at the hospital were season ticket holders at the theater, so when Dr. Gupta and I ran into each other at the gym and he asked me out, I accepted. I laughed as Marcus left me the most desperate message on my answering machine the following day.

"I know where you were last night. I can't believe you were out in public with another man. My wife out with a motherfucking terrorist, cumin-eating fucker."

"You mean your ex-wife!" I shouted at the answering machine, happy I had succeeded in hurting him. I wondered where Crystal was when he was leaving me those desperate messages.

It was now obvious that Marcus wanted me back. Whenever I was feeling particularly spiteful, I would answer his calls and make a point of describing how exciting my life was now that I was single again. I also put on a happy face and talked about my busy social life, whenever I ran into someone who I knew would tell Marcus about it. But inside, I was a sad woman.

After about a month or two of pretending to be happy, the urge to make Marcus jealous had dissipated. I realized that hurting him was not what would make me feel better. It was time to put my energy into more productive things. It was time to focus on myself.

Marcus did continue to pursue me, though. So much, in fact, that I ended up changing my number to a private listing. I felt sorry for him, just a little. He hadn't really meant to hurt me. He just got caught up. Poor thing was just going to have to charge that to "the game." I was ready to put it all behind me.

Life was okay for me finally, and a lot of that was attributed to the friendship I'd developed with Davis. The offer of working on the Berlin account never came up again, but we did start talking and sending instant messages to each other pretty often. I still didn't know what he looked like and was careful to keep our conversations only on a friendship level, but I enjoyed talking to him. He helped me pass many hours at work, when I should have been doing something else, like working. Davis made me laugh, something I hadn't done much of since my divorce.

Stan came to Atlanta and offered me a position in Germany—It was only for a few months—to help set up the marketing division in the Berlin office. I decided the change of scenery might do me some good, so I accepted.

I was so busy in Europe, I didn't have any extra time for anything besides work, though I did keep in touch with Davis. He proved to be an invaluable resource with the German marketing department. His parents were prior military, so he'd learned German as a child when he lived there.

I was constantly blowing up his phone for help. Even though I had translators to help me out, I used any excuse to talk to him and hear his sexy voice. Some of our friendly conversations became more flirtatious, and some were even dangerously close to sexual, but I didn't mind. I was really starting to like Davis.

The two months in Europe flew by quickly, and after I got back to the States, we continued our daily phone calls and emails. Things started to become even a little more intense. We'd chat and flirt online all day at work then have marathon phone conversations almost every night.

By now, Davis knew everything about Marcus and

the divorce. He told me about his life, which seemed so simple in comparison to mine. It actually made me a little jealous. His life seemed so uncomplicated and drama-free. Maybe that was what attracted me to him, the fact that he just seemed like a regular guy with a normal life. It was somehow comforting to me.

We had so much in common. We both enjoyed performing community service and cared about the same social issues. It was a very safe long-distance friendship. He didn't pressure me for anything, but I was secretly falling for this wonderful man. He would send me flowers at work at least once a week, with cute little sayings like *just thinking about you*, or *to a phenomenal woman*. Marcus had never sent me flowers. Davis was quickly earning points in my book, and each day I felt my heart opening up a little more.

December rolled around, and we didn't speak much during the holidays. Davis said he would be busy with his family, and I would certainly be busy with mine. My extended family of devout Catholics, all sixty-four first cousins, aunts and uncles, always got together every year to celebrate. I also hosted a rites of passage ceremony and a Kwanzaa celebration for some of the girls in the Big Sisters program.

Christmas and Kwanzaa came and went, and I hadn't had a chance to talk to Davis in over two weeks. I missed him and couldn't wait to get back to work to chat with him.

By the second week in January, I still hadn't heard from him, and was starting to become very concerned. I called the Denver office, spoke briefly with Miguel, and filled him in on the latest water cooler gossip circulating in Atlanta.

When I asked him about Davis, Miguel said, "I didn't know you knew Davis all that well."

"Well, it's not like we've met or anything," I said, trying to sound nonchalant. "It's just that he and I were working pretty closely on some things and I hadn't heard from him since before the holidays. I can't really finish this porject on my own," I lied.

"Oh," Miguel said, his voice full of doubt. "I don't know about all of that."

Something about the tone of Miguel's comments caused a little flutter in my stomach, but I ignored it. I just missed Davis and wanted to know why he'd stopped contacting me. "So, what do you know, Miguel?"

"All I know is we've been informed that Davis was having some personal issues and would be out of work for a while."

"Miguel, do you know what's going on with him?" I was so worried, you'd think I was his girlfriend or something.

"Rhea, you're my homegirl. If I knew, I would tell you. Y'all getting a little chummy, aren't you?"

"No, Miguel!" I tried to protest, but Miguel saw right through it.

"He is fine, girl. I am not mad at you. I sho' wouldn't mind getting with him myself, but he act like he don't like fags, though."

"I think he's straight, Miguel." I laughed, wondering about Davis' looks. Miguel and I both had different ideas about what *fine* looked like.

"Oh, I heard Davis is straight, all right. In fact, too straight, if you ask me."

"What is that supposed to mean?"

"Girl, Davis is just a flirt. But when you do him, let me know how it is, so I can fantasize."

"Miguel, you're sick. And for the record, I will not being *doing* Davis. We're just friends."

"It's only a matter of time. He talks about you all the time," Miguel said.

"I told you, we're just friends." I didn't want to admit how happy it made me feel to know Davis was talking about me. I felt a fluttering in my stomach again, but this time I knew it was just butterflies, the kind I felt when I was a young girl with a crush.

"Girl, what you waiting on to get laid? My grandma gets more dick than you."

"Bye, Miguel. I'll give you a call later. Call me if you hear anything else about why Davis had to be out of work." I hung up.

Miguel was crazy. As soon as we hung up he sent me an email in fifty-point font that read: *GIRL!!! GET SOME DICK!* Miguel was as bad as Michelle. They simply could not live without sex. They needed to find a hobby, read a book, write a book, something. There was more to life than sex.

I was really starting to get worried about Davis. I called and left a message telling him I was very concerned and hoped everything was okay with him. Three days passed by. Every time my phone rang, I jumped to answer it, hoping it was him.

When he finally called, it was while I was sleeping at 4:00 A.M.

"Rhea, she's sick." I heard a low, raspy voice, when I answered the phone.

"Who is this?"

"It's me."

"Davis?" I was still groggy.

"Yes."

"What happened? Who?" By then I was awake.

"My mom. She had a stroke."

"When? Where are you?"

"At the hospital."

"Do you need me to come out there?"

"No, I'll be okay. My best friend Mike just flew in from Vegas, but thanks for asking. I just needed to hear your voice." He whispered, "I don't know what I would have done if you didn't answer, Rhea. You have been on my mind for the last few days."

"Oh, Davis, I'm so sorry. What do you need?"

He sounded so sad. It didn't even cross my mind to ask him why I'd only been on his mind for the last few days when we hadn't spoken for weeks.

"Just pray for me," he said solemnly.

"Please call me if you need anything."

Although I'd been so worried about him, sleep was creeping back in suddenly. I guess I was finally able to relax now that I'd heard his voice. I felt bad that his mother was sick, but I was relieved there was nothing wrong with him.

"Okay, I will. And Rhea . . ." There was a long pause.

"Yes?"

"Thanks for listening."

"Davis?"

"Yes." He was still whispering. Maybe he was in the room with his mother and didn't want to wake her.

"I missed you too," I told him, knowing it was what he'd really wanted to say.

There, I said it. Now that I'd admitted out loud that I'd missed Davis, there was no more lying to myself. I was falling for this guy, no matter how many times I'd tried to convince myself I would never have feelings for another man. Davis was special. He'd helped me out of the funk I'd been in ever since my divorce, and now I had to admit to myself that I wanted him in my life.

After Davis called me from the hospital, I waited for him to call me again. I didn't expect that it would take weeks, but it did. I was extra busy at work and with teaching, but I still constantly thought about him.

Finally, I got a call from him again at 2:15 A.M. on January 28th.

"Hello." I was wide-awake, grading papers.

"Hey, it's me!" His mood sounded so different from the last call. He sounded happy again, so I assumed his mother was out of the hospital.

"Davis!" I couldn't hide the excitement in my voice. "Hi, baby!" *Oops, I slipped!*

" 'Baby'? Well, alrighty then. Girl, you keep on like that and next time I'll have you calling me big daddy." He sounded so much better than the last time I'd talked to him.

"Whatever, Davis." I was grinning from ear to ear. If I'd been at all upset with him for not calling me for weeks, my happiness at hearing his voice made me forget all about it.

"So, how are you, pretty lady?"

That evoked a smile.

"Mom is doing better and can't wait to meet you."

"What! You told your mom about me?" I was surprised but also delighted. This confirmed for me that Davis was also starting to have feelings that went beyond friendship.

"Yes. Is that a problem?"

"Well, honestly, I told my parents about you too."

He laughed. "So, since we know each other's innermost secrets and have made it into the sacred realm called the Momma Circle, when are we going to make this thing official and meet face to face?"

"I don't know about that, Davis." Suddenly I was nervous.

"I guess I'll just have to wait, huh?"

"Tell you what—when I'm ready for that, I'll let you know." I really liked him, but I was so afraid of getting hurt. What if I got too attached to him and it didn't work out? I didn't know if I could handle another failed relationship. I might have been a strong, independent woman, according to Marcus, but I was still deeply affected by the divorce.

"Whatever you want, beautiful." It made me feel good to know he wasn't going to pressure me.

My call waiting beeped. "Davis, hang on a second please. I have a beep, and I know it's nobody but my cousin Michelle calling me at this time in the morning."

I clicked over. "Hey, Michelle, what's up?"

"Nothing. Do you think that fifty-five hundred is too much to pay for fake boobs?" She sounded exasperated, as if the world was coming to an end. Michelle was such a drama queen.

"I don't know. Why are you asking me? And I gotta go. I'm on the phone with a man."

"What? Who?" She sounded more excited than I was.

I teased her. "He's going to be my baby daddy. Gotta go." I clicked back over to Davis. "Hey, sorry. That was my cousin Michelle. She was telling me about her fake boobs."

"'Fake boobs'? Are yours real?" he asked flirtatiously.

"All thirty-eight double-D," I replied proudly.

"What! Damn, girl! So, do you like lingerie?"

I knew where this conversation was headed quickly, so I put on the brakes a little. "Yes, but I normally sleep with a big T-shirt on."

"What are you wearing now?" He made his voice deeper, imitating Barry White. Obviously he wasn't about to let me change the subject without a fight.

"Davis, go to hell," I said with a laugh.

"So, how long has it been?"

"Since what?" I asked, knowing exactly what he meant. I just couldn't believe he was asking it, and I needed a moment to decide if I really wanted to go there with him.

"You know what I'm talking about. So tell me, how long has it been?"

I decided it was time to let my defenses down. It was just harmless flirting. "Let's just say there have been a few New Year's Eve parties since I've had some."

"Wow! Really? That's a long time, girl."

"Shut up, Davis. It's not like it's that long. Besides, there's more to life than sex," I protested, knowing I was full of shit. Sure, I kept myself busy with work and volunteering, but I was still a young, vibrant woman, and I did miss the feel of a man's body. Shit, I was horny!

"Well, it's been a while for me too. Do you ever think about me at night, Rhea?"

I responded with a slow "Yes." I had an idea where the conversation was going, but I didn't try to stop it this time.

"I think about you all the time." He paused then lowered his voice. "I also touch myself when I think about you."

"So, are you back at work, Davis?" I changed the subject, suddenly unsure if I was ready to go where he was trying to take this.

"Yeah, I've been back a few days. If I didn't know any better, I'd say you were changing the subject, Rhea." He laughed.

"What are you talking about?" I lay back on my bed.

"Hey, girl, I know you all too well now. But I touch myself a lot when I talk to you. Hell, sometimes even when I think about you." Just like that, he took the conversation right back there.

I was excited and afraid at the same time. I sighed. "Davis, you know how bad I've been hurt. Even though it's been a long time, I'm not ready to make a commitment right now. I'm also not ready for casual sex either."

"I know, but phone sex isn't a commitment, is it?"

He had a point there. "Nope!" I said a little too quickly.

"What are you wearing?" he asked again.

"I'm wearing a T-shirt. Why?"

"Take it off, baby," he said in a seductive tone.

I was beginning to enjoy this. I did as he said, lifting my shirt over my head. "Okay, it's off."

"Now I want you to do something for me."

"Yes, baby," I responded as I got lost in my own thoughts.

There was a battle being waged in my conscience. My Catholic schoolgirl mentality was telling me this was so wrong, but then I could hear Michelle's voice saying, "You need some dick, and it's safe."

"Rhea?" His voice interrupted my thoughts.

"Yes."

"Am I making you uncomfortable?"

I started to cry. I felt so stupid. "I'm sorry, Davis."

"Oh, don't cry, baby. What's wrong?"

"Nothing. It's just that I really like you."

"I like you too, Rhea. I know this may be a big step for you, but there are millions of people all over the world that are doing what we're about to do."

I laughed at the image of phone lines burning up across the country with steamy sex conversations. "Now, that's my girl. Just lay back and let big daddy make you feel good. Okay, baby?"

What a wimp I am. I take sex too seriously. This is just phone sex. Damn, Rhea, stop crying like a freaking teenager!

"Okay, Davis."

"I can guarantee you this much, Rhea—tonight you're going to sleep like a baby."

"Mmm," I moaned.

"Rhea, turn your light off. Then I want you to lay down with your legs open and your eyes closed."

I reached over and turned off my nightlight. "It's off. Tell me what to do next," I whispered.

"Now I want you to put two fingers inside yourself."

"Oh yes, Davis." I followed his command.

"Now put the telephone down between your legs so I can hear your pussy pop."

I did as Davis instructed, and then much more. It was a very long, satisfying night.

CHAPTER 8

The next morning, I was so refreshed from my night of splendor and my first introduction to the world of phone sex, I was on cloud nine. I had only gotten about four hours of sleep, but it was such a deep, comatose sleep that I felt like I'd slept for days. Davis called around 8:00 and woke me up.

After I took a shower and got dressed, he called me back. I talked to him on the phone, from my house to the gas station, and on the commute to work, which, by the way, I was late for again.

I went into the office, and after allocating duties, I had a few meetings to attend. I arrived back at my desk a little after noon.

Davis had left a message that said, "Where are you, Rhea? Call me when you get in the office."

I called him back. "Hi, baby."

"Hey, beautiful."

"How are you?"

"Fine, thanks to you." He chuckled.

"Davis, you molested me," I snickered, while shutting my office door.

He laughed a deep, rich, sexy laugh. "No, *you* molested *me*. How many times did you cum, Rhea?"

"Only three," I responded proudly and plopped down in my chair.

"Not enough. Tell you what—let's plan on touching bases at around nine my time and I'm going to make you scream again."

"I can't, baby. I'm in a wedding this weekend, and my flight leaves at five this afternoon."

"Well, I guess I'll have to jack off thinking about you this weekend, huh?"

"I guess so. Hey, hit me up on email because I'm really running behind. That way I can still talk to you and work."

As soon as I logged on, I got an email from him. He expressed on company email how he wanted to pin me down and bury his head between my legs until I had a total of seven orgasms, since biblically speaking the number seven meant completion. I got so horny, I had to tell him I'd call him en route to the airport. I slept like a baby on my flight.

I had a wonderful time that weekend. My sorority sister, Tina, had a beautiful wedding. It was wonderful to see so many of my friends I hadn't seen since my own wedding. When I first got the invitation, I thought I might get upset at the wedding because some of the people I knew would be there didn't know I'd gotten a divorce. I figured I'd spend the weekend explaining things to people, and I wasn't looking forward to that.

Davis, though he was thousands of miles away, helped me through that. Anytime I got tired of the pitiful looks people gave me, like they thought I was an incomplete woman now that my doctor husband was gone, I would just leave the room and call Davis. Just hearing his voice and the compliments he gave me made me feel good again. I actually left the wedding reception early so I could go back to my room to have phone sex with him.

During one of our conversations, he was actually out at a club with one of his frat brothers. As soon as he heard me on the phone, he went out to his car to talk to me. His boy came looking for him, and when he found Davis, he made him hand over the phone.

Rob took the phone and said to me, "Girl, what you do to my boy? He turning down pussy right and left. He keeps on talking about Rhea. All I hear is Rhea this and Rhea that."

Davis yelled from the background. "He's lying! Rob, give me back my cell phone."

When Davis got back on the phone, I told him, "Thank you, Davis."

"For what?"

"For making me feel like a woman again."

"Rhea, you are all woman," he assured me, and I knew he meant it.

I got back in town on Sunday night. Davis had called a few times. I was so exhausted, but I called and talked to him just long enough to tell him I missed him and to thank him again for being so nice to me whenever I was feeling down. It was funny. I had always prided myself on being so independent, and here I was leaning on Davis for emotional support. And the best part was that I didn't feel bad about not being the strong one for a change.

When I got to work on Monday, there was a huge bouquet of daffodils sitting on my desk. I excitedly opened the card. It read: *Just a little note to say that I missed you this weekend and to tell you that the best is yet to cum. Your Chocolate Prince.*

I was almost in tears. Davis was going to make me fall in love with him yet.

I called him at work, but the secretary said he'd be in a training session until six. I was fiending for his voice, but by the time he'd be out of his meeting, I'd be teaching my class.

Around 3:00 he called me back, while I was out of the office. He left me a message.

"Hey, beautiful, I'm in an all-day meeting today with "our" favorite boss, Stan. I think that white boy has the hots for you. Everything is 'Rhea from the Atlanta office does it this way and that way.' I almost clocked his ass for talking about my girl. Anyway, I can't wait to talk to you tonight. I'll call you around nine. We're going to have a fantasy re-enactment. I'm going to make you scream."

I didn't know what a 'fantasy re-enactment' was, but if it could make me scream, I was sure looking forward to it. I felt so good inside. Davis was starting to ignite feelings in me that had been smoldering for years.

That night, I let my students out early and raced home. I got home about 8:15, took a hot bath and lit candles in anticipation of the intimate evening to come.

True to his word, Davis called at 9:00 on the dot.

I looked at the caller ID. "Hello, Rhea's house of lustful sex. How may I help you?"

"Guess what I'm doing, baby?" he whispered.

"What? Thinking about me?"

"Well, that too, but I'm measuring my dick."

"What?"

Davis was a freak, but I was loving it.

"I'm measuring it now, then I'll measure it after I'm good and hard. I want you to know what you're working with."

"I see. What *I'm* working with? Who says I'm ever going to see it?"

"Well, that's up to you. It's yours if you want it. What do you have on?"

"Absolutely nothing. I'm naked and waiting on you."

"Slow down, tiger. I think I've unleashed an animal." He laughed.

"Yes, you have, my dear," I whispered.

"Damn. Now, that's what I'm talking about! I want you to lay back, close your eyes, and give me your undivided attention."

"Whatever you say."

"Say something to me in Spanish."

I whispered something deliciously nasty.

"I don't know what you said, but it sounds sexy as hell."

"I said I want you to taste me, baby. I want to feel your tongue in my pussy."

"Oh, baby, if I were in Atlanta right now, that's what I'd be doing. I've got big lips too. Okay, close your eyes and relax."

I closed my eyes. "I'm relaxed."

"Rhea, I want you to imagine me there with you right now. We're sipping on champagne. I'm slowly massaging your feet, and I suck each one of your toes. I'm moving my hands up your legs. Are your eyes shut, Rhea?"

I was so excited my body shivered. "Yes!" I shrieked.

"Good. Now imagine the sound and feel of chocolate whipped cream being sprayed all over your body. Then imagine the smell of strawberries, as I put a strawberry in my mouth and our tongues mesh together. Now smack your lips for me and think about our tongues savoring the taste of one another."

"Yes, baby." I began to squirm.

"No, I said *smack*."

I did as I was told and smacked my lips. "Davis, I'm so hot."

He talked over me. "Imagine me taking another strawberry, dipping it in whipped cream and spreading it all over your body. Next, I'm going to slide it from the valley of your earlobe to your breasts. Then I'm going to take this King Cobra tongue and trace the same path and lick the strawberry juices off of you."

I had a feeling of inexplicable contentment overcome me. My skin tingled all over. "I want you so bad."

"I want you too, but don't touch yourself yet. Only when I tell you, okay?"

"*Sí, papi!*"

"Now, I'm going to lick the whipped cream off of you, but first I'm going to rub ice on your nipples. Now squeeze your nipples and say my name."

"Yes, Davis!" I screamed and squeezed my nipples.

"I'm going to take each one of your nipples in my mouth and suck gently, then harder."

My breathing became shallow, and my hips were starting to rise off the bed.

"I'm going to use another strawberry as the brush and the whipped cream as my paint. I'm going to paint a trail down to your moist pussy. Then I'm going to bury my head between your legs and suck on your pussy like a Slurpee."

I couldn't contain my cries of pleasure as he urged me on. I screamed louder and came as he told me how he wanted to bend me over and pound me so deeply that I'd feel his dick inside my esophagus, while he spanked my ass with his fraternity paddle. Just when I was certain the intensity could not get any higher, Davis said he was coming as well. I screamed, and he moaned. Maybe this phone sex wasn't the real thing, but it was damn good!

It was now June, and I'd been having phone sex for five months with Davis Edwinn Hickman. Every night it was wild, unforgettable phone sex. Friday nights were our all-nighters. We would talk literally for eight to ten hours straight.

Every day at work we'd talk on the phone or chat online. He would email romantic poems he had written for me, and at least once a week he'd send me flowers or candy to work. I was getting the best of both worlds—the sweet, romantic Davis during office hours, and the wild, freaky sex partner during our nightly phone calls. He was definitely boyfriend material, and I was falling for him hard. It was only a matter of time before we both agreed it was time to meet in person.

On June 1, Davis mailed me a roundtrip ticket to Denver. The following Friday, I left work early and flew out to see him. I was so excited. At that point, it didn't matter what he looked like. He could have shown up in a wheelchair and I would have been just as smitten with him.

He said he wanted to totally pamper me. He had a small apartment and asked if I would mind if we got a hotel room, since his place probably wouldn't be up to my standards. I told him that I didn't care where we stayed. We could have slept in a cardboard box on a street corner. I just wanted to be with him.

I walked into the airport lobby, after retrieving my luggage, and spotted him right away. He was tall, blue-black, with the most beautiful bone structure I had ever seen. Even if my instincts didn't tell me it was him, I would've known anyway. He was waving the Haitian flag with a picture of Ms. Cleo plastered on a jar, trying to be funny. Gosh, was I embarrassed. That voodoo shit was too fucking funny. I admired him from head to toe. He was Tyrese and Morris Chestnut rolled into one.

"Hi, Rhea." He walked up to me.

"Hi, Davis."

We exchanged brief hugs, and he handed me a bouquet of daffodils.

"Thank you. That was very thoughtful." It was amazing how I could communicate with him via email and telephone but just clammed up when I met him in person.

"You're welcome," he said softly.

We walked out to the parking lot. We were both silent as I followed him onto the parking elevator.

He stared at me for a couple of seconds before I asked, "What are you looking at?" feeling a little uncomfortable.

He kept staring at me.

I was checking him out, too, but at least I was trying to be inconspicuous. Davis had beautiful, silky, black skin. I could see the definition in his muscles from under his shirt. A few hours in bed with me would help define them even more.

He had big, beautiful eyes, curvaceous lips, and a deep dimple on the left side of his face. I was enthralled. I was finally staring face to face with the man who'd had me sticking candlesticks inside of myself, pretending that it was him inside of me. He was gorgeous! Yes, Lawd, this was the kind of man I'd always longed for but never had. A big, chocolate brother. A big, cracklin', bread-eating country nigga that would just throw you upside a wall and fuck the hell out of you. Yep, I had me a big ol' hay baler. And if Davis Hickman made me scream like he did every night on the phone, I would probably marry his fine ass.

He finally answered. "You're beautiful, Rhea."

"And you're a very handsome man, Davis."

I stared him directly in the eye. He looked away quickly. Did he have a shy streak in him? I stuck that tidbit of information in my mental Rolodex in case he ever got stupid. I could use that to my advantage and embarrass him in public if he ever pissed me off.

Okay, now is test time, I thought, as we got off the elevator and headed toward his car. *If he doesn't open the door for me, he's history. If he does, he'll get some pussy.*

He walked toward his door with his keys in his hands then looked at me and winked. He turned around and walked back over to the passenger side of the car to open the car door for me.

Good. At least he had some manners.

After Davis put my luggage in the trunk, I settled in the passenger seat and began to think about my first impression of him.

He spoke first. "I've always wanted me a cute little chocolate girl. One of my ex-girlfriends is from Grenada."

It figures. Now I have to listen to this shit. Rule number one is that you never talk about your past pussy!

I stared at him blankly, rather than telling him

what I was really thinking. I was trying very hard to keep my big mouth in check.

He must have gotten the hint because he changed the subject. "So, what part of Cuba is your dad from?" he asked after paying the parking attendant.

"Havana," I said, trying to sound upbeat.

Davis tried to impress me by mutilating the entire Spanish language. After a few seconds of awkward silence, he asked, "Is your mom's family from a large city in Haiti?"

"Port-au-Prince."

"Is that a big city?"

"It's the capital, Davis," I said mockingly, using the same tone I used when my students couldn't process simple concepts.

"Oh, I knew that," he said sheepishly. "And your grandparents?"

"My grandparents what?" He was still on this kick? Maybe it was just my nerves, but I was starting to get irritated.

"Where are they from?"

"Which ones? I have two sets." *You are a little bit annoying, but I'm trying to be nice to you.*

My sarcastic answer silenced him, so I laid my head back, grateful for a moment to think about what I had gotten myself into.

I closed my eyes and felt something wet under me. I reached underneath my leg and pulled out a wet napkin. I hadn't really noticed his car when I got in. I looked around now. This boy had the nastiest car I'd ever seen! Shoes, baby stuff, food, soda bottles. Didn't he know he was coming to pick me up? *It's not too late to turn around,* I told myself. What lie could I think of? I could tell him I left my luggage and run back inside the airport and hop on the next plane home. Or I could change my phone number and never speak to him again. Nope, couldn't do that either. We worked for the same company. But then again, he was in Denver and I was in Atlanta.

Nah, I'd better not. With my luck, Sebastian will probably end up sending me to the Denver office.

I took a deep breath.

He's a nice guy, Rhea. You said you wanted to get away from Ivy-League stuck-up pretty boys. And it seems you got exactly what you asked for this time.

I could hear my mom now. "Does his family own any property? Where did his grandparents go to college? Oh, Rheonique, I hope they didn't go to a state school."

I swear, my mom was clinically insane, but I must admit, I was a little touched as well. I laughed out loud.

Davis looked over at me laughing and shrugged. "Rhea, first of all I'd like to apologize. My beamer is in the shop and I had to borrow my boy's car. He has a baby. I didn't have time to clean up the car before coming to get you."

"That's okay. I understand." *See, Rhea, stop bugging out,* I scolded myself. I always had been too quick to judge people. It was something I was trying to change about myself.

"So, what do you want to do?" He touched my hand.

I wanted to say, "You!" Instead, I responded with, "I don't know. This is your city. How's a movie sound?"

"Cool. Let's see. Did you ever see *Baby Boy* with Tyrese? It's at the dollar movie."

"Oh no, I never saw it. That sounds great," I lied, trying to sound jovial.

'The dollar movie'! Wasn't that movie about six years old? That shit should be free. Tyrese was a li'l fine-ass Kunta and all, but the last fucking movie I wanted to see in the whole world was some ghetto-ass shit about a nigga that had two baby mommas and lived with his mammy and rode a fucking bicycle. I mean, what kind of women would put up with sharing a baby daddy anyway? They had to be some poor, pitiful, gutter trash.

I checked myself before I spoke my true opinion about his choice of movies. I was determined not to be the big mouth that Marcus had accused me of being. I sat back in the seat and tried to convince myself that things could only get better from this point on.

By the time we got to the theatre, it was thundering and raining. We ran inside quickly, trying to avoid the downpour, but it was useless.

It had taken me a long time to decide what to wear. I had to be very selective for my first meeting with Davis. That mini-skirt was carefully chosen. I found one that wasn't too revealing but was still sexy.

By the time I got into the theater, my clothes were soaked and clinging to my body in all the wrong places.

As bad as I felt, though, one look at Davis's sexy body made me forget all but one thing. I began thinking of ways to make him scream—until he really fucked up the moment.

"Man, we missed the matinee. I didn't realize it was two dollars after five."

Red flag! Red flag! Of course, I knew this was a problem when the man I was with didn't want to pay four fuckin' dollars for a movie. But one look at his gorgeous muscles and I could overlook his cheapness.

"That'll be four dollars," the clerk said.

Davis pulled out a hundred. The clerk couldn't change it, so I handed Davis a ten.

"Davis, which way is the restroom?"

He pointed down the hall.

I went to the bathroom and checked myself out to make sure I looked okay. I ran my fingers through my hair to make my curls a little wavy then checked my nose and teeth to make sure they were clean. *Okay, I'm the bomb.com.* I went back inside the bathroom stall and applied some feminine spray in my private area. *Just in case. You never know.*

I found Davis over by the concession stand, buying popcorn with my change. I was dying of thirst, so I reached down in my purse to find some money for bottled water.

Davis didn't offer to buy it for me, nor did he hand over my change.

Stop it, Rhea. Money isn't everything. Stop acting like Mommy.

As the movie began to play, he started kissing my neck. His hands found their way under my soggy skirt. He stuck his finger inside of me then licked it. I was just ripe for that chocolate man.

"Rhea, just sit on top of me. The theatre's practically empty. I can just slip it inside right here," he whispered.

This fool must be crazy! He thinks after years of being dickless he's gonna ram that big rod inside of me in the middle of a damn movie theatre?

I kissed him seductively. "Davis, I want our first time to be special. I want to be able to touch you all over. And we would have to muffle our sounds because there are people sitting four rows ahead of us."

"Okay. Can we leave now?" He licked my ear.

"Yes, please," I responded breathlessly. I didn't want to see the damn movie in the first place!

On our way out to the parking lot, we couldn't

keep our hands off of one another. He pulled onto the freeway.

I was so hot and horny, all I could do was just lay my head back and close my eyes.

After a while, I looked out the window. Denver seemed like a nice city. Too bad it was raining.

"Hey, I need you to drive. I have a headache. Can you drive a stick?"

"Yes, and I can ride one too." I winked at him.

He pulled over to the side of the road at a gas station. As we ran past each other to switch seats, he squeezed my nipples. Maybe it was just the rain, but I felt my body shudder.

"Davis, what are you talking about? This is an automatic," I said when I got into the driver's seat.

"I was just teasing, but I do have a headache."

"What do you take for your headache? I have Motrin in my purse." I started fumbling around to find it, steering the car with one hand.

"Pussy," Davis said matter-of-factly.

"What?" This boy was even freakier than I thought, but I kinda liked it.

"I have a headache." He pointed down to the hard bulge that had formed inside of his pants. Davis pushed my mini-skirt higher and higher, as if he were on a scavenger hunt. He pulled my thong to one side and sent his tongue searing into my wet vagina.

My foot kept slipping off the gas, as he fingered me deeply while I drove on the interstate. I was milking him out of three or four children with my free hand.

After a few minutes, I saw a sign for a rest area and had to pull over so we could continue.

"The hotel is about another twenty minutes away. I'll drive now." He zipped up his pants and came around to the driver's side once we were finished.

"Thanks. I'm not trying to get lost in this rain." I adjusted my bra.

Some people got out of their vehicle to walk toward the restroom, staring at us like they knew what we had just done.

"Girl, you got my mind spinning." He looked down between my legs and licked his lips as he started up the car. As he started to drive, he said, "I know a high-maintenance girl like you wants a luxury hotel."

About a half-hour later, we stopped at The Ritz of Denver. The sign on the marquis stated each two-bedroom suite came with a wet bar along with concierge service for $149 a night. I was impressed. I started humming along to Sade's "King of Sorrows," which was playing on the local easy-listening station.

Not tonight. I won't be the Queen of Sorrows anymore. Things had gotten off to a less than perfect start with the nasty car and the cheap-ass movie, but the sex was so damn good! I hoped and prayed that nothing else would happen to fuck up the weekend. I couldn't wait to get my hands on this man again.

"I'll be right back," Davis said as prepared to get out and go into the lobby.

"Okay, baby. Give me a kiss."

He leaned over, grabbed me by the back of the head and pulled me forward. His kiss was like fire. It burned and churned my inner soul. It tickled my toes and made my eyebrows singe at the same time. This was either the best kiss I'd ever had, or it had been so long, I forgot what one felt like.

It was still raining, so I dug around in my bag for my umbrella, which was decorated with my sorority emblem.

"You want me to carry that thing with those ugly-ass colors?" he said with a wink.

"Whatever. Don't talk about my sorority, with your country-ass fraternity. Y'all still wear overalls?" We both laughed.

He took the umbrella and went toward the lobby.

Within minutes he was back in the car, shivering from the downpour. He rubbed his hands together and smiled, looking sheepishly at me.

"Well? Did you get the room?"

"No, I didn't . . . Um, it's a hundred forty-nine dollars plus tax, and I only have a hundred dollars."

Okay, this shit was too much. Time to go off. I ain't from Missouri, but it was time to show him! "What? Davis, you invited me here. You don't have money for the hotel? Can't you just use a damn credit card? We wouldn't have this problem if you would have just taken me to your place. I told you I didn't care where we stayed!" I yelled. I wasn't sure why I was getting quite so upset, but I suspected it was because this money issue was slowing us down from getting into a bedroom and getting busy.

"Rhea, calm down. I was just kidding. Of course I've got the money. Truth is, I was rushing to get to the flower shop to get you some flowers and I left my credit cards at home by mistake. But I've got cash. Dang, you can get feisty, can't you?" He smiled at me.

I smiled at him. "Davis, I'm sorry. Sometimes I go off." I could just hear Marcus now, telling me about my big damn mouth. I had to get myself under control.

He kissed me on the cheek. "No problem. I like my women to have spunk."

"I'm glad, Davis, because I've got plenty of that. But as far as me getting feisty, I was not about to offer to pay for the room. That would be too much like paying for dick!"

We both laughed, but the truth was, I was so horny, I just might have paid if he pushed the issue.

CHAPTER 9

We ran from the car to the hotel. I almost slipped as we were running, and Davis put his arms around me to keep me from falling. The electricity between us was enough to light up Yankee Stadium. We held hands as we walked through the lobby, and I admired the surroundings. The hotel was fabulous. There was a three-piece ensemble playing in the lobby, along with a gift shop tucked away in the corner.

Davis stood my luggage up against the corner and went inside the gift shop. He came back with a bouquet of roses.

"Oh baby, that's so sweet. Now I have daffodils and roses." I gave him a hug.

"Rhea, you make my heart smile. I'll do anything for you." He bent down to kiss me.

We stepped into the elevator.

"You're making me wet," I whispered in his ear, as we rode the elevator up to the tenth floor.

"The battle is halfway over then," he whispered back so the other guests wouldn't hear.

We got off the elevator, and Davis tapped me on my butt.

After opening the door to the suite, I ran and turned the heater on. "Oh, I'm freezing."

He helped me strip out of my wet clothes, giving me a look of appreciation when he saw my Victoria's Secret bra and panty set.

"Yes indeed. The biggest butt I've ever had," he muttered under his breath.

"You haven't had me yet," I teased.

"It's only a matter of time, *mi amor*." He grabbed me from behind, cupping my breasts.

I pushed him away playfully. "Stop, Davis. Not now."

He kissed me again. "Why don't you hop into the shower and relax? I'll light some candles then give you that massage I've been promising for months."

"You've got condoms?" I asked.

"I thought you said were on the pill." He looked upset.

"Well, pregnancy is not the only thing condoms prevent, you know. Can I trust you if we don't use a condom? You haven't been with anyone else, have you?"

"Of course you can, and no, I haven't been with anyone else. Rhea, can I tell you something?"

"Sure. What's wrong?"

"It's nothing." He began speaking slowly. "I'm a little embarrassed. My penis is very sensitive. Condoms give me a rash. And honest to God, most of them are too small for me." Davis studied my face.

I tried to remain calm and forced myself not to laugh. *Now, that's the oldest line in the book. He's allergic to condoms? And they're too small for him? Lord, men will say anything not to have to use a condom.*

He touched my face. "Baby, I promise I would

never put you at risk . . . or myself for that matter. I have too much to live for. I swear I haven't been with anyone in almost a year."

"You know I've been hurt before, so please, please don't lie to me."

"Rheonique Ramirez Baptiste LaDay, I promise that I, Davis Edwinn Hickman, would never hurt you." He reached down inside his bag and produced some massage oil. He winked at me.

"I'm still freezing. Let me go take a shower first, okay?"

"Sure, baby," he answered.

I headed to the bathroom with my bag. I stayed in the shower for an hour, trying to assess the whole situation. Doubts were formulating. Was I about to make a mistake? I was so tired of hurting and so tired of not trusting anyone since Marcus. Most of all, I was tired of being alone. I hoped with all my heart that Davis was telling the truth.

Besides, after all the months of phone sex, my body was so ready for the real thing. And damn, he did have a beautiful body. I shook my head as I realized I was coming close to making my decision.

Am I about to raw fuck a man I've never seen before? But he can kiss, though. And I am so horny! I mean, I am his girlfriend . . . sort of.

I felt like I had the little devil and angel sitting on my shoulders. I was tired of being cautious. It was time for me to finally be happy.

"Are you okay?" He knocked on the bathroom door.

I turned off the water. "I'm fine. Just trying to decide if I want to wear a teddy or a negligee. I'll be right out."

"Honestly, Rhea, it doesn't matter. If I have my way, it'll be off in five minutes anyway."

I decided on an elegant long, black sheath with a split up the left side. I exited the bathroom to discover he had transformed the room into a love nest. There were at least twenty votive candles flickering, and daffodil petals were scattered throughout the room. He'd turned the dresser into a little work table with towels, massage oil and honey. The thought of finally having Davis inside of me made me so wet, I had to look down to make sure I wasn't dripping all over the floor.

"What type of music do you like?" He put a CD in the player.

"Anything. I'm flexible."

"Oh, I bet you are." He winked.

I almost had an orgasm right there. I sat down on the bed, bouncing up and down to see if it squeaked. I pulled the comforter down and ran my hand across the soft sheets.

"Nice music. The Gyspy Kings are one of my favorite groups." I was impressed.

"Mine too, but I really dig Native American music, though. It's earthy."

I could tell he was about to go on a tangent about Indian culture to try to impress me, so I cut him off.

"Fascinating. I'll have to check it out some time." Indian culture was the last thing on my mind.

He touched my face. "There are a few songs that remind me of you, though."

"Oh, really?" I kissed his lower lip.

He put in a CD that had "Rhea's songs" written on it. "Touched a Dream" by R.Kelly, "Say Yes" by Floetry, and "Forever My Lady" by Jodeci were written on the burned CD.

"Boy, you better be careful burning them illegal CDs," I teased. "That's very sweet of you, though, to make this for me."

"Rhea, you are so wonderful. I just want to spoil you. I want to give you so much." He took his shirt off.

"You already have." I traced the outline of the fraternity brand on his arm.

He motioned for me to lay down then slowly poured cinnamon vanilla oil on my back. He massaged me with soft, deep strokes. I was so relaxed that I fell asleep.

A short while later, the dinging of the microwave timer woke me. Davis returned with some honey in a small bowl, turned me over, and teased my nipples with his coal black fingers. He sucked them into an erect hardness then dribbled honey on my breasts and licked them gently.

His touch ignited sparks from the inner depths of my soul. I was both afraid and excited at the same time, as he bent me over the bed on my knees.

"Oh, baby, let's try it in another position." There was no way in hell he was going to have me from behind. As long as it had been since I'd had sex, I'd probably start bleeding.

"Oh no, baby. I want you just like this." He reached to play with my nipples.

"I know you said doggie-style is your favorite position, but I'm afraid that you may hurt me."

He sucked a spot near the base of my spine. "Don't worry. I won't hurt you. Bent over is what I want." He rubbed his hands down my spine and grabbed my buttocks, pulling me toward him. "Your skin is so soft."

Davis was pretty big, and my vagina was so tight

that even tampons hurt like hell. I instinctively tensed up and closed my eyes to brace myself for his throbbing manhood. I soon relaxed, though, when I felt his tongue enter me from behind.

"I've never done anyone else like this before, so you should feel privileged," he said.

"Yeah, right. You do that too good to be an amateur." I laughed.

He laughed too then came up for air. He parted my legs like a swimmer who was pushing back water to get to the top of the pool then began to lick me from my clit to my ass.

Just as I was about to explode, Davis turned me around and put on a tongue-piercing clip. He buried his face in between my legs and I tightened them around his neck.

I stopped counting after the tenth orgasm.

"You taste so good. In fact, I can stay down here all night. My God, girl, it has been a while for you. I know I just drank about eight ounces of your fluid." He tried to finger me. "Damn, your pussy is tight!"

He got up off his knees and lay across the bed. "Your turn." He grabbed my hand and slid it up and down his hardened spear. I gladly complied.

Although I wasn't too fond of giving head, I was determined to do my best, even more so after the magic Davis had just performed with his tongue. Besides, all of our phone sex had loosened up some of my old sexual inhibitions. I'd started watching *Sex Talk* on television, trying to get pointers on giving good head.

I yearned for this big, ebony stick in my mouth. His dick was huge and black like a dark piece of antique wood that had been chiseled precisely. His tool was like a polished clarinet about to be played in a symphony orchestra. I wanted to please my man and make him happy, no matter what the cost.

"I want to taste you, Davis. Fill my mouth with your rod." I moaned and sucked his thick, black dick, starting at the tip then making my way down to his shaft, planting small kisses, sucks and nibbles along the way.

As I moved southward, I gently placed his testicles in my mouth until I could feel his magic love juice developing from the inside of his soul. I nibbled lightly on the base of my new toy until I felt him explode inside my mouth.

"I want more," I screamed. I sucked his essence like an ice cream cone, twisting gently and allowing my tongue to discover every indentation, nook and cranny of his rod. I sucked my black god's dick, on my knees, praying for his repeated explosions.

"Oh, baby. I can hold you inside my mouth forever."

I faintly heard Davis whispering, "Yeah, baby. Suck it. I can't wait to be inside of you."

I felt his erection forming again as I caressed the underside of his penis. I gently traced his bulging vein with my fingernails. His long, coal shaft stood eleven inches tall before me. Yes, I would be his sex goddess, his subject. My destiny was to be his slave. I humbled myself before my African prince on my knees. I was willing to do whatever it took to please him. Our souls were in sync as he played with my nipples, kneading them into hardness.

As he moaned, I felt the eruption as it flowed up inside of him, aiming toward me. Suddenly, he burst onto my full Caribbean lips, and I felt the rush of generations of his ancestry cumming full force onto me.

This Mandingo warrior was spreading his seed across my longing lips. I wanted to lap up his love juice like a puppy.

I pushed him back down on the bed. "I want to ride you."

"Damn, you're forceful, baby. Are you sure you're ready?"

"I don't care, Davis. I *have* to have you inside of me." I pushed his head back against the bedpost and positioned myself on top of his penis.

After a few tries, I painfully fit on top of him. He grabbed my buttocks with a little force and pulled me down until he was deep inside of me.

I rode him so hard the people in the next suite began to beat on the wall. I was experiencing a oneness that I had always longed for. We were like horse and jockey at the Kentucky Derby. I was mounted to him like Super Glue.

He began to shake. "Rhea, I've wanted you so long. I've never wanted anyone like this. Damn, you're so sexy."

"I've wanted you from the first time I spoke to you."

The muscles around his mouth were tense, and his mouth was wide open in a state of ecstasy. "This . . . is . . . so . . . good." He moaned. "Ride, big daddy. Ah yes, Rhea!"

I listened to the slurping sound of my honey pot as I tightened and loosened my vagina around his big, black dick, a technique I learned, compliments of the book, *How to Make a Man Scream.*

The way I slurped his nipple in my mouth like a Slurpee was what sent him over the edge. I let out a big "Oooooooh" and we exploded together. I was so backed up that I let my love juice flow down his thick, juicy black thighs.

"Ah, don't move." He began shivering.

I started gyrating back and forth then rubbed my wavy tresses across his nipples. Within minutes, he was ready again. I braced myself for the next explosion.

Now I knew that Davis Hickman was my soul mate. Over the phone we had already developed a great friendship, and now our bodies had joined together like we were made for each other. It was a perfect fit. There was something so spiritual about our sex. I knew that no matter what happened between us, we'd always have a tie that could never be broken.

I love you, Davis. I wanted to scream it at the top of my lungs. Would I scare him off? Maybe I'd tell him the next time.

We lay in each other's arms, exhausted. "Damn, girl, that was the tightest pussy in the world. You almost broke my dick off."

"Well, baby, it's been way too long, and thank you very much." I planted light kisses on his succulent lips and rubbed his back with the tip of my freshly manicured fingernails.

"I'm not done yet." He got on top and plunged deeply inside of me.

I wrapped my arms around my new lover and my best friend.

Davis was definitely the best lover I'd ever had. He had me climbing up walls. The things he did with his tongue should be illegal. The myth about dark-skinned brothers had indeed been tried, tested and confirmed. I'm here to testify that it's true. Let the church say amen!

After a short rest, Davis ran out to the store. He came back about fifteen minutes later with Popsicles, strawberries and whipped cream. He stuck the Popsicles inside of me. My warm walls melted the frozen mass into a tasty love punch, and he slurped up every drop.

I took two Popsicles, aligned them side by side with his penis, and sucked them. Then he made little mounds on my breasts with the strawberries and whipped cream and enjoyed another lustful feast.

I had so many orgasms, I lost count. I finally collapsed into an exhausted sleep, but Davis wasn't quite finished, I guess.

We had been sleeping with my back to his front, in a spoon position. While I slept, Davis had somehow managed to work his way in, and I was now awakened to the feeling of him plunging deeply into me. He pulled my hair and held on for dear life. Just as he was about to explode, he pulled out and emptied himself on my back.

"Oh, baby, why are you wasting good cum? You should have cum in me."

"Rhea, I've got lots of cum for you. I knew your conservative ass was a freak!"

"Yes, I'm your freak." I tried to ram my finger up his ass.

He pushed my hand away. "Hold up, baby. I ain't into that kind of shit."

"Just testing." I laughed. *Yes, it was a test! Good! He's not bisexual. Marcus was into fingers in the ass, and it did make me wonder about him.*

The next morning, we went to the hotel lounge for brunch and listened to a live jazz band. Then we went back to the room and had sex for the rest of the day.

Between bouts of sex in the afternoon, we watched C-Span and discussed politics. He kept antagonizing me about my political preference.

"You republican or democrat?" he asked after I'd made a negative comment about black republicans.

What kind of a stupid question is that? I just told you what I thought about black Republicans, so why would you have to ask if I am one? I thought. I must have still been tired from all our passion, because I sure was cranky all of a sudden. *Calm down, Rhea. The man is trying to be nice and carry on a conversation with you. You better keep your mouth under control so you don't lose this man just like you lost Marcus.*

"Democrat," I answered without any of the nasty attitude I'd been thinking about.

"Oh really. I'm surprised a rich girl like you knows anything about the plight of us working Negroes."

"Well, Mr. Hickman, on occasion I do slum down in the ghettoes with the commoners." I changed the subject, before he said anything else that would annoy me. "I'm starving. What do you want for dinner?" I grabbed the room service menu out of the top drawer.

He winked. "A salad."

"That does sound good. I love Caesar salad. What's your favorite type?"

"A chocolate salad." He began to nibble on my round buttocks until I begged him to stop.

After about six more rounds of sex, I could barely walk. I got up to take a bubble bath, hoping to soak away some of the pain.

"Ow!" I screamed from the bathroom.

"Are you okay, Rhea?" He knocked on the bathroom door.

"I'll be okay. It just hurts when I pee. Damn, Davis, I swear you split me wide open!" *It didn't hurt this much when I lost my virginity! Especially with Hassan's li'l-dick Taliban ass!*

"Hurry up and take a bubble bath so I can fuck

your brains out again. After that we'll take a shower together, and I'm going eat your pussy."

"In the shower?" I asked curiously.

"Yes, ma'am. I'll have you hang onto the shower rod so you can wrap your legs around my neck."

"I don't think the shower rod is sturdy enough." I couldn't take any more. My coochie was stinging.

"Rhea, stop yelling. I'll talk to you when you come out. I'm going to bring a chair to the bed later on tonight and eat you out again and again."

"I'm ignoring you. You're out of control!" *This guy is a freak!*

Davis came into the bathroom and sat beside the tub. He looked deeply in my eyes. "Rhea, you are so wonderful."

"So are you." I smiled.

He bent down beside the bathtub to kiss my forehead. "Hey, I've got to make a few phone calls."

"Take your time. I'm relaxing. I'll be in here for a while."

He was about to leave, but paused and said, "Hey, before I go, I have something for you."

"What?" I asked apprehensively. There was no telling what Davis was capable of.

He left briefly and came back with a brown package. When he opened it, he pulled out a huge black dildo. "Let me see you suck it, Rhea." He sat down on the toilet seat and put it in my mouth. I sucked it seductively then Davis stuck it between my legs.

His dick stood at attention. "I want to see you do it. Show me what you do when we're on the phone at night."

The warm bath had soothed my pain enough that I could handle it. Plus, I was turned on again by the mention of our wild phone sexcapades. I took it from him and stuck it inside myself. "Oh, Davis," I called out.

He stroked himself with one hand and played with his nipple with the other one.

After he became good and hard, I motioned for him to come closer to the edge of the bathtub.

I rested my back against the bath pillow, fucked myself with the dildo, and Davis fucked me in the mouth at the same time. He took his dick out right before he came, and exploded all over my breasts.

"Get out! At this rate, I'll never be able to take a bath," I told him when we were done.

He turned to leave and whispered from the doorway, "Rhea, you're the kind of woman that every man dreams about."

"Is that so?"

"You're so smart and beautiful enough to be a supermodel. Every man wants a corporate woman by day and a super freak at night. I know you'll please your man, and your man only."

I thought for a moment. "That's true, Davis. I've never cheated on anyone I've ever been with. Have you?"

"Hey, we can talk about this later. Let me go make these calls, Rhea."

I was too exhausted to be concerned that Davis had completely ignored my question. I ended up falling asleep in the tub. I woke up about half an hour later to freezing bath water and wrinkled skin. I climbed out and dried my body, pinned my hair up, then wrapped up in a thick terrycloth robe.

As I entered the living room of the suite, I saw Davis on the couch, practically whispering into the telephone. When he saw me, he hung up quickly.

I felt a fluttering in the pit of my stomach. *Red*

flag! Red flag! I looked at his face, but I couldn't read his expression—no guilt, no nervousness, nothing.

He came over and tried to kiss me. "You smell great, Rhea. Your hair is beautiful, pinned up like that."

I pushed him away. "Who was that on the phone?"

"My mama."

I tried to read something in the tone of his voice, but he was very calm and nonchalant. He tried to kiss me again.

"Oh." I pushed him away.

"I was just calling to check in."

'Check in'! Are you under house arrest or something? I didn't see any beeping devices attached to your legs! Just as I was about to comment, the telephone rang. I wondered who could be calling. I know I didn't tell anyone where we were staying.

Davis answered the phone. "Hello? Oh, hi." He turned to me and whispered, "It's my grandmother."

I listened to his side of the phone conversation for a few minutes, and believe it or not, it did sound like he was talking to a grandmother.

Either this guy is a great actor, or he really is on the phone with his grandma. Now, this is something new for me. I can't say I've ever been with a man in a hotel and he gave out the number to his momma and his grandma.

"Rhea," Davis said, "my grandmother wants to speak to you."

My eyes flew wide open in disbelief. How embarassing. I had just had sex with this man in every conceivable position, and now I was supposed to get on the phone with his grandmother! What the hell was I supposed to say to her?

As it turned out, I didn't have to say anything. As soon as Davis shoved the phone in my hand and I said, "Hello," she gave me an earful.

"Hey, baby. I just want to tell you I love my grandson, and he doesn't need no more babies," she said in this sweet little old-lady voice.

"Oh? No *more* babies." I looked at Davis, my stomach suddenly feeling very queasy.

"Is there something you want to tell me?" I yelled at him without bothering to cover the phone. I didn't care what his damn grandma heard.

He grabbed the phone from me and said, "Grandma, I love you. I'll call you later." He hung up the phone and looked at me with a stupid grin on his face. "My grandmother sure is a trip. She's not all there, you know. What did she say to get you so upset, Rhea?"

"Your grandmother said you don't need no more babies." I was infuriated.

"Girl, my grandma is crazy. She's eighty-five, and always getting me confused with my cousin Darren."

I had to stop and think for a minute. The flock of vultures in my stomach calmed down to a few butterflies. Maybe it was possible that she was confused. She did sound old as dirt.

I rolled my eyes at him. "Okay, Davis, but if I catch you in a lie, I'm going to kill you."

He wrapped his arms around me. "Why would I fuck up when I've found the woman of my dreams?" His lips found their way to the most sensitive spot on my neck, which he had discovered while we made love the night before.

I rolled my head back and let his tongue travel from my neck down to my breasts. He caressed them gently with his tongue and his hands then slid my robe over my shoulders and onto the floor.

I stood before him naked. He got on his knees and worshiped my body with his beautiful full lips for an hour.

Once I was satisfied, he said, "I know you're sore, honey. You go ahead and get some rest," then tucked me into the bed and sat with me until I fell asleep.

Sunday night, Davis asked me to stay with him for the rest of the week. I called in to request personal days from work and rearranged my other commitments as well.

Davis went to work every day and came back to the hotel every night. It was the most blissful time I had ever spent with any man. Davis pampered me so much. He washed my hair, gave me a pedicure, and every night after sex, I could expect a full body massage. He loved going down on me so much that he fell asleep one night in between my legs.

He took the following Friday off work so we could spend the day together. We visited the African American museum, and he treated me to a day spa. We went salsa dancing at a club called La Tienda. I was elated that Davis had arranged for me to meet the famous drummer Ruben Blades, who was part-owner of the club.

Davis was by far the most rhythmless black man I had ever met. After a few glasses of wine, I decided to give him a show and let him see what a true West Indian girl could do. I danced a few merengue and rumba dances with an older Panamanian gentleman, while Davis looked on in approval. Then I took him over in the corner while the band played a nice long salsa ballad by Jerry Rivera.

Once we were over in a dark booth by the exit, Davis sat down first. I straddled his lap, facing him, then bent down to kiss him, making sure I positioned my butt on his penis. Our eyes locked, and my heart skipped a beat. Davis had this sweet, little-boy look, almost like a cute puppy that just wags along behind you.

As he reached forward, pulling me to him for a deep kiss, I knew that I was in love. My favorite song, "*Suavemente*" by Elvis Crespo, came on. I leaned in close and traced the muscles in his back with my fingernails, grinding my hips into his lap. Damn, he was fine! He got so hard that we left. We couldn't even make it back to the hotel, so we pulled over at a rest area and handled our business.

The next day we did it again in a public place. This time it was in broad daylight, on a hiking trail at his favorite park. We were like teenagers discovering our sexuality.

Saturday night was our last night together. After making love, I was so exhausted I fell asleep instantly.

I was awakened by his penetrating stare.

I smiled and snuggled into his broad chest. "What's wrong?" I asked after a few seconds.

"Nothing." He traced his fingers over my lips.

"Why are you looking at me so intensely?" I sat up.

"I don't know, Rhea. You're very intriguing, and by far the most fascinating and beautiful woman I've ever been with. You have so much going for you. Why do you want me when you could have any man you want?"

"Don't put yourself down, Davis." I put my head back down on his chest.

"I'm not. It's not like everyone else I've been with was a loser. It's just that you come from a different world. Your parents have more money than everyone I know combined. I'm just curious why a girl from a family like yours would want me. I have nothing to offer you."

"Damn, Davis, you act like we're some sort of interracial couple and this is the Jim Crow South." I had never made a big deal about my family's wealth, so I didn't understand why this was an issue with him.

"You have to admit we are on a different socio-economic level. Why give it up to *me* after all these years of celibacy?"

Because I love you!

Though my heart was screaming those words, my response to him was, "I don't know, Davis. At first it was our friendship that was so special. And now . . ." I let the words linger in the air and rubbed my hands across his broad chest.

"Let me ask you something." He stroked my hair.

"Sure, baby. Anything."

"What would you do if, say, you ever got pregnant?"

I took a deep breath. "Wow, that's a tough one. But I don't think I'm ready for kids right now. My life is just too demanding. I would have to say that I would probably have an abortion, but since I've never been pregnant, I couldn't really give you an answer." My curiosity got the better of me. "Why?"

He shrugged. "Just asking. I really care for you, Rhea. It's almost like you're too good to be true."

Oh shit! Where have I heard that before?

CHAPTER 10

Davis came out to visit the following weekend. I couldn't wait to see him again, and he told me all week on the phone that he felt the same way. From the moment I picked him up at the airport, my body felt full of electricity. His touch set me on fire, and once we got into my house, he had me in every room twice. I had never before felt a connection like this with anyone.

Unfortunately, I discovered that this heightened passion also made me very sensitive. When he made the smallest comment that I considered ignorant, I would get totally irritated. When we weren't having incredible sex we got into some pretty interesting conversations about all kinds of things. One particular conversation about welfare had me totally pissed off, though. We completely disagreed about whether modern welfare was creating a permanent underclass. I thought his take on the whole issue was so stupid that I finally had to just walk away from him. I went into the bathroom to take a shower, trying to ignore him when he followed me in.

"Damn, baby. I'm going to start calling you my little chocolate salsa," he said as he started to caress me. I guess his way of making up after our first fight was to have more sex. "You're sweet like candy but spicy like salsa." His tongue traveled down my belly headed for his favorite place.

"I don't eat my own pussy, so I wouldn't know what that tastes like," I said sarcastically.

"Smart ass." He smacked me on the ass playfully then flicked his tongue in just the right spot.

Damn, Rhea. Why do you care how this man feels about welfare when he can use his tongue like this? Just shut up and enjoy yourself! I leaned against the shower wall and let Davis do his thing.

Over the weekend, I started to see a pattern. Any time we had a disagreement on any topic, I would get irritated, and Davis would always know just the right way to distract me. Needless to say, I had many, many orgasms.

Sunday morning I dropped him off at the airport then went to church. I missed Davis the second he got out of the car. He called Sunday afternoon when he got home. On the plane, he'd written a poem for me entitled "Rhea's Eros," and he read it to my answering machine.

I listened to it over and over with a silly grin on my face. I couldn't believe what was happening to me. After my divorce I didn't think I'd ever be with another man, and here I was falling in love. I called him back but got his answering machine. I left a message thanking him for the poem, but I stopped just short of telling him I loved him.

That evening, I fell asleep watching TV. Davis called me back around 10:00. We talked about how wonderful our weekend was and laughed together over the silly arguments we'd had.

"I like that you can get feisty, Rhea. I can't stand a girl with no opinions of her own," he told me.

"Well, I'm glad to hear that. I've been told that my mouth was too big." I thought of Marcus' words and how they'd hurt me. I was glad that I had stopped myself a few times from really going off in front of Davis. I guess I showed him just enough strength, because he seemed to like what he saw.

"Well, I don't know who told you that," he said, "but I sure like a girl with a big mouth."

From that point on, the conversation turned in a totally different direction—my favorite direction to go with Davis. In no time, he had me moaning and screaming into the phone. Once he introduced me to the world of phone sex, there was no turning back. This was becoming a nightly experience for us.

As I regained my composure after a big wave of pleasure, I heard a noise in the background on Davis' end. I heard a door slam and a female's voice yelling something. I couldn't make out what she was saying, but she didn't sound too happy.

Davis said abruptly, "Gotta go, baby. I'll call you back."

I stared at the phone in my hand for a few seconds after I heard the dial tone. I hit the speed dial for his number. "Davis, what the hell was that all about?" I demanded.

"Oh, that's my roommate's girl. She just came in,

and I didn't want her to hear us having phone sex," he answered.

Oh, but you could have sex with me in broad daylight in the damn park? How much sense does that make? "Davis, you are a grown-ass man. Besides, you never mentioned anything about a roomate before."

"Rhea," he said with a sigh, "everybody doesn't have the money that you have. I didn't necessarily want to admit it to you, but I live with my line brother, Eric, and his girl comes by from time to time. Why are you getting so angry?"

Damn. There's that money issue again. I must sound so bougie when I go off over these stupid things. "I'm sorry, Davis, it's just that I—"

"Rhea, I'm in love with you. Don't you know that?"

"I'll talk to you tomorrow baby, okay?" I just had to get off the phone. I felt so stupid.

"Okay, sleep tight, beautiful."

He was so sweet. Even though I had just embarassed him into admitting he was too broke to live by himself, he was still being nice and understanding.

Monday morning on the way to work, I decided to try to make peace with him. I called and asked if he wanted me to come out the following weekend. "I can show you just how sorry I am for being so stupid last night."

"That sounds good, Rhea, but I have to go out of town for a few weeks."

"Is everything okay? You sound kind of depressed."

"Everything's fine. It's just some family stuff." He sighed heavily into the phone.

"Are you sure you're okay? You sound funny."

"I'm fine. Rhea, you are the most considerate person I've ever met. That's why you—" He stopped abruptly.

"I what?" He was starting to make me nervous.

"You're what every man dreams of," he said softly.

"That is so sweet of you to say." *Especially after the way I flipped out on you last night,* I thought.

"No, I wasn't just saying that. I meant it," he said.

"Then why do you sound so sad?"

His tone made me think he wasn't telling me something. You know, like he really meant to say, "You're what every man dreams of except . . ."

"Rhea, I've gotta go. I'll give you a call later."

I hung up totally confused. What he said was really sweet, but I wondered why he seemed so upset. Maybe my little outbursts were starting to get on his nerves and he just couldn't bring himself to say it. I drove to work feeling bad that I could be pushing him away with my mood swings.

When I got to work and booted up my system, there was an email waiting that gave me an explanation, and it was definitely not what I expected.

Dear Rhea,

I really care for you tremendously. In fact, I've fallen in love with you. You're smart, funny, and everything that I've ever wanted in a woman. But there is something that I have to tell you. I know that I'm taking such a cowardly approach by sending this to you via email, but I was too scared to say it on the phone.

I have a two-year-old daughter, and I didn't know how to tell you this before. I'm sure you remember the girl that you heard in the background. Well, that's my daughter's mother. I know you're probably livid now, and I'm very sorry. I just didn't know how to tell you.

I never meant to hurt you, baby. I can explain everything when I get back. It's a long story and I have a lot of issues with my baby's mother. Hopefully you can find it in your heart to forgive me for not being honest.

Although we started out just as friends, I think about you all the time. I would still like to take our relationship to another level if you can find it in your heart to forgive me.

Love, Davis

I nearly fell off my seat! That lying, dirty dog was having phone sex with me while his baby mama was in the same house? Either he was a professional liar, or she was not the brightest star on the Christmas tree. Fuck Davis Hickman. In fact, fuck all niggas. I needed to start dating white men!

I stayed in my office for the rest of the morning, trying to figure out how I could have been such a fool. I thought about my first trip to visit him in Denver. All the baby stuff in the back seat of that car was probably his after all. And now I knew the reason he wanted to stay in a hotel instead of taking me to his home.

Davis called me at work a few hours later. I told my secretary to refuse all calls from him. I blocked his email from my Yahoo and hotmail account and just deleted anything he sent me at work.

For a month, I ignored him. Davis called every night. Each time I saw his name on the caller ID, I let my answering machine pick it up. As soon as I heard his voice on a message, I would delete it. I refused to listen to his sorry ass begging me for forgiveness. I was pissed at myself for letting another man hurt me, but even more disgusted that a small part of me actually missed Davis. It got so bad that I was making myself physically sick.

Ignoring his calls and emails didn't seem to deter him. He just kept trying—until one day in August, when I decided that the only way to make him stop would be to cuss him out.

"Hello," I answered.

"Listen, baby. Before you hang up, I'm being completely honest, Rhea. There is nothing going on between us. She's in college. She's only twenty-one and needed a place to stay temporarily."

I remained quiet as I thought, *I guess he really did have a roommate. He just neglected to tell me it was the mother of his child!*

"I want to tell you the real story, Rhea. Can we see each other the weekend after next?" he begged.

"Nope. I'm busy then. But I'm free next weekend," I challenged him.

"Well, that's not good for me, Rhea," he said quietly.

"Oh, what, your baby mama's going to be there?"

"No, she left last week."

"You make me sick." I hung up.

CHAPTER 11

I felt like I was going out of my mind. The less I talked to Davis, the more I missed him. He did try to call for a few weeks after I hung up on him, but I just wouldn't answer. I would stare at the phone, wishing I could turn back the hands of time. I wanted to go back to before I knew about his child. I wanted to be able to pick up the phone and hear him whisper sweet nothings in my ear, just like he had been doing for months before I learned the truth. My heart was aching, and I didn't know how much longer I could stand the loneliness.

That's when he sent me a letter. I tried to resist reading it, but I couldn't. I think I secretly wanted to believe that something in that letter would make everything all better and we'd be able to start all over. Maybe the letter would contain some explanation good enough to make me trust him again.

As I read the letter, it was like I could hear his sexy voice telling me all about his daughter, Ashley. He said his parents kept the child while Terri, the baby's mother, was finishing school. He included photos of the little girl. She was beautiful. She had innocent eyes that practically shouted *Please forgive my Daddy*, but I was not about to fall for it. I stuffed the photos back in the envelope and dropped it in the trash. I refused to deal with another lying, cheating dog. Davis could have told me about his daughter from the beginning and everything would have been fine.

I tried to stay busy. I had a zillion projects at Sebastian that I was working on, in addition to my book club, sorority and other volunteer obligations that constantly kept me going. The pain of Davis's lies got a little easier to deal with. I even got over the fact that I was no longer having nightly phone sex with him. After all, I had been celibate for a long time after my divorce, so I knew I could deal with it again.

Things finally felt like they were getting back to normal, until August 23, when I heard his voice on my answering machine. Miguel had called me that same day, and though I had forbidden him to even mention Davis's name to me, he felt I should know that Davis's mother had suffered a stroke. I tried to pretend like I didn't care, but a part of my heart ached for him. I knew he was close to his family, so he must have been devastated. That's why I didn't delete the message when I heard his voice.

"Rhea, it's me. I know we haven't talked in a long time, and I know you probably don't ever want to talk to me again. I just wanted you to know that you don't have to worry about me bothering you on the work email anymore. I resigned from Sebastian today. My mother is sick, so I'm going to move back in with my parents. They live three hours away from Denver, so I'll have to find a new job once I get settled. Well, I just wanted you to know . . ." His voice trailed off and then I heard the dial tone.

It took all my strength not to call him back. As mad as I was at him for his lies, I could hear the pain in his voice, and a part of me wanted to be his friend and comfort him. I resisted the urge. I knew that, once he moved, I'd no longer have his home phone number, so I could let go of any feelings for him and move on with my lonely life.

Of course, he didn't make that easy. He called and left a message the following Sunday to let me know that he had made it to his parents' home safely. He left the home number, and though I didn't write it in my address book, I didn't delete the message either.

I was shocked when I got home the next day to find that Davis's mother had called and left me a message saying she wanted to speak to me. She said Davis told her about what happened between us, and she apologized for him. He really loved me, she said. "Please return my call, Rhea. I know Davis gave you the number."

It really pissed me off that Davis was getting her involved, especially if she was sick. Some guys would do anything to try to get some ass. I called to confront him.

"Hello?" A female answered. She sounded too young to be his mother, and I knew he didn't have any sisters, so I wondered who the hell was answering the phone at his mother's house.

"May I speak with Davis?"

"He's not here. Who is this?" She sounded like she was getting ready to take an attitude with me. She almost got cussed out.

Maybe she's just a simple bitch with no home training. I'll have to remember to get her an application for the simple

*bitch parade too. But I don't know who she is yet, so let me
hold my tongue and try to be nice.*

"This is Rhea," I answered in my most professional
voice.

"Oh hi, Rhea. This is Terri." Her voice softened.

*The baby mama Terri? And why does she sound relieved,
as if she thought I was someone else? What the fuck is she
doing there?*

"Uh, Terri, is Davis there?" I struggled to maintain
my composure.

"No, he's not. I'll have him call you back." She hung
up the phone before I could say anything else.

I wanted to throw the phone across the room. I
felt like such an idiot. How could I have ever fallen
for him?

Davis called back a few hours later, trying to sound
like nothing was wrong. "Hey, Rhea, I miss you. I'm
glad you finally decided to call me back."

"Davis, I was calling to cuss your ass out, but you
are not even worth my time. What the fuck is Terri
doing answering your phone?"

"Rhea, it's not what it seems. She's here visiting
Ashley, that's all. And besides, I told her all about you."

"I bet you did, you trifling dog." I hung up.

Two more weeks passed. I kept myself busy at
work, even working from home on Labor Day. Davis
was playing some kind of mind game. He would call
and leave messages on my machine at home, when
he knew I was at work, then leave messages on my
cell phone at night, when he knew I'd have it turned
off. I guess that was his way of trying to get me to call
him back, but I didn't.

Finally, he left a message telling me that I needed
to know the truth. He claimed he loved me, he was
suffering without me, and he wanted us to have a

committed relationship. I deleted that fucking message so fast. I had been played, yet again. I'd poured out my soul, my heart, my body to this man. If nothing else, I thought we were friends, but he seemed to think it was all a game.

One day during the middle of September, he called my home to leave another message, not knowing that I was home sick that day. I couldn't keep anything down and my head kept spinning. Checking the caller ID had become second nature to me, but I was so disoriented from my illness, I picked up the phone without looking at it.

"Hello."

"What's up, Rhea? I expected to hear your answering machine message again." He sounded upbeat.

This bastard is still acting like nothing happened! Terri must've gone back to school, so now he's lonely.

"Nothing."

"You don't sound good. Are you sick?" He sounded concerned, but I knew it was an act.

"Nigga, you ain't concerned about me. I've got the flu. Now get off my phone so I can go back to bed."

"That sounds good to me," he said.

Did he really think that was going to turn me on? "What do you want, asshole?"

"Hey, you don't have to get an attitude and talk to me like I'm dumb."

"Oh, but you are if you think that you can try to come back like everything is fine."

He ignored me and said, "You're sick? Are you throwing up? I hope you're not pregnant."

"Fuck off, Davis. I hope you don't think that shit is funny."

"I'm serious. My mom had a dream about fish the other night. I never told you this, but that last night we were together in Denver, I felt something happening. I know it sounds crazy, but it was something so special, like we had created a new life. I saw little white lights."

"Well, I'm not the one your mother dreamed about. What are you doing? Going down your harem checklist? White lights! Negro, please. Call the fucking *X-Files*. Maybe they can track down the lights."

"I'm serious, Rhea."

"Davis, leave me alone." I hung up on him.

Another week passed by, and I'd been in bed for seven whole days, sick as a dog. I hated doctors and medicine, so I'd been taking Echinacea, trying to get over this on my own. When I couldn't take it anymore, I finally went to the doctor, where I got the shock of my life. He did a routine blood test and told me, "Well, your white blood cell count shows that you did have a virus, but I think there's another explanation for your queasy stomach." I had no idea what he was talking about, and I guess he knew that from the blank expression on my face. "You're pregnant, Rhea," he explained.

Oh, shit! I mean, I hadn't been feeling well, but I never suspected I was pregnant. My cycles had been sporadic my whole life. I'd sometimes go months without a period, so I wasn't alarmed when I missed a few this time. Maybe I should have listened to Davis's ass when he said his mother had a dream.

While I was at the office, I went ahead and got tested for HIV and any other STD that nasty-ass nigga could have given me. The doctor talked to me for a while about how to have a healthy pregnancy and gave me the name of a good obstetrician. I was still in shock, when I left the doctor's office with a prescription for prenatal vitamins in my hand. I called Davis as soon as I got back home.

"Hello."

Thank God he answered.

"Davis, I'm pregnant." I just blurted it out.

"Look, I figured you were. I don't have any money to send you right now. With the move and all, I'm a little strapped for cash. But I'm still waiting on a few checks from Sebastian and my 401K balance. If you'll pay for the abortion, I'll pay you back next month," he said as calmly as if we were chatting about the weather.

"What?"

"Look, Rhea, why do you have to give me a hard time about this? I know you've got plenty of money from that rich family of yours. I told you I'll send you the money as soon as I can get it."

"That's not the point, Davis."

"Well, then what is?"

I hesitated, still not believing what I was about to say. "Would it be so bad if I kept the baby?"

"Don't even think about it, Rheonique. I can't afford another baby. And besides, you said if you ever got pregnant that you'd have an abortion."

"I said *probably* have an abortion. I did a lot of thinking on the way home from the doctor's office, and now that I know there's a life inside of me, I don't think I could go through with it."

"Rhea, you're talking crazy. How is a career woman like you gonna raise a baby all on your own?"

"That's just it," I said quietly. "I don't want to be alone. Every child deserves a chance to be with its mother *and* father. Maybe we could give it a try, Davis. Maybe we could be together."

"Girl, please!" He laughed. "You've barely spoken to me in months, and now you wanna talk about being together? There must be something wrong with your hormones now that you're pregnant, 'cause you're talking crazy."

"No, Davis," I insisted. "I think it's the opposite. I think it was my hormones that made me overreact when I found out about Terri. I mean, you said she means nothing to you. And I think it's admirable that you're taking responsibility for Ashley. Most fathers wouldn't do that. I want you to be a father to our child too."

"Rhea, stop tripping. You know as well as I do that we could never really be together. Your little social class structure would be turned upside down if anyone knew that Rheonique Ramirez Baptiste LaDay, daughter and heiress to the LaDay cosmetics fortune, had a baby out of wedlock with a commoner."

"That's not true. I don't care what my family says anymore. I love you. I'll even marry you if you want." I tried not to cry. I don't know if it was my hormones making me so emotional, but I knew I was terrified by the thought of having this baby alone. I now knew that I would never be able to have an abortion, but I didn't want to be a single mother. In my heart, I wanted to find a way to work things out with Davis. "I love you, Davis."

"Give me a break! One week ago you were cursing me out and hanging up on me, and now you're telling me you love me. Forgive me if I say you're full of bullshit." The phone went dead.

I cried myself to sleep that night, and for several nights afterwards.

A few days later, I felt strong enough to go back to work. I came home to an unexpected message on my answering machine. "Rhea, this is Davis's mother, Mrs. Hickman. Davis told me everything. I just want you to know that I think you're doing the right thing. That baby you're carrying is my grandchild, and I couldn't stand it if you had an abortion. I know Davis has feelings for you. He's scared about being a daddy again, but he really does want to be with you. Please call me back so we can talk. I want to do what I can to help you."

Two days later, I finally gathered the courage to return her call.

"Hello." A young female answered. The voice was not the same as the one on my answering machine, so I knew it wasn't Mrs. Hickman. I assumed it was Terri. She was probably just visiting Ashley again. This time, I didn't feel threatened by her.

"Hi, Terri. This is Rhea."

"Oh, this isn't Terri. This is Noel." She sounded like she had a little attitude, but I answered her politely. I had younger cousins, so I knew that teenagers hated to be interrupted when they were on the phone. She was probably just on the other line with her little boyfriend.

"Oh. Hi, Noel. Are you one of Davis's cousins?"

"No, I'm his son's mother," she said with even more attitude than before.

"'His son's mother'?" I nearly choked on the words. *What the fuck?*

"That's what I said. His son's mother. Who are you?"

"Noel, this is . . ." *Keep it together, Rhea! Don't break down. Don't you dare cry in front of this little bitch.* "Can you have him call Rhea as soon as he gets in?" I was shaking so badly I could barely stand up.

* * *

Davis called about an hour later. I snatched the phone, ready to cuss his ass out, but he started talking fast. "I was going to tell you. I swear I was, but then you called and said you were pregnant and didn't know what to do. You see, Terri and Noel were roommates. When me and Terri broke up, Noel and I started kicking it. She got pregnant, and that weekend I told you not to come, it was because she had my son that weekend."

This isn't real. It has to be a bad dream.

"What? So, let me get this straight. You had baby mama number one there one week. The next week, baby mama number two has a baby? Then you get me pregnant, and now I'm baby mama three. Do we all get motherfucking T-shirts or something to wear to the baby mama convention? Davis Hickman, you are trash!"

"Rhea, that's not fair, and you know it. It's not like you put up much of a fight when I said I didn't want to wear a condom. You can take some of the blame for getting pregnant, you know."

Damn, he had a point, didn't he?

"My parents are keeping my son now. Noel is only here to see him," he offered as an explanation.

"What the fuck kind of shit do y'all have going over there? You got two baby mamas that go to the same school, and your parents are raising both of the babies? Y'all some strange motherfuckers." I thought about the message I'd received from Mrs. Hickman. Shit, she was probably happy I was pregnant so she could keep my baby too!

"I know it sounds strange, but I can explain. Please, please, I'm begging you. Let's meet face to face so we can talk."

I don't know if it was because I was carrying this

man's child or if the prenatal vitamins were causing an allergic reaction that somehow depleted my common sense, but I felt myself weakening for Davis. I was not the same strong person that would sit and laugh at those stupid women on talk shows. I was slowly becoming a Jerry Springer guest.

"I need to see you, Rhea." He began crying.

There just has to be some type of explanation. I need to at least let him try to explain.

"I need to see you too, Davis, so we can talk. I'll come this weekend."

"Noel is coming back to visit our son this weekend. It wouldn't be good for me right now if anyone found out about you being pregnant."

"Well, if you're not sleeping with either one of your baby mamas, why does it matter?"

"It's just—I don't really have any legal paperwork for custody. I only have oral agreements that my family will keep the kids until they get out of school. I just don't want to have a situation where I could potentially lose my kids."

"Well, I'm not showing yet, so you don't have to worry. I'll keep your little secret for now. Besides, I'd like to meet your mom." *Damn, I am becoming pathetic.*

"No, boo. Just wait, okay?" he pleaded.

"Okay." I tried to sound disappointed. Maybe if I took the less direct approach I could get him to agree. No such luck.

"That's my girl. Hey, so when are you going to have the abortion?"

"Davis, I'm keeping the baby. My decision has nothing to do with you. I know what I said before, but now I don't think it's right to kill a child."

Davis went off. "You know what, Rhea—every year for the past three years it has been some shit in my life keeping me from getting to the next level. I'm telling you now, you'd better get rid of it. As far as I'm concerned, I only have two kids."

He hung up then called back about five minutes later. I refused to pick up.

Between the crying and the sucking snot sounds he was making on my answering machine and the baby inside of me giving me morning sickness, I'd had enough of the Hickman bloodline for one day.

"I'm sorry I yelled at you. It's just that I wouldn't have slept with you had I known that you were against abortion," he said in a pathetic, whiny voice. He filled up my entire answering machine memory with that 'woe is me' shit.

On any other occasion, I would have called one of my girls so we could laugh about a man leaving crying messages like a bitch. I was too embarrassed, though, to let anybody know about this debacle.

As I thought about my situation, I started feeling really stupid. He was right about one thing—I had to accept the fact that I was just as much to blame for the pregnancy. And I did tell him that I would have an abortion if I ever got pregnant. If I had told him I wanted kids, would he have worn a condom? *Hell no, Rhea! He didn't ask me my views on children until the last night we were together, after he'd already ejaculated inside of me a million times. Who in the hell does he think he is?* I fell asleep with these conflicting thoughts running through my head.

I woke up the next day around 5:00 A.M. Thank God it was Saturday. I was too exhausted to even think about getting out of bed. It was time to take care of me and my baby. At exactly 8:00, I called Tasha's mom and cancelled my Big Sister appointment. I was going to resign from teaching at the adult education center the following Monday. This morning sickness was kicking my butt, and I really needed to rest.

The telephone rang around noon.

"Hello," I answered cautiously. I wasn't in the mood for Davis and his bullshit.

"Hi, princess." It was my father.

"Hi, Daddy. How are you?" I tried to sound like my usual upbeat self.

"Fine. I was just calling to see how my favorite daughter was doing."

"Well, your *only* daughter is fine." I laughed for the first time in days. It had only been a few short weeks since I'd spoken to my dad. The thought of his sardonic sense of humor and his upbeat attitude always made my sorrows melt away.

"How's Mom?"

"She's Mom." We both laughed.

My mother was Miss Black World 1964. I think sometimes she thought she was still the reigning beauty queen, because she expected people to always be doting over her. Actually, Mom would fit in real well in India, because she was a firm believer in the caste system. "Everyone has their station in life," she always said. If Davis thought I was stuck up, he'd have an aneurysm if he ever met Veronique Baptiste LaDay.

Dad was flying into Miami that afternoon. He had a four-hour layover in Atlanta and called to take me out to dinner.

Two hours later, at the Atlanta Hartsfield Airport, I heard my named being called out over the P.A. system.

"Rheonique LaDay, please meet your party at the Delta baggage claim area."

After ten minutes and a few "excuse mes," I squeezed myself through the crowd and found Dad.

"Hi, baby!" He hugged me and gave me a kiss on the forehead then looked me up and down. "Girl, your hips look like they're spreading. You'd better leave those Doritos alone."

My heart skipped a beat. My father and I had a special bond, but was it really possible he sensed something? "Oh Daddy, why do you still tease me like I'm a little girl?" I said playfully to conceal my nerves.

I looked at my father. In my eyes, he was still the most handsome man in the world. At age sixty, he still had women fawning over him. Roberto Ramirez, CEO and chairman of LaDay cosmetics, was the most charming, intelligent man on the planet. Funny, he never wanted to fly on a private jet like a lot of CEOs. He said he wanted to mingle amongst the masses. Unlike my mother, he was totally down-to-earth. My Dad was my best friend. I wondered if I had a little girl, would she and Davis be so close?

"Is everything okay, Rhea?" He knew me so well. I never could hide my feelings from him for very long. I damn sure would try, though, because I was not ready to tell him that his little girl was pregnant.

"Yes, Dad, let's get out of here." I gave him a big hug.

"What was that for?" he asked, surprised.

"For being the best daddy in the world." Davis was not going to dampen my afternoon with my father. "How does Enoch's sound? They make a mean paté."

"Oh, I'm sorry. I called and made reservations at Adolph's for seven o'clock. I know how much you like their lobster."

"Adolph's is great, Dad. They have a wonderful spinach artichoke dip that they serve with Wasa crackers."

"So, what kind of music are you into lately?" he asked after we got inside my new Jaguar convertible.

He'd helped me do the wheeling and dealing for this latest toy. He began looking through my CD case. My repertoire of music ranged from Yani to Ludacris. Dad settled on Sade, and out blasted the lyrics "Somebody already broke my heart." I immediately thought of Davis.

"What's wrong, baby?" he asked again as he touched my shoulder.

"Oh, nothing. I think I need new glasses," I lied and wiped away a tear. I squeezed his hand. "I'm glad you're here, Daddy."

Adolph's was by far the best seafood restaurant in the area. The shrimp was imported from Hilton Head, and the crab was shipped in fresh daily from Casco Bay, Maine.

We walked into the lobby and waited for the host to acknowledge us. The host was engrossed in a conversation with a patron.

"I'm a singer. This is my day job until I can get a record label to sign me," he said in a phony southern accent. He reminded me of a black version of Miguel, gay and proud.

After a few minutes of listening to him lie about himself, I'd taken about all that I could of his little performance. I cleared my throat. "We have reservations, two for LaDay."

The host gave me a look that said, *You'd better be glad I'm not cooking your food because I'd spit in it.*

Dad laughed as the singer led us to our table.

I'd always heard that when a woman is pregnant her sense of smell is heightened. I soon found out that was not just an old wives' tale. I was nauseous and lightheaded as soon as we sat down. The smell of seafood was sheer torture. My head felt like it was on the guillotine block, ready to be chopped off.

After three trips to the bathroom, I was sure I was close to death. "Daddy, I don't feel well. I think we need to leave." We paid for our drinks and left.

"Dad, do you mind driving?" I asked.

"Sure, sweetie. Are you okay?" He touched my forehead.

I nodded, praying he'd believe me when I said, "I'll be okay." I tossed him the keys.

As we were pulling out of the parking lot, he called Mom on his cell phone to let her know he'd made it into Atlanta safely. "Rhea's not feeling well," he added.

"Your mom wants to say hi." He passed the phone to me.

"Hi, Mommy." I tried to sound happy.

"Your dad says you're ill. What's wrong? And I'd prefer if you would speak to me in French. You and your brother never use your French language."

My mother could be such a bitch sometimes, so harsh and demanding, and this was no exception. I could barely think straight, and she wanted me to start speaking in a language I rarely used, except in her presence.

My parents always had this ongoing feud as to whose language should be spoken primarily in the household. Mom thought her native French language was more regal. Dad thought his native Spanish language was more practical.

"Just the flu, I think," I said quickly in French. My heart started racing. There's something about mothers that makes you nervous when you lie. It's almost like you're transparent and they can see right through you. Dads will believe anything; however, a black mama knows the real deal.

"So, why haven't you called lately, darling?" she asked.

"Just been working," I replied meekly.

"That's funny. I've called your office a few times. Your secretary told me you've been out ill."

"It's no big deal. Just a little stomach virus."

She was silent for a long moment before saying, "Is that so, Rhea?" She didn't believe a word I said.

I held the phone away from my ear, knowing she was not going to give up that easily.

"Don't ignore your mom," Dad yelled loud enough for her to hear then winked at me.

"Were you holding the phone away from your ear, Rheonique?" she asked.

Okay, I'd done it. I was always Rhea unless she got pissed. I rolled my eyes and gave Dad an evil look.

"No, ma'am. I was about to sneeze and didn't want to hurt your ears by sneezing into the telephone."

"Don't lie to me, young lady. I'm your mother. I gave you birth. I know when my little daffodil is fibbing. And furthermore—" She sounded as if she wanted to say something important, but stopped herself abruptly then changed the subject.

"Well, look, hon. I've got to run. The massage therapist will be here momentarily. You know, the funniest thing happened. I had a dream about fish the other night. Oh, well . . . It's probably nothing. Maria's immoral daughter is probably pregnant again."

Maria was the maid, and her daughter, Ponia, who was twenty-six, had six kids.

"All right, Mom. Love you. Bye."

"Rhea?" she said before I could disconnect the call.

"Yes, ma'am." I was so afraid, my voice was trembling.

"Please call your brother, and telephone me Monday after you've found a physician to tell you what type of *virus* you have," she said rather smugly. Damn.

If she hadn't figured it out already, it was only a matter of time before she would know my secret.

I was starting to get nauseous again and began praying silently that I wouldn't puke until after he was out of the car.

"I'm sorry for ruining dinner, Daddy."

"It's okay, sweetheart. I'll just get something to eat at the airport," he said then kissed me goodbye and left to catch his flight.

I had to pull over on the side of the road at least six times while I drove home.

As soon as I got home I puked again, took a bath, and fixed a nice, healthy dinner of crackers and seltzer water. That was about all I could hold down. I put *Motown Sings Sinatra* in my CD player and rested on the couch with my dogs.

My mind wandered back to the phone conversation with my mother. Did she know? And if so, how? I couldn't believe how pathetic I was, behaving like a high-school kid. I was a grown-ass woman with plenty of space for a baby. In fact, my house was so large I could rent out five bedrooms and still be comfortable. I didn't need my mom's approval to have a baby. Or did I?

"Call your brother." Mom's voice kept resonating in my ears as I closed my eyes to sleep. I would call Toussaint the next day.

Something told me to turn my ringer off for the night. About fifteen minutes later, I heard my answering machine turn on. Yes indeed, I'd thought up the devil. I laughed out loud as I listened to my brother's voice.

"Hi, Rhea. This is your long-lost brother. Give me a call whenever you can. Take care. By the way, Marcus called me. Why won't you return his calls?"

"Aaah!" I punched the pillow on the couch and woke up Rosencrantz. He barked at me then jumped on the floor.

Toussaint really knew how to piss me off. He was always looking out for Marcus. In his opinion, Marcus could do no wrong. "He's my frat brother," Toussaint would always say, whenever I said anything negative about Marcus.

My brother and I never had a normal sibling relationship. Toussaint always treated people like pawns in a chess game. He, like my mother, lived by the philosophy that people should stay in their respective places, and of course, his place should always be on top.

One summer, I brought home a little girl I'd met on the playground. After being questioned, it was determined by Toussaint that she was not on our level because she didn't have a father at home. He said so to the girl's face. I cried then looked to Mom to scold him. Instead, she nodded her head in approval at what he was saying. In fact, she looked downright proud of him.

Actually, if Toussaint weren't my brother and I met him on the street, I probably wouldn't like him very much. He was still single at thirty-six, which was not by coincidence. My brother would only date a certain type of woman. She had to be rich, beautiful, and educated. It wasn't too hard to find a woman to meet those qualifications, but it didn't take long for most of them to figure out his last requirement. Above all, his woman had to be subservient. When they finally figured this out, each woman in his life had turned and run the other way.

Toussaint wanted a corporate June Cleaver, an idea that matched as well as two left shoes. I laughed when I realized that must be the same kind of woman that Davis Edwinn Hickmann thought he was getting in me.

The answering machine clicked off after Toussaint left his message. I might think about calling him back in the morning, and then again, maybe I'd never talk to anyone ever again. I rolled over on my side and curled up with my dogs, realizing how truly depressing my life was becoming.

CHAPTER 12

Monday was such a busy day at work, I was glad to have an excuse to leave early. I had a doctor's appointment. I was so excited about my first ultrasound, although I felt guilty that I was more than three months pregnant and just beginning to get prenatal care. I made up for it by buying and subscribing to as many magazines as I could find on pregnancy and childbirth.

It was a lonely ride to the doctor's office. Months earlier, my commute didn't seem so long because I always had Davis to talk to. Now I felt guilty that I'd sort of pushed all my other obligations, friends, and sometimes my family away since he came into my life. I went into the office and spotted a nurse that used to work for Marcus. She smiled, so I knew my business would probably be on the 6:00 news.

Once the doctor came in and performed the ultrasound, I got some news of my own that nearly killed me. I almost fell off the table when the doctor pointed out two babies with two little heartbeats. Their sex

could not be determined, but there were definitely
two little heads and two little hearts on the screen. I
gasped when I saw it, not out of joy, but out of fear.
What in the hell was I going to do with twins? I had
less than five months to prepare, and I was totally
alone. I was in total disbelief.

They looked like aliens. What would I do if it they
looked like little gnomes or hobbits when they came
out? Maybe I could put a big hat on their heads to
cover them up. Was there plastic surgery available for
babies? But if all else failed, maybe they could be rap-
pers. I mean, the Ying Yang twins did well for themselves.

Stop, Rheonique! You're not ugly, and neither is Davis.

Still, I wondered what my babies would look like. I
already knew what my mother's expectations would
be. I could hear her saying, "What if they have nappy
hair? What if they're too dark? Now, Rheonique,"
she'd say, "you know you can't bring any ugly babies
around here." Funny, my grandfather was black as
coal, but because my mother was light-skinned, Mom
still had some sort of color complex.

God give me the strength to deal with this situation.

Two weeks later, Davis called me at midnight. I saw
his name on the caller ID but answered anyway, hoping maybe we could call a truce. I thought he should
know that I was having twins.

"Hello?"

"What's up? This is Davis."

"Hello, Mr. Hickman."

"Oh, it's like that now, is it?"

"Yes! What the fuck do you want, nigga?" So much
for calling a truce. My hormones had my moods swing-

ing all over the place lately, and all of a sudden I was full of rage.

"I was just calling to let you know I'll go with you to have the abortion." He sounded like he thought he was doing me a favor.

"Fuck you, Davis! I ain't having no fucking abortion."

"What is your problem, girl? I don't want to have kids spread out all over the world. With my first baby I had to go through so much bullshit." He sighed. "You don't understand, Rhea."

I was good and pissed. "If you went through it, it's because you put up with her shit. Besides, I'm a grown-ass woman. I wouldn't be playing custody games with you like these young-ass girls you like dealing with. I just want you to want to be a father."

"I hate to say this," he told me, "but I didn't even want the second baby, and sometimes I find myself looking at my own flesh and blood with contempt. I don't want another baby that I don't know if I'll ever *be able* to love. Hell, I don't know if the second one is even mine."

I held my tongue on that. If Noel was nasty enough to sleep with her friend's man, there was no telling how many other potential fathers there were. *But Davis better not be implying I've been with anyone else but him! Shit, I was practically a nun when I met him, as long as I'd been celibate.*

"Well, just pretend my baby is not yours either. I'm going to bed."

"Okay, look, Rhea. Don't hang up. It doesn't have to be like this. If you're really going to keep this baby, I'd like for us to talk. Do you think you could come out here?"

"Oh, is it my week again so soon?" I asked sarcastically. "We are on the baby mama rotation, right?"

"I don't want anything. Just to talk, okay? I'll fly you out on Saturday."

"Why in the hell would I come see your ignorant, lying ass? Give me one reason why." I was developing a splitting headache.

"Have I cussed you out? Have I raised my voice at you?" he asked.

"As a matter of fact, I don't think you have, you punk-ass bitch. At least not tonight."

"Rhea, are you that angry at me? When did you start talking like some old ghetto trick?" That comment hurt a little, since in most situations I was able to maintain my class, but Davis just seemed to bring out the worst in me. It was that passion thing again. All that fire and passion I felt for him in the beginning had transformed into an anger just as strong.

"Since I found out that you were a ghetto-ass, baby-making loser." I hung up and turned off the ringer.

I went into Sebastian the next day and handed in my resignation. I needed some time to deal with the mess I'd made of my life, and I didn't want anything to distract me. Besides, it wasn't like I needed the paycheck. My parents had set up trust funds for me and my brother when we were younger, and I still had enough money in mine to live well for the rest of my life.

Within ten minutes, Stan was blowing up my phone to find out what was going on. I didn't tell him I was pregnant, but just that I had some personal issues that required my full attention right now.

He advised me not to make a rash decision. "Why don't you just take some vacation time, Rhea? Take a few weeks to think about what you want to do."

I agreed, realizing that it was probably best not to burn my bridges just yet. That way, I could always go back to work if I chose to after the babies were born.

When Davis called that evening, he started begging me again to go to Colorado, just to talk. I accepted, but made it clear his ass would be paying for my ticket. "I have an appointment on Friday morning, so don't make my flight reservations before four," I instructed.

Davis picked me up at the airport late—no kiss, no hug, no hello. He didn't even help me with my bags. "How was it?" he asked after we got into the car.

"What? The flight?"

"No, your appointment this morning," he said as if I should have known what he was talking about. "Do you want to talk about it?"

"Um, no. But if you really want to know, the doctor said the corn on my big toe had nothing to do with being pregnant." *Why the hell is he asking me about my appointment anyway?*

"What are you talking about, Rhea? When you said you had an appointment this morning, I thought you meant to have the abortion."

"What? You must be deaf. I have told you too many times that I will not be having an abortion! And furthermore, you didn't even bother to call to see if I was okay since you thought I'd had an abortion."

He was such an ass! I impersonated him. "How was it, Rhea? Like it's a fucking piece of chicken or something. How was the abortion, Rhea? How would you rate it on a scale of one to ten? Like you're a goddamn abortion connoisseur. " I slapped his face as hard as I could.

He clenched his fist. "Why did you hit me?"

"Because you're an ignorant-ass bastard, Davis." I

looked down at his hand. "Nigga, you better unball your fist, with your punk ass."

He straightened his fingers. "You are going to fuck up my life, Rhea. I swear, Terri is crazy. She's going to take my baby away from me."

"Take her to court. You have the baby now anyway. Just put it in writing. I'll give you the money."

"No!" he protested. "I don't want my daughter to hate me one day." He began pounding on the steering wheel.

"What do you mean?" I checked my hair in the mirror and tried to pretend I didn't see the look of disdain Davis was giving me out the corner of his eye. Terri might have scared him, but she was nothing to me.

He didn't answer me, and we rode in silence all the way to his house. I fell asleep until Davis pulled into the driveway of a modest, single-level brick home. Out came a little boy, who gave me a hug as I got out of the car.

Oh, Lord. Now, I know Davis said his son was just born. Please don't tell me this is another child I didn't know about.

"That's my nephew, Nicholas," Davis said. "My older brother can't keep himself out of jail, and the boy's mother ain't worth shit. Little Nicholas had been put into foster care, so my parents adopted him." This place was starting to sound like a damn daycare center.

There was a little girl standing behind Nicholas. I approached her. "And who are you, pretty girl?" She shrugged. "You must be Ashley. Your dad has told me so much about you." I gave her a big lollipop.

She took her pacifier out of her mouth and stuck the lollipop in then grabbed my left hand.

Nicholas grabbed my right hand and led me up

the driveway. These two sweet little children made me momentarily forget this horrible situation I was in. I hoped my babies would always have that same ability to make me feel better.

I walked inside the house and finally met the woman who had claimed to be so happy that I was pregnant by Davis. His mother, Willie Mae Hickman, was the most beautiful woman I had ever seen. She had very dark black skin, with high cheekbones. She looked like a beautiful Indian matriarch.

She spoke first. "Come here, baby. I've been waiting so long to meet you. You are such a pretty little thing."

We hugged, and she touched my belly. "Hi there. I'm your grandma."

I held back tears.

Mrs. Hickman was the only other person on the planet besides myself that happily acknowledged my children. I really wished I could confide in my family, but the timing hadn't felt right yet.

"Thank you, Mrs. Hickman," I whispered.

She motioned for me to sit down on the couch. "Have a seat, Rhea. We don't have much, but make yourself at home."

Suddenly, I felt at peace, a feeling I hadn't felt in a long time. The house was tidy, not extravagant like my parents' home, but there was such a sense of love. Now I understood why Davis quit his job when his mother became ill.

"Hey, gal, you must be the newest baby mama." I knew who that deep voice belonged to. Davis had told me his father always said the first thing that came into his head, no matter how ignorant it sounded.

"Hello, Mr. Hickman." I extended my hand and stood up.

"Girl, call me Ernest. We're family now."

I was grateful for the warm reception I was getting from his parents, until I noticed the look Ernest gave his son. You know, the one that says, *Yeah, I bet you tore that pussy up*. Now I knew where Davis got it from.

We exchanged hugs, and Ernest looked down at my belly. "You look like you carrying kind of high. I think it's going to be a girl."

Just then, a baby began crying. Willie Mae left and came back with a little chubby baby. "This is your little stepson." She laughed and set him in my arms.

"Hi, little Davis." I touched his soft little fingers. I couldn't believe the way I felt, holding this baby. I expected I would feel some kind of resentment toward this child, but there was none. I fell instantly in love with the baby, and tried to pretend I didn't see them checking me out. I know they wanted to see how I interacted with the kids.

Willie Mae said, "Oh yeah, you got that natural mothering instinct. I can see you're going to be a good mother."

Davis, on the other hand, didn't seem impressed, and was behaving extremely inhospitably toward me.

Well, what the hell did you invite me here for, then?

His parents noticed his sour attitude and tried to make amends for their son's curt behavior. I actually started to enjoy the way they scolded his ass like he was still a damn child. After all, he was acting like one.

Meanwhile, I had a blast with the kids. We played outside; then I helped Ms. Hickman with dinner. I gave all three kids a bath, read them a bedtime story, and taught them a prayer in Spanish.

I went to sleep that night hoping Davis would have a better attitude the next day.

The next morning, Davis was just as foul, so I stayed out of his way. He kept coming around me, trying to pick a fight. Since I was in his parents' home, I tried to remain ladylike and refused to respond to his obnoxious remarks.

After a while, though, I just couldn't take it. I'd taken enough of his crap for one day. He had some nerve to invite me to visit then treat me like a dog. If nothing else motivated him to act like a decent human being, I'd think that since I was carrying his baby, he would show some respect.

When he made a snide remark about how he should open up a daycare center with all the kids he was going to have, I replied, "Aw, poor Davis. Maybe you could trade in your car for a twelve-passenger van. Surely you'll have another baby mama next year."

Willie Mae walked into the living room, while Davis and I were arguing. "You all stop that now." She tripped over the telephone cord and almost fell. She picked up the phone. "I can't believe the telephone didn't ring one time today. It's normally ringing off the hook."

Davis took this distraction as his chance to get away from me, now that I wasn't taking his verbal abuse. "Beats me, Ma." He glared at me then walked out of the room.

Willie Mae sat down on the sofa with me. She picked up the cordless phone to make sure it was working. That's when she discovered the ringer was turned off. She turned it back on. "I wonder who did that?"

At first she thought it was the one telephone, but then she checked and discovered that every phone in the house had been turned off. She turned each one back on then came back and sat with me.

We watched some mindless reality show on television, and I was glad to see there were still people in this world with problems crazier than mine. Davis actually came in and watched with us for a while, but when the telephone rang at exactly midnight, he jumped up to answer it and left the room, whispering into the receiver.

At 12:15 the phone rang again. Davis must have answered it from another room, because he never came back into the living room with me and Willie Mae.

I fell asleep on the couch.

Willie Mae woke me up some time later. "You go sleep in Davis's bed, baby. He can sleep on the couch." She handed me a beautiful, handmade blanket. It was a rich, dark red tapestry print with lots of Afrocentric colors woven into circles.

"That's beautiful, Willie Mae. Did you make it?"

"Yes, I did. I was pregnant with a little girl right before I had Davis, and I made this for her. She passed away."

"Oh, I'm so sorry."

"Don't worry about it. Tell you what." She kissed my forehead. "I want you to keep this blanket and give it to my grandbaby. There's something special about you. I like you already. I don't have as much money as your family, but the least I can do is give my new little baby this blanket." She squealed. "I'm so excited about the baby, Rhea."

Should I go ahead and break the news about the twins?

Before I could say anything, she started up again.

"And don't worry about Davis. He'll come around. He acted like this with both of his other baby mamas, but he loves those kids."

"I don't know, Willie Mae. He was pretty pissed when I said I wouldn't have an abortion."

"Well, I really like you, and I can't wait. I really am happy that you didn't have it." She hugged me. "You need rest. Don't worry. I'll deal with my son."

I looked up at the clock at the end of the hallway. It was 2:45 A.M. I excused myself and went to Davis's room. When I passed by the childrens' room, I heard Davis whispering in there. He was still on the phone! I didn't even bother to go in and say anything to him.

When I got in the bedroom, I couldn't resist snooping around his bedroom. I opened the closet and found a bright red teddy hanging in there. In his top drawer I found the biggest dildo I had ever seen in my life. It was much larger than the one he'd used on me.

I wondered which of those nasty girls that shit belonged to. *This shit better be old, because if I find out he's been using it on someone recently, his ass is dead.*

I was afraid of what I might find on the sheets if I pulled the covers down, so I put Willie Mae's blanket down and slept on top of the bedspread.

What the hell was I doing there? I could hear my Great-Grandma Ann now. "Child, that house is full of lust demons."

Yes, Grandma Ann, and it was lust demons that got me in the situation I'm in now.

I fell asleep quickly, but not for long. At around 4:30, Davis crept into the room and woke me with his head between my legs. I was still groggy from sleep, but when I realized that the warm sensation I felt was his tongue circling my clit, I tried to sit up.

"What the hell are you doing?" I whispered, not wanting to wake anybody else in the small house.

"Shhh. Just sit back and enjoy it, Rhea. I'm so sorry I was so mean to you today. Let me make it up to you," he said between slurps.

As much as I wanted to protest, his tongue was performing miracles. Before I knew it, I was rolling around, moaning, begging him for more.

I'd heard that pregnancy can make some women extremely horny, and I guess I was falling into that category. I totally forgot about his nasty attitude, the secretive phone calls, and the dildo in his dresser drawer. At the moment, all that mattered was getting me some.

"Damn, girl, this is the best sex I ever had," he said as he climbed on top to enter me.

When we were finished, we lay in the dark together for a while. He whispered to me, "Hey, it's after midnight. It's my birthday. This is the best birthday present that I could ever get. I love cumming in you, Rhea. I love pregnant pussy."

"That's obvious," I said with attitude. Now that I'd had something to satisfy my lust, I was starting to feel stupid for putting up with his funky attitude and still giving up the pussy.

"What's obvious?"

"That you love pregnant pussy. You have a new baby every year."

"That's not very funny, Rhea?"

I turned over. He was stupid.

When we woke up the next morning, Davis asked if I would like to take a drive to the mountains. He seemed to have turned over a new leaf. Even after my sarcastic comment before we fell asleep, he was still treating me with respect, like he did before he found out I was pregnant.

I decided to go with him, thinking it would do us

some good to get away together to talk things through. Maybe there was some hope for us after all.

We drove to the mountains and rented a cabin then went to an outdoor amphitheatre to watch a play.

Later, Davis took a nap, so I went out and bought him a birthday cake and some candles.

Once I got back to the cabin, I did the unspeakable—I made him a steak. To my pregnant senses, the smell of it cooking was enough to make me want to barf, but I soldiered through it.

We spent the rest of the week at the cabin, and things went pretty smoothly. Of course, we had plenty of sex, and that always kept Davis in a good mood. We avoided the subject of my pregnancy as much as possible, since neither one of us really wanted to fight.

Before I found out about his other kids, and before I was pregnant, Davis and I had been getting along so well. I think both of us just wanted to escape back to that time again, and the best way to do it was to avoid any touchy subjects.

Willie Mae was so happy when we returned to her house and she saw how well we were getting along. "See," she said to me. "I told you not to worry about Davis. I know that boy loves you."

A part of me didn't want to leave when it was time for my flight back to Atlanta. I really liked the kids, and other than the fact that his family referred a little too often to my wealth, I liked his parents too.

I began to imagine me, Davis, and all of the kids living together, having a barbeque, living life. That fantasy didn't last long, though. *Who am I fooling? Even if I were the perfect stepmom, I'd still have to deal with two other women. Oh Lord, Rhea, where have your standards gone?*

There was a time in my life, not too long ago, that I would not have accepted a man who had children. When I married Marcus, I was headed for the perfect life as a doctor's wife. We would live in a big, fancy house, drive expensive cars, have beautiful children, and be the envy of every other couple. Then reality hit. Not everything was as it seemed, and mister perfect doctor turned out to be a cheating dog.

Maybe it was time to re-examine my standards. Yes, Davis did have some babies, and no, his family didn't have money, but there were other things that were more important. Davis made me laugh when I thought I would never laugh again.

Watching him with his kids, I knew he would be a good father, not like Marcus, whose ass was always at work. Plus, Mrs. Hickman was so down-to-earth, not stuck up like my own mother. Maybe she could teach me a thing or two about relaxing. And of course, there was the sex with Davis, which was so damn good I didn't know if I could ever give it up.

As I sat on the plane flying back to Atlanta, I began to give serious thought to the possibility of moving to Colorado.

CHAPTER 13

We visited one another every other weekend for the next two months. The money Davis had saved while working at Sebastian was pretty much gone, so I started paying for all the plane tickets. I didn't mind, though, because we were happy together. He had started to show interest in my pregnancy and actually seemed excited when I told him we were having twins. I was getting closer to his other children and his parents, and I could imagine us having a happy life together.

I stopped going to book club meetings and avoided my friends like the plague. Cheryl's grandmother had died, and I was relieved that she spent a month in Arizona.

It was becoming impossible to hide my belly. I lied to my parents and told them I'd be out of the country on assignment for Sebastian. That way, I wouldn't have to go visit them, and my mother wouldn't try to call the Atlanta office looking for me. I didn't want her to find out that I had taken a leave of absence from work.

I called my parents just often enough so they wouldn't suspect anything. I changed everything about my daily routine, even switching grocery stores for fear I'd run into someone I knew. I never answered my home phone number, only my cell.

I could only avoid everyone for so long, though. One weekend, after returning home from visiting Davis, I saw Cheryl's car parked in my driveway. Although I lived in a gated community with a guard, she was listed as family and had a sticker on her car to gain access into the housing development. She also had a key to my house.

I knew my time was up. I couldn't hide anymore, so I took a deep breath and opened the front door.

She was on the couch in my living room. "What the fuck?" She held up copies of the *Parenting, Baby,* and *New Mom* magazines I'd left on the coffee table. Then she looked down at my belly. "Oh, Rhea, why didn't you tell me?"

I had no choice but to tell her everything. The façade was finally over. It was time to face reality.

"First of all, are you crazy?" she asked after I told her the story. "He's sleeping with one or both of them, and you're stupid to believe he's not."

"Well, maybe . . ."

"Well, maybe hell! Why does he have to *choose* the weekend to see you if there's nothing going on? I'm telling you, Rhea, those two little babies you're carrying is not the end of the world. You are too old with too much going for you to be competing with some little young-ass twenty-one-year-old girls. And his ass must be retarded, as old as he is, for messing around with them in the first place." She took a deep breath.

"I can excuse their stupidity. They obviously have been sharing him for a while, but what is your stupid-ass problem? Girl, you better get it together. You are highly educated, you're beautiful, you have a big-ass house with no mortgage. Hey, you got something I would love to have—good credit!" Cheryl was talking a mile a minute. "Sounds like he gets off on that 'Captain Save-a-ho' shit. You don't need him. You're not on the same level, Rhea. I'm telling you, keep the twins, drop the man."

"Well, his mom and I get along great." Even I knew this argument was weak, but I wasn't ready to step out of the little fantasy world I'd created over the last few months to face the reality of the situation.

She threw her hands in the air. "Damn, Rhea, I thought you were smarter than that. Yeah, sure, you get along great, as long as you're kissing her son's ass. Don't be no fool, girl. Mention child support and see if his parents won't go along with him, even if he's wrong. Whatever child support he should be paying, you will be taking away from their household. And another thing—if you stayed in his parents' house and screwed him, his other baby mamas probably did too. I hope you don't think you're special."

"Cheryl, she wouldn't get mad at me," I protested weakly. "She's really down-to-earth."

"Like I said. Piss him off and see if his mom won't take his side."

"She promised me she would always be around."

"Rhea, when did you become so stupid?" She rolled her eyes. "And tell me something else. Has the father of your babies promised he would always be around?"

I remained silent. Davis had never made such a

promise. But then again, I had never asked him to. In fact, I was careful not to pressure him about anything whenever we were together. We had been getting along so well, and I didn't want to mess that up.

After all I had been through over the last few years, I just wanted to be happy. If that meant avoiding any uncomfortable topics, including the reality that we were about to be parents, then dammit, I would avoid those subjects. I had been floating along in my little fantasy world the last few months, and Cheryl was messing it up with her big mouth.

"Cheryl, you're wrong on this one. Davis's family is not going to abandon their grandchildren, even if Davis and I don't end up together. After all, they're raising all their other grandkids."

"Don't even get me started on that, Rhea. Shit, what are you gonna do—become a momma to all them kids?"

"Cheryl, can we please change the subject? I have a headache."

"A headache! You keep on with this ghetto drama and a headache is going to be the least of your worries."

I started to cry. Cheryl was normally mild-mannered, and if she felt that strongly about the situation, I could only imagine what Michelle was going to say. This was exactly why I hadn't told anyone before now.

"Come on, Rhea. At least with Marcus you got money when it was over. What are you gonna get besides a broken heart and a li'l bit of child support when this shit blows up in your face?" She gave me a hug and held me as I cried.

"I love you, girl. You don't need him. He likes them needy ho's. That 'I can't take care of the baby. I need some money' kind of girl. Those people wouldn't know what to do with a strong woman like you."

Maybe there was some truth to what Cheryl was saying. Both of Davis's other baby mamas could barely take care of themselves, let alone their children, and his parents actually seemed to like it that way. They sure talked enough shit about those girls, bragging about how they rescued Terri when her mother put her out on the street during Christmas break because she was pregnant. And Noel, they told me, was literally barefoot and pregnant. Her mom dropped her off on their doorstep with just the clothes on her back.

Ernest loved to tell the story of how they bought the girl some shoes to wear that day and let her stay until the semester started up again. They all made a big deal about how much they helped those girls.

Maybe Davis did want a woman to need him. Maybe that was why they all seemed so uncomfortable about my money—it gave me an independence the other girls didn't have.

One thing was for sure. I certainly wouldn't need them to take care of my babies, like those young girls. All I needed was to feel loved, but now Cheryl was putting doubts into my head and messing up my fantasy world. Shit! My head felt like it was going to explode!

"Let's go get that baby some food, girl," Cheryl said when my sobbing subsided. "You look beautiful, and you're going to have a beautiful baby." She handed me a tissue.

I wiped my eyes. "Thanks, Cheryl. You're a good friend, even if I don't always like what you have to say."

She stood up and stretched. "Rhea, you'd better get it together before I call your mama myself. You're lucky Michelle is gone to Europe for a few months; otherwise she and your brother would get together and kill Davis."

I laughed through strained teeth. She was right about Michelle and Toussaint. They would not only plot but, with the help of my uncles, would probably kill him for real.

We went to lunch at a deli not too far from my house. I couldn't stand the smell, so after eating a few bites of a veggie sandwich, we ordered cheesecake and took it back to my house.

"This is what you do," she said in between bites of cheesecake. "Issue him a challenge. Tell him you need to know what's up, and that if he doesn't tell his other baby mamas, you will."

"Okay, Cheryl, I will," I answered, not really sure that I would. I was just hoping that would shut her up.

"How are you going to tell your parents?"

"That's a good question. I don't know. I just don't know."

CHAPTER 14

My attitude toward life sucked. I hated everything, and my life had been reduced to sleeping and eating all day. And as if my life could not get
any worse, I did the dumbest thing ever and issued
my challenge to Davis.

"Either you tell them or I will," I demanded.

"Rhea, you don't trust me, do you?"

*Why do men always try to put the blame back on the
woman?*

"I'm serious, Davis. I'm giving you one week." I
hung up, feeling proud of myself. Everything would
finally work out. We would get married and probably
have another baby in a few years. We would have
some issues at first with the other two baby mamas,
but eventually we'd get it together. I would let both
Terri and Noel know I loved their kids like they were
my own.

A week went by, and though Davis admitted he
hadn't yet told them, I had faith that things would
work out. I was madly in love with Davis Edwinn

Hickman, and I knew that in the end we would be together.

I decided to surprise him with a visit, so I flew out to Denver and checked into a hotel. I called his parents' house to let him know where I was. I figured we could spend the weekend together in the hotel doing all kinds of nasty things to each other's bodies.

"Hello."

I almost dropped the phone when I heard Terri's voice. "Terri? Put Davis on the phone, please."

"Who is this?"

"This is Rhea."

"Hold on," she said with fake politeness then dropped the phone.

She came back within seconds. I knew she hadn't even gone to tell him I was on the phone.

"Rhea, he says he's busy."

"What? Look, Terri, please tell him I need to speak to him now." I was trying to stay calm, trying to convince myself that she was only there to visit her daughter.

"Rhea, Davis told me about you. He said he was trying to be your friend. He felt sorry for you because of your divorce, but you're taking this friendship thing way too far."

"My divorce? I've been divorced for years! And as far as friendship goes, I'm six months pregnant by Davis. Does that sound like he's just trying to be my friend?" This man was trying to insinuate I was stalking him like some *Lifetime* movie.

"Davis told me that he never slept with you. He said you got him drunk and tried to force him to have sex, but it didn't happen."

"Well, obviously he lied to you, just like he did to me," I told her.

Then Terri said something that surprised me. "Tell you what, Rhea," she whispered, "I'm going to take his car and come meet you somewhere. You and I have a lot to talk about. Call me on my cell in an hour." She gave me the number and hung up.

Maybe this girl wasn't quite as dumb as I thought. She wasn't going to pull the typical ghetto shit I would have expected from her, you know, those stupid young girls who find out their man is cheating and want to fight the other girl, instead of putting the blame on the cheating man. No, it seemed like Terri wanted to meet me so we could become allies. Then again, maybe she wanted to beat my ass. I didn't know what to expect.

Time stood still. Exactly one hour later, I dialed Terri's cell phone.

"Hello."

"Terri, this is Rhea."

"Tell me what hotel you're at so I can come meet you."

I thought about it for a second and decided it wouldn't be smart to tell this girl where I was staying. I still didn't know what she was up to.

"Actually, I'm starving. Can we meet at a restaurant?"

"Sure," she said. "Meet me at Apple World. Do you know where it is?"

"I can ask at the front desk. I'll see you there." I hung up and got ready to leave.

I got to the restaurant early and looked over the menu. I wondered if they served organic lettuce. I know most places washed the insecticides off the lettuce, but from what I'd seen so far of this restaurant, some of the employees looked like they might need to be washed off with a water hose.

"Ma'am"—The waitress interrupted my thoughts—"Would you like to order something to drink while you wait for your party?"

I looked up. Lord have mercy! This lady had bleached blond hair and something green in her teeth.

"Oh, no thanks," I said, trying not to laugh out loud. "Can I switch to a booth, please, over by the window?" *Preferably something far away from your station so hopefully I can have another waitress.* A window seat would've also given me time to spot Terri and assess my competition when she drove up.

I closed my eyes for a few minutes to marinate in all the drama, opening them just as I saw Davis's car enter the parking lot.

Terri stepped out, took Ashley out of her car seat in the back, and headed for the entrance. She was average-looking, nothing special—no breasts, no butt. I definitely didn't feel threatened by her looks. I just couldn't see her and Davis together.

"Hi, Miss Rhea," Ashley said excitedly when they came in and saw me. She gave me a hug.

Terri was livid. I could see a vein sticking out from her forehead. I swear, for a minute I thought her head was going to pop open like an alien from the movie *V, the Visitors.*

"How do you know my daughter?" She was checking me out too.

"That's my other mommy," Ashley said.

"How many times have you seen my daughter?" Terri was incensed now.

"Quite a bit in the last few months," I admitted, feeling a bit like I was on trial.

She shook her head back and forth in disgust then sat across from me.

Over the course of a two-hour conversation, we both shared tears of hurt. I learned that Davis and Terri had been planning on getting married. They were on their way to the Justice of the Peace, when I'd called!

"He was pushing so fast. I knew something wasn't right. He's waiting on me now. Get this, Rhea. He wanted me to borrow the money from my student loan check to buy the ring from Wal-Mart. He said he'd pay me back when he got his income taxes."

We both burst out laughing.

Meanwhile, my heart was exploding into a million pieces. I felt the twins start to move in my womb, as if they could feel my pain.

Terri must have seem the look on my face because she tried to cheer me up. "I know. Believe me, girl, it hurts. But I'll tell you something to make you laugh."

I smiled.

"Noel told me once that she knew Davis loved her because he was adding her on as a co-user on his Blockbuster account."

I laughed then started to cry again because he'd told me the same thing. When had I become so stupid?

"It'll be okay, Rhea. At least Davis didn't cheat with your best friend. Noel and I used to be so close before she started fucking him." She patted my hand.

"I know. Excuse me." I turned my head away from the table to blow my nose.

"No problem. I'm surprised my nose isn't running either. My allergies always bother me this time of year. But back to what we were talking about. You probably only know his version." She went on to explain how she met Davis online when she was only 16 years old.

What does this guy see in these li'l young girls?

Terri must've been reading my mind. "Rhea, he's only twenty-four, and just turned twenty-four at that. I hope you know that."

"He told me he was twenty-nine."

"Girl, twenty-nine, my ass. I told his dumb ass he needs to go back to school."

"Graduate school, right?" I really couldn't take any more surprises.

"Davis doesn't have any degrees. He never finished undergrad. He only went to college for the frat parties. The only reason why he got that internship at Sebastian was because of his frat brother." She laughed, but my jaw nearly hit the table.

"Did you say intern? Davis wasn't an employee?" *No wonder he never mentioned the Berlin account after that first night.*

Terri stared at me in disbelief. "Damn, he really did feed you some stories, didn't he? He was an intern. He was put on academic probation for the second time, so Sebastian had to let him go. Before that, he was working for an extension of University of Phoenix here in Colorado as a customer service rep but got fired for coming to work late. And get this— they were paying for his tuition."

My heart dropped. I was a fucking idiot. I was the Director of Marketing at a major corporation with a doctorate degree, and I had been sleeping with a twenty-four-year-old intern and all-around fuck up! Why didn't I check him out? It would have only taken one quick call to Human Resources to find out about his status. Was I that desperate? Or was I just so lonely that I got caught up? Maybe I should have stayed in counseling a little longer after my divorce. It seemed liked every day there was another twist or turn to this saga.

Terri went on to tell me the story of how she and Noel were friends since high school and went to college together. I only listened to bits and pieces. I was still in shock. She said that after two years, she and Davis began to have problems in their relationship. She'd confide in Noel, who would instantly get online and tell Davis everything Terri told her. When Terri went home for the summer, Davis started sleeping with Noel.

"Rhea, you can't imagine. We all went to a small college, and he continued sleeping with her when I came back in the fall."

We were both crying.

"But, girl, I took him back," she admitted.

"That's okay. I've done some stupid shit with regards to Davis too." That was an understatement.

"Yeah, but it's not like I never gave him and Noel a run for their money," she said as she wiped her tears. She told me the story of how she beat the shit out of Noel in the school library.

That must have been funny as hell. I'd heard Noel was as skinny as a crackhead and Terri was a pretty thick girl. I could just imagine Terri moping up the floor with that little "bug-eyed, African click-talking bitch," as she called her. Boy, did Terri have a way with words.

Poor Ashley was falling asleep, so we laid her down in the seat. Terri put her sweater up under her head as a pillow.

"Girl, I broke out the windows in that fucka's car too." We both laughed.

That would explain why Davis called her crazy—

because she was smart. Well, this motherfucker did not know that I was about to play the biggest game of all. I was smart like Terri, but I was a rich bitch with a plan. I would use whatever means necessary to bring him to his knees.

I was so mad at myself. How did I get played by a little boy? Davis Hickman was definitely the master of disguises, lies and deception. But as Terri described her situation, I learned I wasn't the only one fooled by him.

"I was pregnant again and wanted to believe he had changed," she said. "He said you guys were just friends and that you were supervising him on a project at work."

Terri was pregnant three months before I got pregnant. Davis made her get an abortion.

Terri let out a sigh. "Rhea, please don't get upset by what I'm about to tell you. It's not good for your baby. But one night when I caught him on the phone with you, Davis said the only reason he was talking to you was because you were crazy and suicidal because your husband left you for another woman. He said he was trying to be your friend. I wanted to ask you so many times when you'd call what was going on, but I didn't. I think I was afraid to know the truth."

"Believe me, Terri, had I known you and Davis were a couple, I would not have ever disrespected you like that. And just so you know, my husband did leave, but only because I kicked his ass out and divorced him. And I have never been suicidal."

"I'm glad. Damn, was I stupid. This boy's phone bill would be so expensive every month in calls to you, and I'd help him pay it. I should take his ass to court for my money."

"Yes, you should. I know I would if it were me." I

thought for a moment. Would I really take him to court? The old Rhea would have taken him to court, set his mammy's house on fire, and sliced his tires. I felt like I was slowly becoming another person, a weak woman who was willing to put up with anything to be with a man.

Terri continued. "Noel was always giving him money too. She let him borrow her student loan check. Girl, he is such an ass. He convinced Noel to try to finance a computer for him even with her bad-ass credit. Then he had the nerve to complain because she had to go to Gateway but *he* really wanted a Dell. And in the end, Gateway even turned her down."

"Oh, he makes me sick!" I said. "All those flowers and the Victoria's Secret lingerie he would send to me. All the poems he wrote. Everything was a lie."

Terri smirked. "Well, you must have a hella pussy, 'cause he ain't never bought me no flowers, and the only lingerie he ever bought was a cheap-ass camisole from Target that he used to keep hanging in his closet. Then I found out he had both me and Noel wearing the same shit. Noel is a size four and I'm a twelve! Girl, that nigga bought the one that said 'one size fits all.'"

"Where the hell did he get the money to send me Victoria's Secret then?" If this wasn't so sad, it would hilarious.

"Rhea, ain't no telling."

"Ma'am, would you like some more water?" the waitress asked.

"Oh, no thanks," I replied.

The waitress was really working hard for her tip. "Let me tell you about our desserts. We have choc—"

I cut her off. "I'll let you know if we decide to get dessert."

"Have you ever slept at his parents' house?" Terri asked after the waitress left.

I didn't answer right away.

"Of course you did. His mom and dad are full of shit."

"Oh no, Terri. I think his parents are real cool."

"Stick around awhile. You'll see just how cool they really are. I wanted to send his mom an email to let her know what I thought of her, then I remembered their broke asses didn't have a computer," she said with a laugh. "Be careful, Rhea. Willie Mae Hickman is a sneaky bitch. Just so you know, every weekend, their home is a revolving door to one of Davis's baby mamas."

That would explain the stain on his sheets the week of his birthday. Terri and I compared notes about the dates of our visits and realized we were practically there within minutes of each other. He'd dropped Terri off at 3:00 the day he picked me up at the airport. I guess he didn't have time to change the sheets. Either that or he was just too nasty.

"So, his parents are in on this crap?" I couldn't believe they knew.

"Of course. They are very clannish. They only like you because you're rich and you haven't done anything to hurt their son . . . yet. But just wait and see what happens if you start giving him any trouble."

"Terri, are you sure about that? Willie Mae?"

"Oh yes, Willie Mae. I'm certain you've seen how she kisses Ernest's ass. I fucking hate his dad."

I thought back to some things that I'd seen and realized Terri was right. I'd witness Ernest yelling at his wife, and she would just laugh it off. He wouldn't let the kids watch cartoons, and he always hogged the TV to watch reruns of *Baretta*.

"He can have a nasty attitude, can't he?"

Terri laughed. "Uh-huh. That's why Davis's brother moved to Hawaii. He ain't shit either. He's got a ten-year-old daughter somewhere in Texas that he don't take care of, his wife is a crackhead, and his ass can't stay out of jail."

I just shook my head in disbelief. Things just kept getting worse.

"But anyway, getting back to the subject. These people knew their son was sleeping with my room-mate. In fact, they let them sleep together in their house before he got his own place, which of course he can't afford anymore.

"I was pregnant, and when I found out about Noel, I talked to his mom about the whole situation. She wasn't even sympathetic. She told me she had known all along and that I should just get over it, be-cause her son was gonna do whatever he wanted to do."

My eyes got wide. This was so different from the way Willie Mae treated me.

"And get this," she continued. "They let Noel come and shack up in their house with Davis. Willie Mae would be on the phone with me the whole time talk-ing about my baby and all the gifts that she was going to buy for Ashley, while Noel's ass was sitting right there at their kitchen table. Then she got angry at me, like I was supposed to put up with Davis cheat-ing. I told her I hoped her cancer would return and she'd die a slow and miserable death, but the bitch had a stroke instead." She laughed. "But to hear them tell it, I was a psycho."

She was right. I had heard from Davis and his par-ents a million times what a psycho Terri was, and how she was the cause of all of Davis's problems.

"Girl, be prepared, because Davis will disappear for days, saying he's reflecting, or he has some family issues. He always has some list of problems to use as excuses, when the truth is his lying ass just be lost up in some pussy."

I wondered about the times Davis disappeared for weeks, like after he sent me the email about Ashley. Whose pussy was he lost in then? Noel had just given birth around then, so technically her pussy should have been on bed rest, so to speak. That meant either she was nasty enough to be having sex right after childbirth, or Terri was still having sex with Davis. I still had my doubts about Terri. She was sitting here talking all kinds of shit about Davis, but I suspected she still had feelings for him.

"Girl, Davis had me on cloud nine with those poems," she said, snapping me out of my wanderings. "I bet he wrote you one called 'Rhea's Eros,' didn't he?"

"How did you know that?" I asked, embarrassed because I already knew the answer.

Terri laughed loudly. "Girl, he wrote 'Terri's Eros' years ago, then 'Noel's Eros,' now 'Rhea's Eros.' I bet if we look at all the poems, it's the same words; he just changed the name."

I had to laugh. He was so stupid. "So, he's not really a poet?"

"Hell no. I turned his ass into poetry.com for stealing their shit. The Library of Congress sent him a warning letter about copyright infringement." Terri hit the table with her hands.

"Well, Terri, do you think he's still sleeping with Noel?"

"Of course he is. That stupid bitch would let him fuck her in the ass then suck the shit off his dick."

Now that comment made me queasy. I couldn't help wondering what made Terri say all these things, when just hours earlier she told me they were heading to the Justice of the Peace. She was about to marry this guy! My facial expression must have shown how I felt.

"Wow, Rhea, you look a little pale. Go get some rest. I'm going to pretend I'm leaving tonight. I'll tell him I have an emergency at school. I'll go get a room then I'm going to call Noel so we can all talk I'll call you later, okay?" She stood up and picked up Ashley.

We exchanged cell phone numbers then I followed her out of the restaurant and watched her get into Davis's car. Did he do to her the unspeakable things that he did to me in that car? For a brief second, I imagined Davis in a casket. Hell, at least my baby would get a Social Security check.

CHAPTER 15

I went back to the hotel, gathered my belongings, and checked out, in case Terri had followed me somehow. I checked in under another name at the Westin. Terri seemed okay, but I still didn't know if I could trust her.

As I sat back on the bed, I began to process everything that had taken place. I was in total disbelief.

"Everything will be okay. Mommy will figure out something." I rubbed my belly. A part of me wanted to disappear and never have anything to do with Davis, but I needed some answers. He owed me that much at least.

I couldn't get too upset over a nigga. I had to think about my children. I took a hot shower and settled back in bed. I read aloud the *Tale of Peter Rabbit* by Beatrix Potter then put Mozart in my portable CD player and placed the earphones over my belly.

"I wonder what you two are going to be like. Who are you going to look like?" Suddenly, an overwhelming feeling of sadness engulfed me. My life was not supposed to be like this. I'd done everything society—and my mother—said I needed to do, and I still ended up in this predicament. I went to college then got married, just like a good little girl. It wasn't my fault Marcus cheated on me. Then I met a man, fell in love, got pregnant, and now I was caught up in this ghetto shit. All I ever wanted was to be loved. How did it turn into this?

Now my twins had two siblings they would probably never meet or grow up with. Why did Davis do this? I wondered if he even realized the consequences of his actions, and how they could devastate all of his children's lives. Did he even care? How would these kids meet? I could see Ashley and my baby sitting across from each other one day at Yale, or if one of the twins was a boy, playing against Little Davis in a football game.

"Hi, I'm Davis Hickman, Junior," he'd say.

"That's my daddy's name. At least that's what my mom told me. I've never met my dad," my son would reply.

"Really? That's my daddy's name too!" Little Davis would say.

"You know, people say we look alike and we have the same middle name too."

"Maybe we're brothers. My dad does have a whole lot of kids."

Even worse, what if one of the twins was a girl and she started dating Little Davis?

Okay! Okay! You're really losing it, Rhea!

There was absolutely no way these kids would meet each other under those circumstances. Realistically, what would probably happen was they would all meet at one of their grandparents' funerals—or their father's, if Davis kept pissing me off.

My cell phone rang. "Hello."

"Hi, it's Terri."

I knew it. I was actually kind of relieved to hear her voice. There was just no telling who could have been on the other line, with the circus that was going on.

"Oh, hi, Terri."

"You're not going to believe this, Rhea."

"Actually, at this point I can almost believe anything."

My Grandma always told me, "You say you haven't seen anything yet? Well, baby, keep on living. You will see a lot before you leave this world."

I braced myself, waiting to hear something insane like Davis was really a woman and had a sex change, that he had another baby mama, or that he was HIV positive.

"Well, I spoke with Noel," Terri said.

"Oh. Is she pregnant too?" I asked sarcastically.

"Nope, but Davis asked *her* to marry him last month. And she said that her mom had gotten a Victoria's Secret credit card and told Noel that she could use it as long as she paid the bill. Well, Noel said she lost it somewhere one weekend while she was visiting Davis. Her mom started getting statements, but Noel went ahead and paid them because she didn't want to hear her mom's mouth. She confronted Davis, and he admitted that he *borrowed* it from her purse to buy lingerie for his mom because his parents were having marital issues."

"Wow!" was all I could say. Noel's mother's card was paying for my underwear?

"She said she didn't question it because his mom is a size eight, and that was the size that he was charging. Personally, I would have wanted to know how he expected his mother to be having sex after she just had a stroke!"

"But, Terri, he had it sent to me in Atlanta. Noel must have known that."

Terri laughed. "Well, I wonder what lie he told her to clean that shit up."

I was really starting to worry about his mental capacity. *Cognitive delayed.* I think that's the medical term for his condition. This boy had serious issues. I vaguely remembered Davis telling me he used to be a preacher as a teenager. Maybe, just maybe, he was being afflicted by demons. I read somewhere in the Bible, I think it's in the Book of Matthew, that if a person backslides, God gives them a reprobated mind so they become immune to evil. Then seven more demons come and take over. That had to be it. He was under the influence of demons.

"I know this sounds bad, Rhea, but I actually got pleasure in telling the little bitch about you being pregnant."

I bet you did! She was beaming through the telephone, enjoying this a little too much.

"Well, anyway, I told her we'd be calling on a three-way call. Hang on, okay?"

"Okay." I couldn't wait to talk to Noel.

She dialed the number. As soon as Noel picked up, Terri began to talk. "Noel, I have Rhea on the line."

"I don't want to talk about this," Noel said quickly, then we heard a click and a dial tone.

What the hell?

Terri yelled, "Oh, no she didn't!"

"What's going on?" I asked.

"That bitch probably called Davis and he told her not to talk to us. She was so ready to talk to you before, and now all of sudden she can't talk. I should have known she wouldn't turn her back on Davis, no matter what I told her about his lying ass. Shit, the girl had sex with him three weeks after she gave birth, just to make sure he wouldn't get too horny and cheat on her. She will do anything for that man."

My cell phone beeped. "Hang on, Terri." I clicked over.

"Hello."

"We need to talk." It was Davis. I hung up. I clicked back over. "Terri, that was Davis."

"What did he want?"

"Your guess is as good as mine. I hung up on him."

The phone beeped again. "Hang on, Terri. Let me cuss this sperm donor out real quick. I'll be right back."

She laughed. "Girl, do what you need to do."

I clicked back over. "Davis, leave me the fuck alone."

"Hey, baby. We need to talk." It was his mom.

"Look, Mrs. Hickman, I don't feel like talking right now."

"I know you probably don't feel like being bothered right now but, Rhea, don't listen to Terri. She's a troublemaker."

"I'm on the phone long distance. I'll talk to you later, Mrs. Hickman."

"Will you call me back?"

"Yes, ma'am, under one condition. I don't want to talk to Davis."

"Okay. He's on his way to work anyway."

Davis had found a job as a singing telegram delivery-man. This boy was going down fast. His latest gig was ringing people's doorbells, singing jingles and hooks, dressed up in all sorts of stupid costumes. To make ends meet, he found a second job working at Hooters, of all places. Nasty fucker was probably on the pussy prowl looking for a fourth baby mama.

I clicked back over. "Sorry, girl. That was Willie Mae."

"I bet she told you not to talk to me, didn't she?"

"Yeah."

"Anyway, back to Noel. She plays that role like she's so sweet. Girl, she is the biggest whore in the state of Colorado. Li'l nasty cunt was cheating on Davis with some ugly-ass, nasty-looking Jamaican named Lee. Now, that's probably *her* baby daddy. That baby got hair just like Lee. She was also messing 'round with some white boy too."

"Davis told me the same thing. Why doesn't he get a blood test to see if he's really the baby's father?"

"Claims he doesn't have the money to get a test. Anyway," Terri rambled on, "Noel is a straight-up skank, a ho in hiding. And girl, you know I was the one to tell Davis his ho was cheating on him. Noel doesn't want to play with me. She knows her mom told her to leave Davis alone. Her mama takes care of her lazy ass because she refuses to work during the semester. It's not like she's on the dean's list. She is not appreciative of anything her mom does. She talks about her own mama to the Hickmans. Rhea, that damn girl is so low down. She was complaining to Willie Mae how she hates taking care of her little brother who's retarded. She said she's ashamed to go out in public with him because he's always beating his chest with his arms and has snot hanging out of his nose. She even laughed when Ernest called her mama fat. Noel is pitiful."

I could tell Terri really hated Noel, but that worried me. I knew Noel had slept with her man, but Terri's anger seemed to go much deeper. Terri was starting to seem like she hated Noel more than she hated Davis. I was really starting to wonder if Terri was still in love with Davis and this was all just an act for my benefit. For all I knew she was just formulating a plan to get rid of me so she could have Davis all to herself.

"But, girl, I tell you," Terri continued, "that bitch was so shocked when I told her about you. That's what she gets. And Rhea, that stank, salamander-smelling bitch wears boots year-round. Not fashion boots, but fucking work boots. In the summer too!"

I was really becoming concerned about Terri's mental stability at this point. There wasn't one thing she didn't hate about Noel.

"So, we need to figure out a way to get this nigga back."

'We'? "You know, Terri, I—"

She didn't let me finish my sentence. "I'm going to retain an attorney here and try to get temporary custody of Ashley. I don't know what will happen because his family and I never had anything in writing, only an oral agreement that they would keep her until I graduated. But under the circumstances, I may need to get a statement from you about all the shit that goes on over there."

"Okay, well, let me know. I'm getting tired." I didn't like where the discussion was headed and was ready to get the hell off the phone.

"Okay, girl. I'll call you tomorrow, when I get back to school." I heard her say under her breath, "Little stank ho." I had to hope she was still talking about Noel at this point.

"Terri, it was nice meeting you," I told her, hoping she couldn't sense that I was starting to have my doubts about her. "Have a safe trip back to school." *And please lose my phone number.*

"Bye, Rhea. Us West Indians need to stick together. See, Davis don't know who he's fucking with. You know how we do it down there. I'll burn a candle on his black ass in a minute."

"I know, Terri. I know." *Putting some voodoo on him does sound like a good idea.*

"Just take care of yourself. I'll be back soon to try to get my baby from this dog. And Rhea . . ."

"Yes." I didn't feel like talking anymore.

"It'll get better. You've got it made, really. You're already out of school and you've got money." She laughed. "Look at the bright side. We can both hit him up for child support at any time before our kids turn eighteen. Girl, we can garnish that bastard's wages and have his driver's license suspended. There are all kinds of fun things we can do to him. But seriously, though, you're lucky you can take care of yourself."

I wasn't feeling very lucky. Terri was the lucky one. I was just getting caught up in this shit, while she seemed to be going on with her life. Or was she?

"And don't worry about Noel. Her blue-collar ass ain't shit. She's not on *our* level."

'Our level'? Now I just wanted this girl to go away. Had I really sunk so low that she considered us on the same level?

"Take care, Terri."

"See ya, Rhea." We hung up.

Later that night, Davis kept calling me on my cell. Around 9:00, I had taken just about enough. I saw a call from a blocked number, so I assumed it was him again, trying to get through. I picked up the phone, ready to cuss his ass out.

"Hello," I snapped.

"Bonjour!" It was my mom.

Oh shit! I am not ready to deal with this now.

"Hey, I'm not at home right now, Mom. Can I give you a call a little later?"

"Well, I've got your brother on the line. Since you two are always conveniently leaving each other messages on answering machines, I thought it would be best if I connect the two of you."

You thought wrong!

Before I could object, Toussaint opened his li'l leprechaun mouth. "Hi, daffodil."

"Hi, Toussaint," I replied dryly.

"Girl, what is the problem? You sound awful."

"Nothing. What's up?"

"Why don't you return my calls?"

"Let's see . . . why don't I return your calls? Maybe because I don't want to hear anything about Marcus, his baby and his baby's mama. Or because I don't want to hear about how he's so miserable without me. Or maybe I don't return your calls because I don't want to hear about how much he wants me back."

"Well, he does."

"Well, he needs to let it go. It's been years."

Mom interjected. "Well, daffodil, I just want you to know that *I'm* okay with what you did."

"What I did?" Did she know about the baby?

"The divorce. I've never said this before, but I'm very proud of you for having the kind of courage that you did. One day, if you ever have a daughter, I hope she's as strong as you."

That was it all it took for me to break down. I couldn't control the tears.

"What's wrong?" my brother asked.

"Rheonique, why are you crying, baby? I thought you'd want me to admit I was wrong about Marcus," Mom said.

"Mommy, Toussaint, I'm pregnant," I whispered.

"What!" They both said it in unison.

My mother spoke first. "Who? Where? How? Well, maybe not how."

Toussaint and I laughed, which broke the ice.

It took me about an hour to tell my mother and brother everything about Davis and the situation.

"Mommy, please let me be the one to tell Daddy," I begged.

Toussaint was livid. "This guy needs to be stopped. I'll call Uncle Pierre today."

I realized my mistake instantly. My mother's family had a history of being involved in unsolved murders and mishaps.

It took another hour to convince them I was okay and it wasn't necessary to involve my uncles before they both hung up. I felt a little bit better, but my mother confused me. I was expecting her to yell or scream at me, but Veronique was completely silent, which scared the hell out of me. There was no telling what was lurking beneath that calm exterior.

I turned my cell phone off. I couldn't sleep, so I fluffed the pillow on the bed, put the headset on my belly and tried to meditate. That didn't work either, so I took a bubble bath. Still, I couldn't sleep. Around midnight, I got back up and flipped through the television channels until I found Lifetime. *The Burning Bed* with Farrah Fawcett was on. Ah, that was comforting—a woman killing a man. How nice.

I tossed and turned all night. My mind kept spinning, thinking about all the things Terri had said. Then my mind started traveling back over every man I'd ever had a relationship with.

Even before Marcus, it seemed like every man I'd been involved with turned out to be using me or lying to me. I came to the conclusion that all the men I'd loved were either liars or whores. The more I thought about them and about Davis, the angrier I became. It was a welcome relief when sleep finally came.

CHAPTER 16

When I woke up around noon, I was on a mission. My little stroll down memory lane hadn't help my mood or my negative feelings for men, especially Davis. I was going to kick his ass that afternoon. Davis had to be taught a lesson.

I called Hooters to see if he was working there that day. The bartender said he would be in at 3:00. I called room service and ordered some lunch then started packing my bag to get the hell out of Denver. I wanted to call the airline to see if I could reschedule my flight from Monday to that night, but first I had to find my itinerary with my flight information on it. Crap. Where was my itinerary? I began to get nervous. Why was I always losing things?

I dug through my purse, praying I could find my flight information so I didn't have to call the airline and wait on hold forever. I found it in the bottom of my purse, along with my cell phone. I turned my phone on and saw that I had four messages from the night before. The first one was from Marcus.

"I know you did it. I just can't prove it. Somebody took an ad out in *The Gay Times* magazine stating, 'Gay doctor needs a thorough rectal exam.' I know you or that crazy-ass cousin of yours did it. This shit isn't funny, Rhea. Those freaks keep calling my office. I had a goddamn transvestite come by my office today for a fucking rectal exam. And he specifically requested no lubrication! This shit is going to ruin my business. My secretary thinks I'm a faggot, and—"

I deleted the message without listening to the rest. Marcus was a fool. I don't know why he called me. He needed to deal with his baby mama and that ugly-ass little gecko of his.

I listened to the second message. "Hi. It's Cheryl. Where are you? I hope you're not with your loser-ass baby daddy."

Delete.

The third message was Davis. "Please call me. I love you."

Double delete.

The last call was from Terri. "Hey, girl, it's Terri. Call me when you get this message. I went by the hotel to say bye before I left, but they said you checked out."

Delete with fear! I'm glad I switched hotels.

My cell phone rang as soon as I closed it.

"Hello."

"Hi . . . Rhea?" the soft female voice said cautiously.

"Yes?" I answered, just as cautious.

"This is Noel."

Why is she trying to sound like a baby? I hate when grown-ass women try to sound all precious and shit on the phone.

"Hello, Noel."

"Look, Rhea, I'm sorry about being so abrupt yesterday. It's just that Terri and I have a bad history."

"Oh?" I said nonchalantly. I didn't want her to know I knew what went on with those two. I didn't need to be in the middle of that shit.

"Well, honestly, Noel, I had no idea you and Davis had *anything* going on."

"Same here." She sounded a little smug.

We ended up talking for about an hour, and the conversation was actually pretty civil. Noel seemed nice enough, but in that short period of time, I could tell that unlike Terri, this girl was desperate. Noel indirectly suggested that we could share Davis, which really shouldn't have surprised me. She'd been sharing him for years with Terri.

My telephone beeped. I was glad to have an excuse to get off the phone with her. She was pathetic. I made a mental note to get her simple ass a packet together for the Simple Bitch Parade.

"Noel, I've got to go. I have another call coming in."

"Okay, Rhea. Bye."

I clicked over. "Hello."

"Hello, daffodil. I could not sleep at all last night. I'm very worried about you." It was my mother.

I was glad she called. I needed to correct the mayhem that was going to erupt in my family because of the circumstances surrounding my pregnancy. I was going to handle Davis my way, but I didn't want my family to kill him.

"Mom, I'll be okay. Really, please don't worry. Everything will be fine."

She remained quiet.

"Mom, you didn't tell Dad, did you?"

She said nothing. I was nervous now. Finally, after what seemed like an eternity, she responded. "No, darling. He's out on the golf course."

"Okay." I was relieved, but only until she started yelling at me in French.

"Rhea, how could you be so careless?"

"Mom, I hadn't been with anyone since Marcus," I stammered nervously. "I'd just started back taking the pill. Davis and I were friends. You remember I told you and Dad about him?" *Damn, I wish she didn't make me feel like a little girl.*

"Yes, I remember. You told us when you met him, but not that you were dating, let alone sleeping with him," she scolded.

"You don't understand. It just happened."

"Rheonique, intimacy doesn't just happen. Do you love him?" Her voice softened a bit.

"Yes, ma'am," I replied meekly.

"Well, too bad. Any man that wants a woman to throw away her baby is not worthy of being loved. Don't worry, daffodil. We'll figure a way out of this."

"What do you mean, 'out of this'? Mom, I'm having twins."

"Rhea, why didn't you tell me this yesterday?"

"Does it matter? Either way, I'm pregnant, and I'm keeping the babies."

"Of course you are, darling. Abortion is a sin. I'm just wondering what everyone will think about two little illegitimate babies."

"Mom, I don't care what people think." *Unlike you, who lives her life based on keeping up appearances.*

She ignored me and said, "It sounds like his family is pretty poverty-laden, Rhea." After a few seconds, she blurted out as if she'd had an epiphany, "I've got

it. This is what you'll do, darling. Find out how much
he wants. I'll send a cashier's check by courier tomorrow, and we'll deal with your father later."

"How much does he want for what?" *Mom must be
on crack.*

"Surely you are not going to pursue a relationship
with this womanizing mongrel. You are going to get
this young man to terminate his parental rights completely. I'll have Uncle Marco do the paperwork, and
as soon as the twins are born, we can finalize everything. But we can try to get as much done as possible
right now.

"Rheonique, you've put me in a very precarious
position, darling. I don't know how I'm going to
stand all the stares. It was bad enough, the humilia-
tion with your divorce. Now a pregnancy from another man out of wedlock. And to top it off, he's
poor, with two other little crumb-snatchers. I pray
he's at least decent-looking. How am I going to be
able to show my face in public now?"

"Mom, I'll call you later." I so was tired of this
whole mess.

"Don't hang up yet, baby. Rhea, where are you?"

"Oh, I'm in Detroit at Nicole's," I lied.

"I was just wondering, because your friend Cheryl
called here looking for you. She said you hadn't
been home in a couple of days."

"Oh, I'll be sure to give her a call."

*That damn Cheryl. She has some nerve, calling my par-
ents' house looking for me.*

"Have a safe trip back home. Love you, daffodil."

"Love you too, Mom." I hung up.

As much as she got on my nerves, I just wanted to
feel her soft manicured arms around me at that particular moment. Veronique was a cunning woman. I

likened her to a tigress that always devoured her prey, no matter what the consequences. I needed my mom's courage and her cunning to help me deal with Davis.

It was getting close to 2:00, so I started preparing to surprise Davis at Hooters. My phone rang again as I was putting the last few items in my carry-on bag.

"Hello."

"It's Terri. Girl, you ain't gonna believe this shit. This freaking asshole just told me he doesn't even know if *your* baby is his."

"What? Look, Terri, I'm on my way to his job to show my natural black ass."

"Good, I'm going to call Noel and cuss her ass out. I know she'll call him at work crying. Then I'm going to keep calling him too. Hopefully his black ass will get fired. Girl, fuck him up for both of us."

"Will do. Talk to you later." I slammed the phone shut, grabbed my bags and headed for the lobby to check out. It was time to show Davis what I was capable of.

CHAPTER 17

Davis knew he was the father. What kind of game was he playing? I had no earthly clue, but if he wanted to get stupid, I would reciprocate accordingly. Seemed like insane baby mamas was all he understood, so I'd make sure I showed him what a real crazy-ass baby mama was capable of doing. This shit was going down in the record book. It was time to get straight ghetto!

When I got to Hooters, Davis was at the bar. He must have known something was up, because he was looking at me nervously. I could tell he was praying I didn't start any shit up in there, because I know his broke ass needed the job.

I was fuming. I began screaming at the top of my lungs like an escaped patient from a psycho ward. "We need to talk!" I yelled as loudly as I could.

Everyone turned around in awe.

There was some drunk sitting at the bar. I grabbed

his pitcher, and beer spilled everywhere. I pointed the empty pitcher at Davis and screamed, "I will bust you in your motherfucking head if you look at me with that 'I-don't-know-who-that-crazy-girl-is' look."

Davis looked mortified.

I continued on with my performance. I hadn't had this much fun since I was the character Eliza Doolittle in the musical, *My Fair Lady*.

"Okay, Davis, you black bitch. You say this isn't your baby, you low-down, pussy-licking, asshole-sucking bitch."

Everyone in Hooters erupted into laughter. There was a group of white frat boys who'd fallen on the floor, holding their stomachs, they were laughing so hard. One of them began to choke, and management rushed over to assist.

"Can we please take this into the office?" Davis was on the verge of tears.

I chased behind him into a little cramped space he called an office.

Country-ass, Toby-lookin' fucka. This isn't no office! My damn shiatsu's cage is bigger than this shit!

"Terri told me what you said, and it's on now. If you thought Terri was crazy, you ain't seen shit yet. You're going to wake up having nightmares about me!"

Davis said the strangest thing in response. "You look so sexy now, baby. Your eyes are beautiful. I just want to bend you over." He licked his lips.

"Bend me over? Somebody needs to bend you over, you faggot!"

He massaged his temple. "Calm down. Let's go outside and get some fresh air, then we can talk about this in a civilized manner."

I followed him, and when he went to turn the doorknob, I kicked the back door open then hit him with the pitcher.

Davis rubbed his arm. "Ow! That hurt!"

"Good, nigga, it's supposed to hurt," I said as I followed him outside. "And that's not it, either. I'm going to fuck you up as soon as I have this baby!"

"Rhea, calm down! Please! If not for yourself, then for our baby." He laughed nervously. "You hit me, which isn't very nice, Rheonique. Our baby is going to grow up and be violent."

"Ain't shit funny, nigga! I don't know why you're laughing. And don't be calling my full fucking name either! You don't know me like that! And oh, it's yours now?"

He lost his cool now. "I never said it wasn't! In case you want to know what's *really* going on, your new best friend just called me. Terri also told me about you guys meeting for dinner and about your little phone conversations. She set you up, Rhea! She called me to tell me you were on your way over here. She wanted me to be prepared, she said, and she wanted me to beat your ass when you got here!"

"What?" I was in shock.

Davis rubbed it in. "Did she tell you she called and begged for me to still marry her? There was only one condition—that I drop you. When I said no, that's when she threatened to call you with this shit."

"What!" Somebody was lying. *Who do I believe? Davis or Terri?* I'd have to sit down and figure that out later, but for the moment, Davis had an ass-whipping coming for being a whore.

I drew back my fist as far as I could and knocked him in his left eye. He was totally taken off guard and stumbled back a few steps.

I was poised and ready to hit him again.

He grabbed my arms as I reached forward, trying to gouge his eyeballs.

That's when it happened. I began to fall.

Davis tried to catch me, but I headed for the pavement, stomach first. I contorted my body just in time, so I landed on my side as my body hit the concrete. Time stood still. I lay in place for what seemed like an eternity.

"Rhea, baby, are you okay?" I faintly heard his voice. For a brief second, I almost succumbed to Davis. I needed his big, strong arms to comfort me, but then I thought of all the shit he had done. So, I did the first thing that came to mind. I spit at him then got down on my knees and scrounged up the scattered contents of my purse.

I grabbed my cell phone and crawled over into a corner like a wounded dog. I began to growl at him like a rabid animal.

Davis looked perplexed and afraid. It was obvious he was beyond embarrassed. The patrons in the restaurant had gathered in the windows and were gawking with amazement.

I finally got up and called 911, then my brother.

"Hello, Dr. Baptiste LaDay here," my brother answered.

"Call Uncle Pierre, whoever you have to. Davis just made me fall. I almost fell on my stomach!" I shrieked into the phone.

"I didn't make you fall. I tried to catch you!" Davis yelled at me.

Suddenly, I felt a sharp pain in my upper left thigh and I let out a blood-curdling scream. Apparently I had fallen on some sort of debris, and something sharp was stuck in my thigh.

"Rhea, are you okay?" I heard Toussaint saying.

I was in too much pain to answer, so I just disconnected the call.

I was in back of a Hooter's restaurant with my baby daddy, who had two other baby mamas, waiting for the police or an ambulance to arrive. Life could not get any worse.

Jesus wept.

CHAPTER 18

A fter taking an initial police report the big burly cop, who could have passed for the local Grand Wizard of the KKK, tried to give me some reassurance.

"Don't worry, darling. I'm going to get some witness statements, and we'll take appropriate action." He gave Davis a menacing stare, like he wanted to kill him with his bare hands. He probably couldn't have cared less about my welfare. He was just happy to find any excuse to put a black man behind bars.

I was loaded onto a gurney and placed inside the ambulance to be taken to the local hospital. They removed the small piece of glass that was lodged in my thigh, so I wasn't in much pain anymore. I wanted to just get to the airport, but they insisted that I go to the hospital and have an ultrasound to check the babies.

The ride to the hospital seemed like an eternity. The medic kept giving me a look of pity, like I was some sort of statistic, and I laughed to myself. It was official. I was assimilated into the world of ghetto-hood. Actually, this shit was past ghetto; it was ghetto fabulous!

How did I go from delivering a dissertation to getting ready to deliver twins for a man like Davis? My mind was slipping. There was something that I needed to do. What was it? Oh, Toussaint. Crap.

I lifted my head up slightly to find my cell phone. The medic stopped me.

Why does this motherfucker with his crunchy black ass have a name tag on that says Blue?

"Ma'am, until we get you checked out, I don't think you should hold your head up."

"Can you dial my brother's number for me? My cell phone is in my purse. Just hit redial, please."

Blue motioned for me to lay still and gave me the phone. Toussaint's voice mail picked up. I didn't leave a message. I would talk to him later.

After getting checked in and taken to a corner of the emergency room, I was given some Tylenol for the dull ache in my leg. I was so tired and stressed from the day's events that I dozed off for a while.

I barely woke up, when they wheeled in the ultrasound machine and checked the babies. Finally, I heard someone say the doctor would be in to see me.

I turned my head and looked up at the clock then looked around to view my surroundings. The dank smell from the dirty bedpan sitting in the corner of the room was bad enough, but the spider web hanging above my head through the cracked ceiling, and the black nurse with the bright red lipstick were enough to make me think I'd died and gone to hell. My God, this was some *In the Heat of the Night* shit!

I laughed silently while I watched the nurse perform for her white co-workers, like a buffoon for a minstrel show.

"Ain't that the cutest little girl?" she said about the child in a nearby bed. "Look at that pretty blond hair. Lawd, I sho' wish *I* had pretty hair."

Why do some black people do that kind of shit? That bitch knows good and well that is the ugliest li'l cleft-lip child in the world. I dare her fat ass to ask me if I think that white girl is cute. I'm not racist or anything, but ugly is universal. That child looks like a lil' mini-monster.

Lord have mercy, the woman had lipstick on her teeth. Everyone was laughing uncontrollably. It was so pitiful. She thought they were laughing *with* her. Poor thing had no idea they were laughing *at* her.

She stopped performing for a moment and looked around to see if she'd gained favor from her white comrades. Her eyes locked with mine, but she looked away quickly.

You need to look away. You should be ashamed!

"Are you okay?" she asked, pretending to show concern.

I could only imagine what she was thinking. Probably something like, *I can't stand these uppity Negroes. That li'l heifer had no idea what it's like to work here with this racism. All she can do is think that I'm an Uncle Tom. She ain't got five kids to raise by herself off of fifteen thousand dollars a year. Look at that necklace. That probably cost half of my salary.*

"I'd like to see if the doctor is on his way in to see me."

"Okay, I'll check." The nurse looked relieved to have an excuse to leave, and I was glad to have one to give her.

A short while later, the doctor walked in and sat

on the edge of my bed. "Hey, sorry I'm running a little late. I'm the only attending physician today." He
looked down at the chart and smiled. "Looks like
your babies are doing fine, so I'm going to release
you. Don't do too much for the next few days, and
unfortunately, Tylenol is the only thing you can take
for pain."

"Am I able to fly?" I wanted to get as far away from
there as possible.

"You should be able to fly after four or five days.
You really need to rest. You took a pretty hard fall.
How's the pain?"

"Actually, it's not that bad."

He looked at my chart again. "Since you are having twins, I'd say rest for at least a week, if you can,
before trying to fly. You may feel fine now, but the
pain may sneak up on you. Also, your iron is a little
low. I would get some ferrous sulfate to supplement
your pre-natal vitamins."

"So, the twins are fine?"

"Yes, both of them. The little boy seemed to be a
little bigger than the girl, but they are fine." He closed
the medical chart.

"A boy and girl!" I shouted happily.

"Yes, a boy and a girl." He patted my leg and stood
up. "Well, take care, young lady. The nurse will bring
your discharge papers in momentarily."

The nurse came back in as soon as he was gone,
much quicker than I expected. "You have a phone
call at the nurse's station. Are you all right to walk
over there with me?" she asked.

*Who could it be? Why did Toussaint hunt me down? I told
him I'd call him back. He always was so damn controlling.*

"Yes, I can walk to the nurse's station." I followed
the nurse and picked up the telephone. "Hello."

"Rhea, it's me. Please don't hang up. I want to be a part of the baby's life, and I'm sorry for everything.

Yeah, I bet you're sorry. All of your pussy just got cut off and you're afraid my family is going to make you the next victim of a drive-by shooting! If I hadn't been in a busy emergency room with a few nurses staring at me, I would have given him a piece of my mind, but instead I kept my answer G-rated.

"Look, Davis, you weren't interested this morning, and I'm tired. Go be with Noel, Terri, whoever. I don't care. I can take care of both of my babies by myself."

There was a long pause.

He began crying. "Twins? We're having twins? I need to be there with you."

"I don't want to see you, and the police are still here," I told him as I saw the KKK-looking officer approaching me. "So, unless you want me to tell them you pushed me so your black ass can go to jail for domestic assault, I'd suggest you leave me the hell alone."

I hung up and slumped down in a chair next to the nurse's station, ignoring the police officer who was now standing over me.

"Miss LaDay?"

"I'm sorry, sir. My mind is elsewhere."

"I understand, young lady. Congrats. I heard you got two buns in the oven."

What the freak! These people need a life. They obviously have never heard of patient confidentiality. God forbid anyone ever contracted HIV!

The idiot cop stood and made small talk with me for fifteen minutes. My eyes were glazing over with boredom. I looked around the emergency room, wondering where the hell the nurse was with my dis-

charge papers. I nearly fell off my seat, when I saw
Willie Mae approaching.

"Ready to go, Rhea?" Willie Mae asked.

I sat there with my mouth hanging open.

"Oh, you're wondering what I'm doing here,
aren't you? Well, Davis told me what happened, so I
rushed over here to help you out. Let me take you
back to the hotel."

I looked from her back to the creepy cop who didn't
seem to want to leave me alone. Finally, I decided that
Willie Mae was the lesser of two evils. "Yes, I'm ready
as soon as the nurse brings me my papers." I faked a
smile.

"How are you?" She patted me on the shoulder.

"I'm fine."

Finally, the nurse showed up with my papers. I
signed them in a hurry so I could get the hell out of
there. We walked to the double doors together.

"I'm parked pretty far out," she said. "Want to wait
here 'til I pull up?"

"Sure," I answered then leaned against the wall
while she went outside.

From where I was standing, I overheard the policeman talking to the Sambo nurse. "I hope she pursues
this. Makes no sense, a sweet-looking girl getting involved with a low-life maggot that works at Hooters.
It's obvious she's not from here. Claudine said she had
insurance, and good insurance, too. Ain't too many
folks 'round here, white nor colored, got insurance."

I coughed loudly to get his attention. His face
turned beet red, when he looked over and saw me
standing there. I rolled my eyes at him and the pathetic nurse and went to wait for Willie Mae outside.

When I got into the car, I told Willie Mae which
hotel I was staying at. "I hope you don't mind, but I

have a headache, so I'm going to try to sleep now, Willie Mae." I closed my eyes for the duration of the ride, hoping she'd leave me alone.

When we reached the hotel, she parked the car and turned off the ignition. I wanted to just open the door and run.

"Rhea?" she said softly.

I opened my eyes. "Yes, ma'am."

"Everything will be okay."

"I hope so."

I had so many questions I wanted to ask her, like why she allowed her son to do this to people. I wanted her to tell me she didn't know Davis was doing this. I wanted to hear that as a woman, she was just as shocked and pissed as I was about the mess her son created.

Instead, she continued with bullshit small talk. "You need to eat, darling."

"I'm okay. I'll be fine." *Why do you care if I eat or not?*

"Rhea, can I tell you something?"

"Yes, ma'am." *She is getting on my nerves!*

"I've been hurt before, and I know how it feels."
Do you really? Try being hurt with two babies!

"Well, Mrs. Hickman, I need to think for a while."

"Do you need me to take you to the airport tomorrow?"

"No thanks. I have a rental car. I may not leave tomorrow anyway. The doctor said I needed to be on bed rest for a few days."

"Rhea, my son is just confused. He's really a good person, and I like you more than you'll ever know. You're the only one that came in and tried to help me out with the kids. You helped me out around the house, even went to church with us. Terri or Noel never did that. If anything, they acted like I was a maid. They only wanted to be with Davis and *their* child, not the other ones. That's always been my biggest fear, that if I died and my son married either Terri or Noel, one of my grandchildren would feel mistreated."

I looked into her sad eyes. "I'm not like that."

"If I got to choose who my son would be with, it would be you."

I wiped the tears as they flowed down my face. I reassured her that if Davis and I ended up together, I'd treat all the children equally.

"I know you will, Rhea." She was crying now.

"I need to go. Bye." I grabbed the door handle.

"Rhea, I love you and I love my grandbabies."

I guess Davis told her it was twins.

"I love you too." We hugged, and I got out.

I went back into the hotel room and cried. I felt like a schizophrenic. One minute I wanted Davis dead, the next I was crying in the car with his momma talking about if we end up together. Was it my hormones that caused me to switch from one extreme to another? I had so many complex emotions going on in my head, it was almost too much to handle.

I called Toussaint back and told him I was fine and that Davis had not pushed me. He said he was on his way over to my house. I confessed that I wasn't at home. "And please don't tell Mom I'm in Colorado." He agreed reluctantly to keep my secret. Toussaint made me promise we would have a heart to heart talk when I got home.

"Rhea, although we have our differences, I love you. All you have to do is say the word and Davis can be taken care of."

CHAPTER 19

I was awakened by the knock on my hotel room door. At first, I ignored it, but then I heard, "Baby, I know you're in there. Please let me in. We need to talk."

"Fuck off, Davis."

"Are you sure that's what you want? I'll sit outside of this door all night if I have to." He pounded on the door.

"I don't give a damn what you do. Leave me alone!"

"Rhea, you probably haven't eaten all day. My grandma is having a get-together at her house, and I'd like for you to go meet my family."

"No thanks. If they're like you, I know I don't want to meet them!"

"Rhea, please! We have to talk. I'm so sorry." He was not going away. That much was obvious. He was just like a spoiled child who always had to have his way.

"Okay, you have fifteen minutes. And the only reason you're coming in is because I don't want the other hotel guests to call downstairs." I opened the door, moved back to let him in, and shut the door.

He looked genuinely sad, but I didn't feel sorry for him. He looked beaten and bruised, but he couldn't blame anyone but himself. Who was Davis Hickman anyway? I thought I knew him. Did I ever really love him, or did I just want to be loved so badly that I'd gotten tricked? I'd have never slept with him if I would've known about his "situation." He knew all about Marcus and what I'd gone through, and he chose to take advantage of me anyway.

"Rhea, I know you hate me."

"I don't hate you. I pity you. You will reap what you sow."

"I'm not a bad person. Everything just happened so fast."

"Speaking of fast, just say what you have to say and get out of here, because I'm exhausted."

"Rhea, I didn't push you down. You fell."

"Whatever. Say what you came to say and leave."

"I was only going to marry Terri because . . . it's hard to explain." He took a deep breath then sat down on the edge of the bed.

"Earlier you said she was the one trying to get you to marry her. Do you think I'm a damn fool? The sweet, generous Rhea that you thought you knew has been replaced by the psycho Rhea. You met her today at Hooters, so please don't come in here with more bullshit. I will cut your fucking throat."

"Rhea, you don't understand. I only—"

The telephone rang.

"Please don't answer that, Rhea."

"Don't tell me what the fuck to do." I picked up the

receiver wondering who was calling my hotel room. "Hello."

"This is Noel. Can you please ask Davis to hurry back home?"

"Your bitch is on the phone!" I threw the phone at him and knocked him in the top of his head.

"Ow!" He took the phone. "Noel, what the hell is your problem? I told you I'd call you later. Rhea is pregnant, and I'm not going to let her get upset anymore."

He slammed the phone down. "I'm sorry. I can't believe her dumb ass did that."

"For once my mom was right," I spat. "You keep trash in the trashcan, *negro basura*! And in case you need translation, *basura* is *trash*, which is what you are. You and your li'l stank ho are beneath me. That girl has no self-respect, calling my hotel room looking for you.

"Why did you even come here anyway? You come over here like you're so fucking sorry. Nigga, you're scared! You know what my family is capable of doing! And back to your li'l African bitch—How did she know I was at the Westin, Davis? Why the fuck would you tell her where I was staying if you're so concerned about not upsetting me?"

He continued to massage his head, where the phone had hit him. "First of all, this is the second time you've hit me in one day. But to answer your question, I told her I was coming over here to see you. She said she had to talk to me. I told her after I left here I would call her back. If you get mad because she called, that's between y'all. She was wrong."

"Cool. So, when I kick her ass, I don't want to hear anything from you. Then you'll piss my brother off, and you don't want to do that."

"Oh, what's going to happen? I'm going to end up like that other ex-boyfriend you told me about?" he snapped.

"Nope, they shot him quickly! They'll torture you then make you bend over and get fucked in the ass by another man. Then they'll kill you slowly and painfully."

"Rhea, you would let them kill your children's father?" He looked frightened.

"At this rate, you're not going to be in their lives anyway, so it wouldn't matter to them if you were dead or alive! Actually, you could do more for all of your kids if you were dead. Do you have any life insurance policies?"

"Don't say that, Rhea. Even if we're not together, I'll be in the twins' lives."

"Shut the fuck up, you lying bastard. You don't do shit for the two you have. You play that role like you're a good father, but your parents take care of Ashley and Little Davis, not you. You ain't shit. I bet as soon as I mention child support, you'll probably move and change your phone number. Your parents will probably go along with whatever you do."

"I would never do that, Rhea. How could you think that?"

"Please. Whenever Noel, Terri or whomever you think you're going to be with this week tells you to drop your kids, you'll do it. Oh, and by the way, you can run all you want, in case the idea ever crosses your mind, but I've got your social security number, so my uncles could always find you within twenty-four hours."

"I would never do that."

"Yeah, right. Talk to me when the twins are starting to walk and you haven't seen them. You probably won't even come to their first birthday party, you despicable asshole."

"Do we have to be enemies, Rhea?"

"We don't have to be anything, and I've been a fool to think we were ever anything at all. I don't know why I never realized this before, Davis. We were two friends that were in lust. At least I was a friend to you. Hell, I still love you, but I was just some more pussy to you." I stopped to take a breath. "I'm tired. I don't feel like talking to you."

He touched my hand. "I'm not leaving until I'm done talking."

I snatched my hand away. "Suit yourself." I crawled back in bed.

"I'm going to lose everything because of all of this."

You're going to lose your life if you keep pissing me off.

"Davis, you don't have shit. You had to move in with your mama. You don't have a fucking degree, you lied about your job at Sebastian, you lied about your age, your children. You steal poems off line to give to women. You stole a fucking charge card from your second baby mama to send me shit. You were fucking us back to back, probably unprotected. You can't keep hurting people. You have to start being honest. If you don't love me, that's okay. But do everyone a favor and stop lying so much.

"If you want to be with Terri or Noel, that's fine. I'll go on with my life, because I had one before you." I was so flustered.

"I do love you . . . I think." He sighed.

"You think!" I threw back the comforter and sat up in the middle of the bed.

"I don't know what I'm saying anymore, Rhea. I don't really love Terri, and Noel, she's just . . ."

"Convenient pussy." I finished for him.

"Yes—I mean no. We're just friends. I've never looked at Noel as the type I'd marry, and Terri has no sense of family. Neither one of them would ever accept the other one's kid.

"Rhea, when I met you, I didn't know you and I were going to hook up. By the time I wanted to tell you the truth about everything, we were too caught up. I didn't want to lose you, so I continued lying. You would have never accepted me if I told you that I was a twenty-four-year-old college dropout with two babies who lost his paid internship with an awesome company because of my failing grades. Also, I never slept with you all back to back. Yes, they came to visit their kids while you and I were together, but I wasn't fucking them. By the time we got together, I'd stopped sleeping with them. I only slipped a few times after you and I started fighting."

"Whatever. Why did you do this to me, Davis? Why all the lies?"

He started to cry. This boy needed some new ammo. I was so sick of him crying!

"Rhea, I'm so sorry for everything. I never meant to hurt you. You made me so happy. I know it sounds crazy, but I wanted to propose to you the first night we were together. As soon as you left that first time, I told my parents I'd found the one. I always wanted to be with you. I just got scared when you got pregnant. I guess I thought we were going to have some time just for us, you know? Then when I realized I was going to have another kid, I don't know, I just lost my mind for a minute. Rhea, don't you understand? I got caught up."

"Fuck you, Davis! I don't believe you. Terri said you were getting ready to marry her."

"It's true," he said, dropping his head in his hands. "Terri is deranged. She said I would never be able to be with Ashley if I wasn't with her."

"Well, be with her then!" I screamed. "Davis, you knew how I felt about relationships. You knew everything I'd been through, and you intentionally deceived me. I fucking hate you. Get out!"

"Please give me another chance. I love you, and I love my babies."

"Is this the same Davis that said I should have an abortion? Boy, go to hell."

He got on his knees and grabbed me, pulling me to him. "Rhea, please let me touch your stomach. I love you, and I'm going to prove it to you, baby."

"Davis, you're full of crap. If you loved me so much, why didn't you jump at the chance when I told you I was ready for us to be together?"

He bowed his head. "Because I had already asked Terri to marry me by then. I'm not saying what I've done makes sense, but I am sorry from the bottom of my heart."

He rubbed my belly then told the twins how sorry he was and promised he'd spend every day of his life proving it to me. He lifted my shirt and kissed my belly. After a few seconds, he felt his babies kick for the first time.

"No matter what happens, I will never put anyone before you two. I will never abandon you, even if your mommy and I aren't together. I swear I will be there when you take your first breath, your first step. I'll be there when your first teeth come in, and on your first day of school. I love you both. I love your mommy too."

He kissed my hand. "I love you, Rhea."

Once again I must have been victim to the overwhelming power of prenatal vitamins and allowed him to embrace me. I swear the FDA needed to do an in-depth study on the side effects of prenatal vitamins.

He got up off his knees. "Rhea, I'm going home to get some clothes. I'll be back in a few minutes."

I just looked at him.

He said, "I know what you're thinking. I'm not going home to call Noel. It's time for me to make some changes in my life, and I'm not playing any more games. I love you. I always have. I only wish I'd been honest months ago, and we could actually be here celebrating our beautiful son and daughter's arrival instead of basking in drama."

"I know, Davis. I wish I could turn back the hands of time too. It's funny you said you wanted to propose to me that first night. I wanted to tell you how much I loved you, but I was afraid I'd scare you off. But this shit is still your fault. You perpetuated all this drama with your lies, your cheating, and your games. And if you walk out that door to go call Noel, don't bother coming back or ever calling me again."

"Rhea, I won't go if that's what it takes to prove my love for you. I know you can't forgive me right now. I know it may take some time, but can we try to find a way to try to start over? I want to move on past this drama."

"I never said I didn't still love you, but I ain't putting up with none of your bullshit and lies anymore. The ball is in your court now." I turned over and went to sleep.

CHAPTER 20

Davis woke me up some time after midnight, and we talked.

"Rhea, I want to spend the rest of my life showing you how much I love you."

"I love you too, Davis."

He went to take a shower. I got down on my knees and prayed.

"Dear God, please help me make the best decision. It's not about me anymore. I have two children I have to think about now. Lord, You said You may not come when we want You, but You're always right on time. Jesus, You know my heart. You know I'm a good person. Please show me if Davis is the right man for me. If he's not, Lord, please send him on his way. Lord, You know I'm not perfect, but You know I try to do what is right. I know my family and friends are going to think I'm stupid if I stay with Davis, but I have to try to make it work for my babies. Then if it doesn't, I can honestly say I did all that I could. This should be the happiest time in my life, but it seems like the worst for me. Thank You for my life, health and strength. Thank You for the gift of life that You've given me, manifested in a son and a daughter. All these things I pray in Your Son, Christ Jesus' name. Amen."

I went to sleep feeling peaceful. No matter what happened now, I had faith that things would work out just as they were supposed to.

CHAPTER 21

The next morning when we woke up, I told Davis I needed some time alone to think. He left me at the hotel, but called all day. He popped back over at around 4:00 in the afternoon, but I sent him away. I told him I would call him when I was ready to see him. From here on out, I was in the driver's seat.

I ordered dinner from the restaurant downstairs, took a bubble bath, then called him and told him to come over at 8:00 to rub my feet.

Michelle once told me that if a man cannot figure you out, then he won't fuck with you because he'll think you're crazy. So, as soon as Davis came in the room, I socked him right in the eye.

I apologized and blamed it on my hormones. He said he understood that it would take me a while to forgive him. I didn't say much to him, and went to sleep while he rubbed my feet.

I woke up a few hours later with a stiff neck.

"Ow. My neck hurts."

He was watching a football game on TV. "Lay down,

baby. Let me give you a massage. I know you're sore."
He began rubbing my neck.

After undressing me and giving me a long, sensual, full body massage from my scalp to my painted toenails, his tongue followed the path that his hands navigated. I allowed my body to give in and enjoy the sensations he was creating.

As he bent me over, I muffled my cries of ecstasy in the pillow. He pumped my valley like an old-fashioned well on a farm, until my water rose, peaked, then overflowed.

I slept like a baby until I was awakened by his tongue in between my thighs around 10:00 A.M. the next morning. He might have been a liar, but more than that Davis was a damn good sex partner!

"What are you doing?" I stretched and yawned.

He looked up at me with a twinkle in his eye. "Eating breakfast."

"Get up. I haven't even showered yet, Davis."

"Okay. If you really mean it." He nibbled on the inside of my thighs then pretended to retreat.

"No, please continue." I teased and pushed him back down. "Hey, stop licking my toes. That's nasty." I squirmed.

"I'm only nasty for you. Girl, you had me so horny when you came and attacked me yesterday. I just wanted to bend you over right then."

"Let's not talk about yesterday." I began to get upset.

He changed the subject quickly. "You have the most beautiful eyes I've ever seen."

"Flattery will get you nowhere, Davis."

"For a minute or so yesterday, I could have sworn your eyes changed colors. I should sue you! You busted me in head with that pitcher, girl."

"Yes, Davis, I was trying to bust your head open."

He quickly changed the subject again. "Are my kids going to have voodoo power?"

"Don't play. If I really practiced voodoo, you'd be dead by now."

He kissed my inner thigh. "You wouldn't kill your babies' daddy. You know why?"

"Why? Give me one good reason."

"Because you're not going to ever find a man that's going to have you screaming in ecstasy like I do. Anyway, I need to finish my breakfast." He put my legs around his neck and went back down for another round.

"Lick it, baby," I whispered seductively.

Yeah, all of this shit you've done, you're going to eat me on demand. And don't even think I'm going to return the favor ever again!

The telephone rang. I reached over to get it, hoping it was Noel, so I could cuss her out.

"Don't get it, Rhea," Davis begged.

"Davis, I'm not dealing with any shit today, and I'm going to put an end to your other baby mamas and their drama."

He got up. "I've taken care of Noel. She won't be bothering us anymore, and Terri wouldn't spit on me if I was on fire."

I grabbed the telephone. "Hello."

"Hi, Rhea." It was Mrs. Hickman.

"Oh, hello." I snickered at Davis, playing with himself.

"Rhea?"

"Yes, ma'am."

"You're in a good mood today." She giggled.

Just come out and say it. You know we had sex!

"Oh yes, ma'am. I feel a lot better."

I tried to listen, but Davis had crawled off the bed.

I was standing up, and he began nibbling my buttocks. I tried to muffle my sounds of delight.

"Rhea, are you okay?"

"Yes, ma'am. I'm fine. I'm—" I cupped my hand over the telephone. "Stop it!" I hissed at Davis.

Willie Mae interjected. "How 'bout when y'all finish what you're doing you have my son call me. And tell that boy to take a cold shower. Y'all keep on like this and you're going to be pregnant every year."

By then, I was totally overtaken as he put my nipple in his mouth and fingered me deeply. Each time he retreated from my vagina, he'd rub my juice on my breasts and suck them. I only half heard what she said as Davis's fingers plunged deeply in and out of me.

She hung up, and eventually the beeping from the phone became a distant sound in the background.

The sounds of flesh on flesh took over as he rammed his muscle deeply inside of me from behind. We copulated like two mad rabbits in heat for the next few hours. I loved to feel him inside of me, and his cum was always like a thunderous volcano. This was what soul mates connecting felt like.

I could feel when his ejaculation was starting to form then travel up his shaft until it exploded inside of me. I'd never enjoyed sex much until Davis. I was totally dick-whipped as his chocolate flesh entered me repeatedly. The silhouette of my big, muscle-bound man on top of me, grasping me by the hair, was the most beautiful sight I'd ever seen.

Afterwards, we lay in each other's arms, exhausted and wet. He tried to bend me over to go for another round only after a few minutes of resting.

"No, Davis. This isn't right. I feel so ghetto! The babies were moving."

"No, they weren't!" He kissed my stomach then got up and grabbed a towel to put in the wet spot. "They were saying, 'Daddy, give me more protein so I can grow up to be big and strong.'" He rubbed my belly. "What are Mommy and Daddy going to name you two?"

He sat up, propped his elbow on the pillow and stared at me. "I love you, Rhea."

"I love you, too, but we've got some serious issues. Don't think an apology and some daffodils is going to erase all this shit. I'm willing to try again, Davis. I want my children to have their father in their life. But I'm not desperate. I'll be able to think a little better when I get back home."

"I know you're not desperate, and I know it's going to take some time. But I'm going to try my best to make you as happy as I did when we first met."

The telephone rang again. I picked up the receiver. "Hello."

"Hey, baby. It's me again. Can I please speak to Davis?"

"It's your mom." I handed him the phone.

"What? When? I'll be right home." He hung up.

"What's wrong, Davis?" I rubbed his back.

"Terri just served me with emergency court papers to try to come get Ashley. She went through child protective services. I don't know how she could do this. I thought you had months to prepare for something like this. I have to be in court next Thursday. I only have nine days to find a lawyer. I told you this would happen! Look, Rhea, I really I can't go through this without you."

Basically, your broke ass is going to need some money! Here we go again with the drama.

CHAPTER 22

I thought the courtroom scenes from the television show *The Practice* were crazy, but they had nothing on the case between Terri and Davis. He laughed when I inquired about the specifics of the hearing. He said the Honorable "Cooter" Butch Dean kept falling asleep throughout the proceedings.

I'd gone with him to meet Matthew Atkins, Esquire, two days before the hearing. Mr. Atkins looked like a cross between Colonel Sanders and Matlock. His lawyer looked as if he had an invisible sign on his forehead that read: *I Hate Black People but I like Green Money.*

I paid the change fee for my flight and stayed in town to support Davis. When Thursday finally rolled around, Davis and his parents went to the courthouse, and I stayed at the house with the kids. I felt I needed to stay around for moral support, just in case things didn't go in his favor. Even after all the things I'd said to Davis about how he would leave his kids one day, I knew he really loved them. It would've hurt him if he lost this case.

I got a call from Terri on Tuesday before the hearing. I lied to her as Davis asked, and told her that I was going home. Her attorney wanted me to give a sworn statement about all the activities that went on in the Hickman household. That would help to assassinate Davis's character, and he would be ordered to let Terri take Ashley with her. She pointed out that I was her smoking gun.

I decided to stay out of the battle between him and Terri. They could fight it out amongst themselves. I still didn't know if I could trust her. His grandmother and aunts claimed they had caught Terri being exceptionally mean to Little Davis. His cousin, Peaches, walked in the bathroom once and saw Terri spanking him. He was practically a newborn at the time.

During one of my phone conversations with Terri, I'd briefly mentioned the allegations to her. She didn't deny it, nor did she admit it. Noel wasn't one of my favorite people either, but I would never be mean to any child.

Terri's attorney tried to portray the Hickman home as an open-door motel. Even if it was, they would have to prove that without my help. They also claimed the kids all took baths together and slept in the same bed. The whole bath thing did irritate me a little. Ashley was a toddler and Nicholas was five. At some point, one would think that adults should not allow children to see each other's genitalia.

Terri's lawyer brought up the fact that Little Davis didn't have a crib and slept with the elder Hickmans, which really shouldn't have been a big deal anyway. I knew that Ernest was taking Viagra, but from what I was told, it didn't work, so it wasn't like they were having sex, with the baby in the bed.

The judge reminded the lawyer that the case only pertained to Ashley, anyway, not Little Davis.

Allegedly, the Hickmans didn't feed Ashley healthy food because she ate Hamburger Helper at least three times a week.

His attorney's rebuttal was that Terri's claims were all unwarranted and without merit. Furthermore, she had no place to raise Ashley but a dorm room. He welcomed the judge to set up home visits to see for himself that Ashley was not being raised in an unfit home.

Judge "Cooter" temporarily ruled in Davis's favor. He made it clear that his ruling was only based on the fact he didn't want to uproot a seemingly happy child out of her environment. He scheduled a permanent custody hearing for the following spring. The judge made it clear that Davis had better be on his P's and Q's, because he was going to schedule lots of surprise home visits.

It was about to be war, and I knew Davis could not handle that wild stallion alone.

The judge allowed Terri visitation with Ashley, so a few days later, she and Davis met at a public park. In a way, I felt bad for her. But then again, I never would have left my child the way she did in the first place.

When Davis returned from meeting with Terri at the park, we took the kids to Chuck E. Cheese's for dinner.

As I was strapping Ashley inside her car seat, my cell phone rang. It had been ringing all day from an unknown caller, and I'd been ignoring it. I needed a day off from all the drama. But after the fourth series of rings, I couldn't take it anymore.

"Hello," I said cautiously.

"This is Terri. I just want you to know that you are a low-down, dirty bitch. If I can't have my baby, you won't have yours either. I know you're still there with Davis. You'd better stay the fuck away from my child. She only has one mother, and, bitch, that ain't you."

She hung up. I shut off my cell phone in case she tried to call back.

Oh God. What had I started? Now that bitch was after me too!

How did Terri know I was in town? Was she watching us? Terri was completley out of control, and now I understood that the last thing I needed was to be her enemy.

CHAPTER 23

The kids were all worn out from the trip to Chuck E. Cheese's and had all fallen asleep in the car. After putting them to bed, I helped Willie Mae clean up, and then Davis and I went back to the hotel. Child protective services would be scrutinizing everything Davis did. Terri and her camp would surely be looking for anything to use against him. Any impropriety on his part could be detrimental to his upcoming case, so there wouldn't any more overnight stays at the Hickman house for me.

Once we got to the hotel, I turned my cell phone back on. Again, I'd received a lot of unknown calls. I now refused to answer anything, unless it had a name or number connected with it.

I sat down on the bed and began to process the day's events. I was so mad and frustrated. My inner voice told me the madness was not about to be over anytime soon. I was glad I was leaving on Sunday. Only three more days to go.

"Aaaaaaaaargh!" I screamed at the top of my lungs out of frustration.

Davis yelled from the shower. "Rhea, are you okay, baby?"

"No! People keep calling me and won't leave a message."

"Don't worry about it." He got out of the shower a few minutes later and tried to grab me.

"Get off of me. You're wet." I pushed him away and threw him a towel.

"I'm about to make you wet, all right," he said as he wrapped the towel around the lower half of his body. Under normal circumstances, that would've been a turn-on, but I was pissed.

"How can you say, 'Don't worry about it?' This shit isn't over, Davis."

"Hey, I wasn't being nonchalant. What I meant was I want you to relax, Rhea."

"Whatever. Let's not talk about this now. I'm starving."

"You want a sausage?" He dropped his towel.

"That's gross! You know I don't eat meat. Seriously, my stomach is killing me."

"I'm hungry too." He licked his lips and stared down at my vagina. I tried to ignore the creamy wet mass that only Davis could produce with his sexy lips.

"Davis, you're making me wet." I kissed him deeply and massaged his back. "But I need some real food."

"Okay, what do you want?" He grabbed me from behind, cupping my breasts.

"A cheesecake, pickles, and some red clay." He turned around and stared at me in total disbelief.

"You sure that's what you want?"

"Yes, that's what I want."

My cell phone rang. We stared at one another.

Since when did answering a phone become such an arduous task? I took a deep breath. "Hello."

"*Hola*, Rhea! *Qué paso?*" It was Michelle.

"Hey, cuz. What's up?"

"Who is that?" Davis mouthed as he started getting dressed.

"It's Michelle," I mouthed back.

"Rhea, are you with Davis?"

"Yes."

"We need to talk. Get rid of him!"

"Huh?"

"*Ahora!*"

"Okay. Hang on."

What's going on now?

"Hey, Davis, the babies are starving. Can you please go get our food now? And Michelle says hello."

Michelle hated him. I'd been emailing her bits and pieces of my relationship with Davis. She thought he was total pond scum. She spoke to Cheryl quite a bit, so she probably knew everything anyway.

"Tell her I said hi." He patted his pockets, looking for his keys. "Found them. Okay, baby. I'll be right back."

"Okay. Drive safely."

Michelle laughed. "'Okay, baby'? What, y'all getting married now?"

I wanted to laugh, but I didn't want Davis to think we were laughing at him.

He said, "Rhea, I love you," as he walked out.

"I love you too," I mouthed.

Michelle was in stitches. "'I love you'!" she screamed hysterically.

As soon as he left, I looked out the peephole then

stuck my head out the door to make sure he'd gotten onto the elevator. I walked back toward the bed and looked out the window. That's when I saw a man walking away from his car. Or maybe I was imagining things. After all, it was dark outside. The man probably just got his car confused with Davis's.

"Michelle, that's not funny. We do love each other. We're having some problems, but we'll work it out."

"'Problems'? Bitch, you've got more than problems." She was still laughing. "Cheryl told me everything, and if you think you have problems now, you're going to go into premature labor when I tell you about this shit."

I climbed back in bed. "What is it, Michelle? Hold that thought. My back is a little sore. I need to find some Tylenol."

"Y'all need to stop doing it doggy-style."

"How do you know how we do it?" I laughed.

"You emailed me that was his favorite position, remember?"

"Oh yeah, I did."

I forgot about that! I need to stop telling her all my business.

"Are you very sore from your fall?"

"What fall?" *How did she know?*

"Rhea, don't play stupid. I know what happened at Hooters."

"How do you know?"

"I don't know how to tell you this, but . . ." She paused.

"What, Michelle?"

Her tone had changed from jovial to solemn within a matter of seconds. "Okay, you have to promise you won't say a word to anyone, okay?"

"Michelle, you've forgotten what family I'm a member of. You know we know how to keep secrets. What's up?"

Michelle was probably going to tell me something trivial about one of our cousins.

"Okay, who had an abortion now?" I laughed half-heartedly.

"Rhea, it's my dad and Toussaint."

"What? What happened?" I sat straight up in bed.

"They're going to help Terri." It took me a minute to make the connection.

"Terri? How? What are you saying, Michelle?"

"What I'm saying is they've agreed to help her financially with her court case and anything else she needs."

"What do you mean? I'm confused."

"Rhea, you're not stupid. Your boyfriend is being targeted."

"Why?"

"Because of all of this shit. Terri also told them how immoral Davis was and that he's a horrible father."

"Will this drama ever end?" I was on the verge of tears.

"Well, I just found out. Enrique overheard Dad on the phone with Toussaint and swore me to secrecy." Enrique, my younger cousin, stayed with Uncle Pierre during the holidays and college breaks. He was the project child in my family. His dad was deceased, so everyone sort of adopted him.

"Michelle, how did they find Terri?"

"They didn't. She found them."

"How?"

"You can thank Davis for that one. When his slick

ass was lying to Terri about your relationship, he told her all about our family."

"How did she find them?" I repeated.

"Think about it, Rhea. How many Toussaint Ramirez Baptiste LaDay M.D.'s are listed in the Atlanta directory?"

Stupid Davis. You don't know what you've done. "Michelle, what do they want?"

"I'm not sure, but I'll snoop. I'm sort of at a disadvantage this time, kid. There's not much that I can do from Europe."

"Michelle, do my parents know?"

"Of course not. Veronique might possibly go along with this shit, but your dad . . . you know he wouldn't allow this to happen. Does he even know you're pregnant?"

I smiled. My dad would never let them get away with this. "No, but I'll deal with that. All I need to do is talk with Daddy. Toussaint doesn't think I have the guts to tell Daddy I'm pregnant, so I'll just beat him to the punch."

"Don't be surprised if someone tries to buy Davis off so he'll terminate his parental rights."

"Mom already tried to get me to do that."

"Rhea, this is a mess."

"Michelle, do you think they would really hurt him?"

She paused for a brief second. "Yes, and I say that only because Terri made it seem as if Davis beat you up. She also told them everything that you've ever told Davis about us."

"Like what? What did she tell them?"

"Well, Rhea, let's just say my dad knows you suspect him and Uncle Tomas in Anthony's death."

"How could Davis tell that? I trusted him."

"According to Terri, Davis put up some sort of guise and made you out to be an unstable, rich girl he was trying to befriend. Are you sure you want to know everything that he said?"

"No, Michelle. I can only imagine."

Davis couldn't be trusted and I was stupid. I should have seen the handwriting on the wall after he told me all of Noel's and Terri's business. I never should have said a word about my family.

"Rhea, he told Terri about some of the illegal things, and she made sure she told Toussaint."

Things were really starting to crest downwards. If Terri even implied she was contemplating blackmail against my family, she, her family, and maybe even Ashley would never be safe.

"Oh, it gets better," Michelle told me. "Terri called Noel's mom and filled her in on the drama. Terri, Noel's mom, and your brother were all on a three-way call and were trying to devise a plan to keep 'the predator'—which was Noel's mom's name for him—away from his kids."

I was in total disbelief. "Michelle, I don't know what to do."

"Nothing. Fuck that nigga." She laughed.

"I just need to think and decide what I need to do." I was getting a headache.

"Maybe Toussaint just wants you to get back with Marcus."

"That has nothing to do with it," I snapped at her. "It's all about Toussaint, even when we were kids. He always has some ulterior motive. I just don't know what it is this time."

"Rhea, let's change the subject. How are my little cousins doing?"

"They're fine. Girl, they are getting bigger every

day. We haven't decided on any names yet. They are so precious, Michelle. You should see them on the ultrasound. My little boy is so big, and my daughter has her little legs crossed in the womb."

"I'm glad you're happy, Rhea. Do you love Davis?"

"Yes, I love him. I love him more than any other man I've ever been with. I don't expect for you to understand, but I want my kids to have their father around. Maybe someday we'll get married." I began to calm down a little.

"Don't get your hopes up with everything that's going on."

"You can say that again." I sighed.

"Tell you what. Think about what you want to do and email me. This international call is costing me a fortune."

"Thanks. I will."

"Get off this phone and rest. Don't let this drama upset you. You didn't do anything wrong."

"You're right. Let me get off of here and try to dry my eyes before Davis gets back."

"Love you, *chica*. Hey, scan the ultrasound photo and send it to me."

"Love you too. I'll email it to you."

Michelle could care less about an ultrasound, but I loved her for at least trying to make me feel better.

I gave Davis the biggest hug when he got back. He was sitting on the bed with a bouquet of daffodils and a whole cheesecake. He'd actually driven twenty miles out of the way to get some red clay. He was so sweet.

"What was that for?" he asked.

"For being the love of my life." I traced his lips

with my fingernails and sighed. Michelle's news had totally made me lose my appetite.

He whispered in my ear. "I love you, Rhea."

"I love you too." I forced myself to eat, and for the first time since my chocolate prince touched me back in June, I lay listless and unexcited as he made love to me.

"Rhea, what's wrong?" he asked afterwards.

I was crying silently in the dark. "Nothing," I answered. Davis had a big mouth. I wasn't going to tell him anything.

"You look tired. Let me give you a foot massage. That should help you rest."

"Thanks. My feet *are* killing me."

The last thing I remembered after my foot massage was him putting his mouth to my belly and telling the twins how he couldn't wait to hold them in his arms.

Davis woke me up around noon the next day. He said he had to go home and would be back later. I took advantage of my free time and slept for the rest of the afternoon.

He returned around 6:00 and said that he wanted to go out.

"Go out? Where?"

"I don't know. I feel like dancing."

"Remember how much fun we had that night we went Salsa dancing?" I laughed.

"Oh, I do. I remember when you were moving and swaying your hips to the beat. You looked so confident and beautiful, like you didn't have a care in the world. I'm so sorry. I know I'm the reason why your life is in turmoil right now."

"All I ask of you is that you be honest with me. No more lies or secrets, okay?"

"Hey, that Latin music is what got your Daddy all hot and horny, and that's how you two got here," he said as he rubbed my belly.

"Don't try to change the subject. I'm serious."

He put two fingers up in the air. "Scout's honor. No more secrets. Come on, pretty girl. Let's go dancing."

"Actually, that's not such a bad idea. Let's go."

I'd gotten a sudden burst of energy after resting all day. I put on a dress that was a tad bit too big, hoping my protruding belly would go unnoticed. We went to a nice French restaurant for dinner.

"Davis, you're not going to believe this." I laughed as we were pulling into the parking lot of The Spot, the local club.

"What, baby?" He parked the car and came around to open the passenger side door for me.

"My friends and I would always make fun of the pregnant ghetto girls at the club. Now I'm one of them." I giggled.

"No, you're not, Rheonique. Believe me, I know what you're talking about. Me and my frat brothers would trip out because all the fine girls at the club would always be pregnant. But this is completely different."

"Whatever you say," I replied sarcastically.

"Seriously. This isn't really a club. It's a lounge atmosphere. It's a non-smoking environment, you have on a nice maternity dress, and you're with your future husband, who happens to be your two babies' daddy." He kissed me.

"Is that so, Mr. Hickman? 'Future husband,' eh?"

I still felt ghetto. I was seven months pregnant at a club.

The thought of waking up in his arms every morning sent a warm fuzzy feeling down my spine. How we got from him fucking all three of his baby mamas last Sunday to marriage the following Friday was a total mystery. He needed to get his shit together with those two other women first before we even thought about marriage. I'd had one terrible marriage, and I wasn't trying to go down that road again.

I was only comfortable at The Spot for about an hour. I was completely out of breath after dancing the cha-cha slide.

"Davis, I'm ready to go. The babies are kicking."

"I'm glad you said it, Rhea. I'm ready to go, too. Besides, I'm horny again."

"Whatever you can get while I'm asleep is fine with me. I'm pooped, and not in the mood."

I crashed as soon as we got back to the hotel and was half-asleep as Davis tried to get some from the side. That boy was always looking to get some, no matter what shape I was in!

CHAPTER 24

It was approximately 2:30 A.M., when the telephone rang.

"Baby, get the phone," I muttered, half asleep.

"It's probably a wrong number," Davis answered groggily and knocked the phone off the hook. Neither one of us picked it up.

A half-hour later, there was a loud pounding on the door.

"What the hell?" Davis jumped out of bed.

Oh, shit! I prayed it wasn't my family and the goon squad.

"It's hotel security!" a male voice yelled through the door.

Davis threw on his shorts and went toward the door.

Oh, God! Please don't let my family kill my boyfriend!

I let out a sigh of relief when he opened the door. It really was hotel security.

"Mr. Hickman, there's been an emergency at your house. You need to call home."

"What happened?"

"Don't know. I was just told to tell you to call home."

"Thank you, sir." He closed the door.

"Davis, let's go." I started looking around for my clothes in the dark.

"We don't need to call?"

"No, let's just go!"

"Rhea, stay here. I'll call you as soon as I find out what's going on."

"No, I'm going with you." I got dressed and grabbed a change of clothes.

We raced to the car and kept dialing the house but couldn't get through.

"I hope everything's okay. I don't know what I would do if something happened to either one of my parents or one of the kids."

I rubbed his shoulder. "Calm down, Davis. Everyone is fine. But if you don't concentrate on the highway, you're going to kill us."

He stepped off the gas a little. "You're right. I'm glad you're here with me. You're my lucky charm." He squeezed my hand.

"I'm your sugar mama," I joked, trying to calm him down.

"No, you're my third baby mama, and the love of my life." He smiled. "Rhea?"

"Yes, Davis."

"Did you want to kill me when you found out I was only twenty-four?"

"No, I didn't," I said quickly.

"Really?" He looked surprised.

"I didn't want to kill you. I wanted to torture you slowly."

"Girl, please. You love this young dick." He laughed. "And, sweetheart, for the record, I'm sorry that I lied about my age." He smiled at me, and I smiled back. Had I known his age, I wouldn't have gotten involved with him. He did have a point, though. I did love his young ass.

There were three police cars in the driveway, when we turned the corner onto Blakely Lane.

Dear Jesus, please, please don't let the Baptiste LaDay family have anything to do with this mess.

Davis stopped the car and ran up the driveway. He looked back and saw me struggling to get out, so he ran back to help.

"I'm sorry, Rhea. I forgot about you." He smiled.

I fanned him away. "Go on in the house. I'm okay." I took my time walking up the driveway.

"Daddy!" Ashley ran to him. He picked her up and held her over his head.

"What's going on?" Davis asked his parents, who were sitting on the couch, talking with a female police officer.

"Put me down, Daddy. I want Rhea!" He put her down, and she ran over and gave me a kiss.

"Someone broke in," a male officer stated as he was coming down the hallway.

"What?" Davis and I both said in unison.

"What did they take?" Davis looked around.

"That's the funny thing." Another policeman emerged from the kitchen. "Nothing was taken."

"I don't understand," Davis said.

I do. This was my family's way of sending a message!

Davis sat down and yawned. "Daddy, tell me what happened."

"There's not a lot to tell, Davis. It's just so weird." Ernest stood up and stretched.

"Did electricity go off?" I asked.

"As a matter of fact, it did." The female officer looked at me in amazement. "How did you know?"

Everyone looked at me suspiciously.

"Oh . . ." I paused and looked around the room, trying to think of a lie. "I saw the clock blinking on the VCR."

Davis looked at me with a look that said, "We'll talk later."

My babies were either restless or hungry. One or both of the twins kicked very hard. Everyone could see the ripple effects through the front of my dress, which caused an eruption of laughter throughout the room.

"Davis, you must not have fed them babies today." Ernest laughed. He and his son exchanged a manly smile.

Nasty motherfucker!

"Go lay down somewhere, girl. I don't want you to have them babies too early. My nerves can't take no more," Willie Mae said with a laugh.

I was grateful for the chance to leave the room. I needed time alone to snoop. I walked out of the living room just as the two male officers were leaving through the front door.

After a few minutes, I went into the kitchen and took the battery out of the cordless phone. I wasn't the least bit surprised, when I found the telephone bug. I snatched it out. I tucked it securely in my bra just as Davis walked in.

"Rhea, what's going on?" He saw me fumbling with my bra.

"What do you mean?"

"Looked like you were sticking something in your bra."

"Something like what, Davis?" I snapped.

Seems like you running your big mouth to Terri about my family was the biggest mistake you could have ever made!

"Nothing, baby. It was just my imagination. Hey, don't get upset with me." He gave me a hug. "I'm just tired."

And I'm not? You selfish son of a bitch! You won't help your mom around the house. You won't do anything with your kids. You and your dad sit around and make your mom wait on you hand and foot. Your mom still does your laundry, and her ignorant ass puts up with y'all treating her like Molly the Maid. And you're tired? I'm carrying two of your babies, and for the past week have been taking care of the other two plus your nephew. Then to top it off, you want pussy every fifteen minutes. I can't take too much more of this everyday dick shit!

The fear I now felt after my family sent this warning combined with my raging hormones put me in a foul mood. Though I didn't say a word to him, Davis must have known I was thinking some pretty mean thing. He treated me gently so as not to get his head bit off.

"Rhea, I know if I'm tired you must be exhausted. Hey, tell you what. Let's go to my room. I'll put on some nice soft music and give you a massage."

"Oh, that's okay. Davis. I'm not tired." I needed more time to look around the house. Besides, Davis's horny ass was just looking for another excuse to fuck.

"Are you sure, Rhea?" He looked disappointed, like a damn starving dog.

"No, thank you. I'm going back in the living room," I said adamantly.

"It's almost five in the morning. You need your rest," he protested.

"I'm fine, Davis. I'm well rested."

"Well, I-I . . ." He stammered, trying to find an excuse to get me to the bedroom.

"Well what, Davis? I'm not tired, and I can help out when the kids wake up."

"And they'll be up soon," Willie Mae said from the doorway. "I just put Ashley back to bed. Thank you, Rhea. It's about time we had another woman in this family. Them other two heifers never helped me out. They never even spoke to me in my own house half the time."

That's your stupid-ass problem! Ain't no way in hell my son would be fucking his women in my house, right up under my nose, and I'd be washing his nasty, cum-filled sheets.

"Rhea, you're a good woman. I hope my son marries you."

If she only knew what I was thinking about her. She was to blame for a lot of this shit, so I wasn't real keen on her at the moment.

She smiled. "Hold on a minute." She brushed my hair from out of my face.

"What's wrong?" I pulled back quickly.

"Girl, all this hair. It keeps falling down."

No, your son has a fetish with my hair and likes to rub it across his nipples.

Willie Mae took a ponytail holder out of the kitchen drawer. She motioned for me to turn around so she could put my hair in it.

"Girl, them babies are going to have a head full of hair."

"I know. Don't remind me. I don't know how I'm going to do two heads every day."

"Hopefully you and Davis will live close enough that I can help you out. Y'all can keep the little boy. I'll take the girl."

"Oh no, thank you. They can come visit, but I'll keep my own babies." *You're not gonna have my babies around this psycho ward. They can come visit, but they sure as hell can't stay.*

The front door slammed shut, indicating the policewoman had finally left.

Everyone headed off into their respective places. Ernest went back to bed, Davis got on the computer, and Willie Mae was sorting laundry out in the garage. Ashley and Nicholas woke up, so I made them pallets on the floor in the living room, where they could watch cartoons. I put Little Davis in his playpen, gave him a bottle, and went back in the kitchen.

I needed to snoop around to find out what else was planted inside the house. I managed to somehow get down on my knees to unscrew the faceplate off the socket. I was getting around pretty good, considering I was pregnant. Luckily, the faceplate came off without a struggle. I didn't see anything, however, which didn't mean that there was nothing there.

I stood up and rubbed my back. There was nothing I could do to combat any of the surveillance crap. So, until I had some concrete evidence, I wasn't about to get upset. I knew my limitations. The thought of taking on the Baptiste-LaDay clan with their warped sense of family unity was a feat I just couldn't handle.

Uncle Pierre had the most up-to-date surveillance equipment. If he'd teamed up with his goon squad friends, I knew they would be an unstoppable team. The Hickmans were not safe. Since the house was bugged, there was probably a wireless video system hidden somewhere. I'd seen the latest equipment that my uncle had used to blackmail a government agent a few months prior. He'd purchased a wireless video and audio system that came with a GPS vehicle tracking device.

I was pretty sure that the little power outage had allowed whomever to set up a main docking station in the fuse box. That would allow them to monitor everything that was done and said in the house. It wouldn't surprise me if GPS vehicle loggers had been installed on all of the cars, which could track them up to 1,000 miles. The guy I'd seen leaving Davis's car from the hotel window was probably the goon they used.

I contemplated going to the police, but even if I did, they would never be able to detect the microscopic devices, with their antiquated equipment. I wondered if the police dusted the fuse box for fingerprints.

Willie Mae walked back into the living room, where I was sitting on one sofa, watching the kids who had fallen back to sleep in front of the TV. She talked so loud she woke up the baby. I told her I'd take care of everything, and she should go back to bed.

I took the baby in the kitchen, fixed him another bottle, and sang to him, hoping he would go back to sleep.

"Jesus loves the little children. All the children in the world," I sang.

Eventually, he closed his eyes. I took him back in the living room and put him in his playpen. After patting him on his back for a few minutes, he began to snore.

I almost tripped over my purse on my way back inside the kitchen. Just then, my cell phone rang. Luckily, the volume was low enough to not wake the kids. *Who's calling me this early in the morning?* I answered nervously.

I almost fainted when I heard the muffled male voice. It had been deliberately distorted.

"Rhea, hope you got the daffodils that were left on the back porch."

I looked out the kitchen window and got dizzy from what I saw. A pair of Davis's underwear had been splattered with red dye, and they were on the back steps with a knife stuck in them. Next to them was a bouquet of daffodils. They'd been dyed black.

I became so dizzy, I felt like I was going to pass out. I had to hold onto the doorknob to keep from falling. This was a professional, because they worked fast. I knew the police had checked the front and back yard for the intruder, and these things had not been out there. Somehow, the caller had managed to place these things in the short time since the police left.

"What are you looking at out there, Rhea?"

It was Davis! I froze.

How can I clean up the mess without being detected? Think fast on your feet, Rhea. You're a LaDay! You come from a long line of liars and schemers.

I quickly closed the curtains.

Davis came up behind me and began to suck on my neck. He whispered, "Damn, baby, you smell good. I can't get enough of you." He pushed his penis up against my buttocks and began gyrating.

"Davis, I feel sick."

"Come on. Let's go to my room," he suggested, ignoring what I'd said. "I want some so bad."

"Davis, I don't feel very good."

"What? But baby . . ." He looked like he wanted to cry.

I faked a few gagging noises.

"Are you okay, Rhea?"

"I'll be fine. Let me go outside." I turned the doorknob. There was absolutely no way he would follow me outside. This boy's stomach was so weak, he got sick changing shitty diapers.

"Are you sure you'll be okay?" he asked again.

"Yeah, I don't want to get sick in this kitchen. I shouldn't have eaten that French food."

He felt my forehead. "Well, you don't have a temperature."

"Tell you what, big daddy—Go in your room and lay across your bed. Then I want you to jack off and say my name. I'm going outside to get some fresh air, and I'll be back in a few minutes to rock your world," I whispered softly.

He turned quickly to leave the kitchen.

I smiled at my plan. Davis was so easy to manipulate, when it came to anything sexual. He'd be masturbating for at least ten to fifteen minutes.

I went outside and cleaned up the flowers, pretending not to notice the white van parked down the street. I came back inside and sat on the couch to watch TV. Davis came out of the room and asked if I was ready to go to the hotel. Obviously, he was ready for more sex. No surprise there.

We woke up his mother to tell her we were leaving.

When we got back, I showered after my alleged sick episode and went to sleep. We stayed in bed all day Saturday.

That evening, we went to the mall, and I had to get some props. I surprised him that night by dressing up in a Catholic schoolgirl uniform, with the short skirt, the long socks, and two ponytails in my hair.

I tried to take at least two layers of skin off his ass, while I spanked him with a paddle.

CHAPTER 25

After a quick lunch on Sunday morning, Davis waited with me at the airport until my flight left. I got back into Atlanta at exactly 5:00, picked up my dogs, and went straight home. I was so exhausted when I got into the house. I lit a fire in the fireplace and crashed on the couch.

I called the Hickmans to let them know I'd made it home safely. The kids wanted to speak to me, so after making my rounds and speaking with Davis briefly, I hung up.

I was both mentally and physically drained but couldn't fall asleep immediately. There were just so many things to ponder. How did a weekend excursion turn into a two-week ordeal? Whoever was behind the schemes almost gave me the impression I would suffer the same fate as Davis if I tried to intervene.

I decided to try to enjoy the simple things in life. I'd always wanted to plant a winter garden full of flowers and foliage but never had the time while working at Sebastian. It would have suited me just fine to relax and sip hot milk for the next few months, but my father had different plans for me.

"Rhea, I haven't seen you in months. I miss you," he said when he called.

"I know, Dad. I've just been really busy."

He didn't budge. "Well, no matter how busy you are, family is always most important. So, book a flight, and I'll pick you up at the airport."

"Where's Mom?" I tried to change the subject.

"She's out, Rhea. Is something going on?"

"No, sir. Why do you ask?"

"Well, your mom and brother have been acting very strange whenever your name is mentioned lately."

"Daddy, they're both strange people. They're Haitian." I chuckled.

"And you're not?" Dad laughed.

"I like to think that my genes come from your side. I try to pretend that I'm one hundred percent Afro-Cuban."

"Very funny, daffodil. Your mother would have a heart attack if she heard that."

Wouldn't that be nice if she did have a heart attack? I chided myself instantly. *Lord, please forgive me for thinking bad thoughts about my mother!*

"Daddy, I've gotta go. I'm late for aerobics," I lied.

"Yes, go on to the gym, Rhea. The last time I saw you those hips and butt were starting to spread as wide as the sun."

"Dad, that's not very funny."

"Sorry, princess. Love you, baby."

"Bye, Daddy. Love you too."

I was in a very precarious situation. I knew I had to eventually tell my father about my pregnancy, but I was waiting for the right time. Was there ever going to be a right time?

Two days later, I finally got the courage to tell him. He wasn't overly excited, but wasn't as disappointed as I thought he would be either. Dad was indifferent. He wanted to meet with Davis before he came to any conclusions.

"Rhea, I'm not happy about this, but you are an adult."

"Thanks, Dad. I knew you'd understand."

He sighed. "I just wish you would have told me earlier. Were you that afraid to tell me?"

"No, Daddy. It's just that I've been so embarrassed."

"Why? Because of who I am? Rhea, I come from a country where people eat out of trashcans. I don't want you to feel ashamed of your children. Your babies are not mistakes. Maybe bad timing and maybe with the wrong person, but no child is ever a mistake."

"Daddy, you are the most wonderful person on the planet, and I love you more than anything." Feeling relieved, I promised to make plans to visit my family soon.

Dad called the next night to say I should come as soon as possible. My *abuela* had taken ill, so he needed to take an emergency trip back to Havana. He wanted me to come the next day so he could see me before he traveled.

I made my reservations and packed my bags immediately.

He picked me up at the airport and was silent the whole ride back to the house. He and Mom must have had a fight about me.

Maria, the maid, greeted me in the kitchen and commented about how pretty I looked.

Mom walked downstairs, saw me, then turned around and walked the other way without speaking.

She barely looked at me and looked disgusted to see my stomach.

Toussaint had the nerve to walk around acting as if nothing was going on. As if he'd never spoken to Terri and wasn't plotting against Davis.

I finally confronted my mother at the dinner table that night. "Mom, what is the problem? You've barely said anything to me today."

"Rheonique, under the circumstances, it would be in your best interest if I said nothing to you. You are a big disappointment. I raised you better."

"Better than what, Mother? To have unprotected sex? Did I ask you for anything? Am I moving back home to bring my little illegitimate babies here to burden you?"

She stared at me. "I'm not having this discussion with you now. And you'd better watch your tone."

"Watch my tone or what, Mom? Now is when I need you more than ever. Have you asked anything about these babies? Have you planned a shower? Have you even told anyone? I'm a grown-ass woman with a doctorate degree. What in God's name are you ashamed of?"

She stood up and got in my face as if she were going to hit me.

Dad jumped up from the table.

She spoke barely above a whisper. "You are a screw-up, Rhea. You have always commingled with trash, and you see where this finally got you?—Two little babies that are going to become statistics."

I left the table in tears. My feelings were so hurt. I'd gone out of my way to be exceptionally nice to her all day. I'd tried to look as good as I could, wearing a beautiful black maternity dress with matching shoes. Nothing was ever good enough for my mother.

Toussaint came up to my room and said that Mom didn't mean to make me upset. Dad followed shortly thereafter and told me everything was okay.

Why didn't he come to my rescue? I was so happy I didn't live near my parents and had my own house. I couldn't wait to leave the next morning.

On the drive back to the airport, Daddy said that as soon as he got back from his trip, he wanted to meet Davis. "I'll fly out to Atlanta to go with you to an ultrasound appointment."

"I love you so much." I began crying as they announced the boarding call for my flight. "Please don't let Mom poison you against Davis. There's a lot going on, but when you get back, we'll talk. I know he can make me happy, Daddy."

"Oh, pumpkin. You'll always be my beautiful little dark princess."

"Thank you, Daddy, so much. Please have a wonderful trip and tell everyone about the babies."

"I will, baby. Tell you what, princess—I'll fly back into Atlanta from Cuba and spend a week with my beautiful daughter. We can set up the nursery together. I can't wait to finally meet the infamous Davis Hickman."

That made me smile. I hoped Dad liked Davis. "I love you, Daddy. That will be so much fun. I'll start thinking of nursery themes."

I boarded the plane, relieved that at least Dad was in my corner. Maybe I should have told him about the plot against Davis.

Mom would be livid that Daddy would be returning from a long trip, and instead of coming straight home, would be coming to visit me. Good.

CHAPTER 26

As I neared the end of my seventh month of pregnancy, it seemed as if I'd gained another pound every day. My stomach looked like a big watermelon. Davis said he didn't care if I got as big as a house. I knew he was full of shit, but it was still sweet.

Davis and I were still seeing each other every other weekend. I knew he couldn't afford it, so I paid for his flights to come see me.

He quit the weekend job at the singing telegram service so he would have his weekends free. He worked during the week full-time at Hooters and helped his parents with the kids. Things seemed to be falling into place.

Davis had suddenly become very considerate of my feelings. He took extra measures in order to wait on me hand and foot. I guess being pregnant by him wasn't so bad after all. He did seem genuinely sorry for the madness he'd created, and actually things had seemed to be pretty drama-free for a while.

The twins were becoming so lively and getting bigger every day. We couldn't decide on names, so we just called them Boy and Girl. Davis would read out loud to them, and I'd sing to them every night.

We purchased all of the large items—the cribs, car seats and playpens. Since we couldn't decide on a unisex theme, we opted to have two separate nurseries. Our little boy's nursery theme would be Winnie The Pooh, and our daughter's was Peter Rabbit.

I got on the registry at several department stores, and between my friends and my sorority sisters, both Boy and Girl would have enough clothes to last until they went to kindergarten. Since no one but Cheryl knew about my pregnancy, though, I was going to wait until after I gave birth to have the showers.

My life really wasn't too bad. Davis frequently talked about marriage, but I was still very cautious. My biggest concern was that he didn't seem to be as eager as I was to end all the drama. Every conversation centered around how to get revenge on Terri. I kept quiet about it until one day Davis just started taking things to another level. He called me, behaving very strangely.

"Hello," I answered.

"Hey, baby?"

"What's up, baby? What time are you getting in on Friday?"

"I think my flight gets in around three."

"Crap, I have an ultrasound at three."

"Can you re-schedule? I want to be there." He sounded anxious.

"I doubt it. It took me forever to get this appointment."

"Don't worry about it, Rhea. I'll make the next one. By the way, I've got the money for the flight this time, and I'll take a taxi to the house. Rhea, thanks for everything, baby."

"Where did that come from?" I asked, perplexed. Davis was up to something. What did he want? He had never offered to pay me back for anything.

"Nowhere, baby. I just want you to know how much I appreciate you. Thanks for letting me come to your house every other weekend to escape," he said wistfully.

"Oh, baby, don't worry about it. I kind of like playing house," I joked.

"Amen to that. We still need to break in the guest bedroom downstairs, but I loved it out on the patio by the pool." He laughed.

"I bet you did. My ass had goose bumps on it for days!" I laughed.

"Hey, I need to talk to you about something."

"What's up?"

"I think I may lose this court case. I'm worried."

"Baby, don't worry. Everything will be fine."

"Rhea, I'm afraid if Terri wins she's going to take Ashley back to Grenada."

"Boy, stop. You're paranoid. What about school? She wouldn't run away and not finish school."

"She could go to school in Grenada. She threatened to take her out of the country when she was born. Terri will do it."

"Davis, you'll win. Don't worry about it."

"I don't want to take any chances, Rhea."

"What are you saying?"

"I'm saying, do you think your uncles have any contacts that could—"

"That could what?"

"You know . . ."

"No, I don't!"

"I don't have a lot of money right now, but I want her out of the way—permanently," he whispered.

"Davis, do you know what you're saying?"

"Yes. I want her dead!" he declared.

"Don't talk like that, please. Both of our phones could be tapped."

The phone started making funny noises. I got off in a hurry.

Davis just didn't get it. There was no chance of me getting my family to take care of Terri, especially since he was most likely a target already. Terri would not be their victim, because she was already their accomplice.

As I thought about my family, I realized things had been too quiet. Since I left my parents' house, Toussaint had not even tried to contact me. Terri, and even Noel, seemed to just disappear out of our lives. It was just too good to be true. In my heart, I knew that any day something was bound to happen. It was just the calm before the storm.

And sure enough, Davis and I were both served with court papers the very next day. I was returning home from getting a pregnancy massage, when Davis called with his news.

"Rhea, I can't believe this crazy bitch!" he yelled from the phone.

I was in my car, waiting for the security guard to open the gate at the entrance to my neighborhood. The guard approached my car with something in his hand.

"Davis, hang on. The security guard is stopping me for some reason."

"What's wrong, Rhea?"

"I don't know. Hold on."

Michael tapped lightly on the window. "Hey, Rhea." He showed me a large envelope. "I had to sign for this. The guy said he had been trying to deliver this for weeks, but he hasn't been able to catch you at home."

"Thanks, Michael." I took the envelope and waved goodbye then picked up the phone again. "Davis, let me call you right back when I get inside the house."

"Don't hang up, please! I'll hold. And hurry up, Rhea. I need to tell you what Terri did."

"Okay, suit yourself." I pretended I'd lost the telephone signal and hung up on him.

As soon as I got in my house, I filled my 7-Eleven mug with crushed ice from the icemaker. I sat down and opened the envelope. In it were court papers, stating that I was being sued by Marcus.

I dialed my attorney and left a message for him to call me back ASAP. Then I called Davis back before he had a heart attack.

Davis finally clicked over after my fifth time dialing. "Look, Noel, I'm sorry. My phone kept beeping. I didn't mean to hang up on you."

"Noel!" I was incensed.

"Oh hi, Rhea," he said nonchalantly.

"What the fuck?" I yelled.

"I called Noel because it seems like you were too busy to talk, and I needed some advice."

"You fucking bastard!"

"Slow down, baby. I also needed to see if she was going to still come here to visit."

"What?"

"I told you she wanted to see the baby. She wants to come here for a week or so between semesters."

"What?" I said again in total disbelief.

"Rhea, you're my woman. Noel knows that. You have nothing to worry about."

"Why in the fuck does she need to come there at all? Why can't her little African ass pick up the baby and go home? That is what college students do. They take their asses home!"

"I don't know, but anyway, I needed advice. Since you were too busy for me, I called Noel."

"Davis, that was blatant disrespect. And for your information, Marcus is suing me."

"Welcome to the club. Terri got some type of emergency hearing set up for the twelfth. For the life of me, I don't know how that crazy bitch got the money for a new lawyer. She's trying to make arrangements to get Ashley for the whole summer." I knew where she got the money. Probably from my mother or brother.

My phone beeped. It was my attorney, so I got off the phone with Davis. I was angry enough to kill either Davis or Marcus. Hell, I could do a two-for-one and kill them both!

Marcus was suing me for $5,000 for items he claimed I'd destroyed. I'd repeatedly sent him certified letters to retrieve his golf clubs and the rest of his shit that he'd left, but to no avail. Marcus would always set an appointment to come by the house then he'd cancel or just wouldn't show up.

My lawyer assured me that this was a frivolous lawsuit and not to worry about Marcus and his unfounded claims.

Marcus wanted any excuse to see me. I could have just given him the money, but it was the principle. I wasn't giving him shit.

The lawyer assumed I'd gotten the paperwork weeks before, and told me to be ready to go to court soon.

I read the 23rd Psalm and went to bed.

CHAPTER 27

The more bullshit erupted in my life, the more depressed I became. Dad was still in Cuba, and every time Mom called, she made sure to tell me that I was the talk of the entire LaDay clan. She assured me that she hadn't shared our embarrassing news with anyone, so I could only assume that between Toussaint and my Uncle Pierre, the rumors had spread like wildfire.

Everyone in the family knew my babies' daddy was either unemployed or in-between menial jobs. He had two other baby mamas, and had beaten me up at Hooters. I was the ultimate disappointment as far as my mother was concerned.

Davis invited me to spend a weekend in Colorado. I was so big and round, but I was in excellent shape, so I decided it was still okay for me to fly.

He picked me up at the airport, and when he hugged me, I could tell he missed me just as much as I had missed him.

"Hey, baby, it's only been two weeks, but I've missed you, Rhea." He smiled.

"I know, Davis. I couldn't wait to see you either."

He apologized about calling Noel, and promised it would never happen again. We went back to his parents' house. Ernest was being his usual grouchy self. His problem that day was that he didn't want to have to buy any diapers for Little Davis because Noel and her fat-ass mother didn't send any money for the baby.

Ernest did have a valid point. They should have been contributing monetarily, but in the interim, the baby needed diapers.

Ernest was really getting on my nerves, so I loaded all three kids in Davis's car and took them shopping. *I'd rather deal with small kids than immature adults any day.*

After a two-hour trip and a two-hundred dollar charge at Toys "R" Us, I took the kids to Macy's. I bought Little Davis his first suit. He was so round, and the suit was a tad bit tight, so he would only be able to wear it a few times. But he had a little brother coming in a few months who would be able to wear it, so I got it anyway. We'd still get some use out of it.

Noel was pissed that I was spending time with the Hickmans, so she picked the baby up the next day. She was going to bring him back before she went back to school the next semester.

The day after that, Terri came and picked up Ashley. Davis had agreed to let her spend an extended period of time with Ashley, in hopes Terri might agree to drop the court case.

I went with Davis and his parents to his grandmother's house, but I couldn't take all the loud talk-

ing and ignorant people she had invited over that
night.

Davis and I left early.

When we got back to the house, an overwhelming
feeling of sadness engulfed me. I suddenly became
very depressed. Everyone in my family hated me, and
I missed my daddy.

I began to cry. Davis was sitting down inside his
closet, arranging his shoes. He pulled me down to
him. He stroked my hair. "Don't cry, Rhea. This time
next year we'll be married, the twins will be crawling,
and I'll have all of my kids together. We'll all be together as a family."

Davis held me as the tears flowed down my face.
"Stop crying, baby. It'll be okay. If your family can't
accept us, we'll start our own family traditions. We'll
have big holiday dinners, and we can buy the girls
matching dresses and the boys matching suits." He
pulled me back a little and kissed my forehead.
"You'd better take advantage of this peace and quiet,
girl. Can you imagine how rowdy our house is going
to be next year?"

I smiled at the thought of me cooking dinner,
chasing all the kids around while Davis watched football and yelled things like, "Rhea, the twins are in the
garage! Ashley got into your makeup again! Nicholas
and Little Davis are outside riding the dog like a
horse!"

I faintly heard Davis.

"We'll have Ashley, Nicholas, Little Davis and the
twins." He was counting out loud on his fingers.
"Damn, that's a houseful!" He smiled and sighed.
"Rhea, we'll be a happy family, I swear."

Davis pulled me down so that I sat on top, facing

him, and we made love in his closet. There was something so different this time about our lovemaking. It was so serene, so special. I had never felt so close to him. While he was depositing himself inside of me, I opened my eyes and saw little bright stars flickering. There was a sort of quickening inside of my stomach, as if something supernatural was taking place.

Davis noticed it too. "Rhea? Something just happened. I don't know what it was."

"I know, Davis. It was weird. My family is from the islands, so I don't question anything."

"Rhea, that's the same feeling that I had, when the twins were conceived."

"What do you mean?"

"Remember that night on our first trip in June when you woke up and I was staring you?"

"Yes." I was puzzled.

"I felt like I had impregnated you. That's why I questioned you about what you would do if you ever got pregnant. I didn't make a big deal about it because I wasn't really sure, but I had that feeling then, just like I do now."

"I don't know, Davis. Something just happened, though."

He kissed me deeply and helped me stand up. "Hey, want to watch TV with me?"

"No, I'm going to take a shower and go to bed."

I slept until the next day.

When it was time to pick up Ashley from Terri's mother's house, Davis, naturally, had no gas money. I paid for the gas and rode with him. I slid my head down in the back seat while he ran up to the door to get Ashley.

When we got home and unpacked her bags, we

noticed that Terri had thrown away all of the clothes that I had bought for Ashley. Since Davis had been having dreams about black snakes devouring him in his dreams, I made him throw away the suitcase. I didn't trust Terri, especially after the comments she'd made about voodoo.

I went back home, and within two days, Davis called, saying he needed to borrow more money. He wanted to enroll Ashley in a daycare center so his mother could get some rest, Little Davis had to go to the doctor, and Nicholas wanted to take karate lessons.

"Davis, enough is enough! Those bitches need to pay child support, and so does your brother!"

"I know. My brother is locked up again. I promise, Rhea, I'll pay you back as soon as I get my income tax money."

"I'll put a check in the mail, and in the memo section I'm going to put *loan to be repaid.*"

"Thanks, Rhea. You know I'll pay you back when I get some money."

"I don't doubt that you *want* to."

"I feel so bad asking you for money. You know I would go back to the singing telegram job, but then I wouldn't be able to see you so much on the weekends, baby."

This boy was pathetic! How did he go from being groomed for corporate America to doing menial jobs, singing hooks like Nate Dogg? Surely the temp agency could find something else for him to do besides dressing up like animated characters, especially in that Dora the Explorer costume. It looked terrible on him. He didn't look so bad in the Blues Clues costume, though. It actually accentuated his figure.

He was so fucking sad when it came to money. He

would fill up his car at the gas station and pretend to leave his wallet. Then he'd leave his driver's license as collateral. The Quick Stop sent the Sheriff to his parents' house after the fourth time. They told him the next time he pumped gas without paying they were going to post his picture at all the gas stations within a thirty-mile radius.

"Davis, pay me back whenever you can." I didn't know whether to laugh or cry.

"Can you please wire it into my mom's account?"

"I think I threw the info away from the last time," I said in disbelief.

"Hang on. Let me get it."

Davis had better not ever piss me off. I have too much of his family's personal information.

"On second thought, Rhea, don't send it yet. I think her bank account is in the negative. Let me check with her first."

"Okay, Davis. Just let me know." I sighed.

The whole family is retarded. The sign on the front of their house should say The Pathetics *instead of* The Hickmans.

CHAPTER 28

As the final six weeks of my pregnancy approached, Davis came to visit me for another weekend. He brought three big bouquets of daffodils and proposed. I told him I would accept his proposal only on one condition.

"What's the condition? I'll do anything you want. Just please say you'll marry me."

"I don't want you to be friends with Noel anymore. It's obvious that she wants more than friendship. I don't have a problem with you all talking, in terms of Little Davis, but that's the extent of it. I'm not going to share you."

"Share me? You don't have to share me. I'm all yours, baby. Noel knows that you're my girl. Do you want her to just stop talking to me altogether like Terri did?"

"Yes, I do."

"Rhea, I'm not going to let you give me an ultimatum."

"Well, then your answer is no."

Davis slept in the guest bedroom the rest of the weekend.

Mom called right after I dropped Davis off at the airport Monday morning. She said Daddy's trip had been delayed and he wouldn't be returning to the States until March. I really was not in the mood for her fake ass.

"Is everything okay in Cuba?"

"Yes, he said everything's fine. Your grandmother is doing better. But he's still very upset about the trade embargo that the U.S. has on Cuba; otherwise he said he would have made a killing selling cosmetics."

"Well, that's real nice, Mom." There was an awkward silence.

"Rheonique, I've always wanted the best for you. You know that, right?"

"Yes, ma'am."

"Rhea, what I'm trying to say is that I'm sorry if you felt as if I have mistreated you in some sort of way."

You're sorry if I felt like you mistreated me? Do you mean now or my whole life? Mom, you will never change.

"Noel's mother and I have been talking."

"What! Why did you call her?"

"I didn't. She called me."

How did she get my parents' number? That fucking Terri and Toussaint! Noel's sneaky ass knew what was going on too!

"Mom, I don't feel like talking right now."

As soon as I hung up, I knew I'd made a mistake. I needed to know what was going on, but my hot-headedness had gotten in the way again.

I almost called her back, but just as I was dialing, Davis called collect. I accepted the charges.

"Hey, Rhea. My dad said he found a nine-bedroom house for only five hundred and fifty thousand dollars. That way we could all live together."

"Davis, your flight hasn't even landed in Denver yet. Are you calling me from the plane?"

"Yes. So, what do you think about the house, Rhea?"

Fuck Davis and his family! I was not going to buy a house for me, him, our two babies, his kids, his nephew, and now his mammy and pappy. Besides, I had a perfectly good house in Atlanta. He could move his ass here if he really wanted to be with me and the twins.

"Davis, I don't feel good. Call me when you get home. And don't call collect."

"Rhea, are you okay? How are the twins?"

"They're fine, Davis!" I shouted.

"I think they know their daddy's voice," he said softly.

"I think so too. They always squirm and kick whenever you read to them." My tone softened.

"Rhea, I'm going to be a good father, I promise."

"I know. Now get off that damn phone before you cost me any more money!" I made a kissing sound into the phone then hung up on him.

I collapsed onto the couch and thought about what I could say to my mother when I called her back. I needed to know what they were planning so I could stop them before anyone was harmed.

The phone rang, interrupting my thoughts. *This better not be Davis again.*

"Hello."

"Rhea, where are you? Court is going to start in half an hour." It was my attorney, Daniel.

Terri had dropped her emergency hearing and

decided to wait until the summer to pursue her case against Davis. Why couldn't I have been so lucky?

"I'm on my way, Daniel!"

Just as I got inside the courthouse, the bailiff was walking out of the courtroom. "English versus Ramirez Baptiste-LaDay case has been postponed fifteen minutes," he announced.

Dan pointed at his watch, asking why I was late. I pointed at my stomach as an excuse. He seemed a little annoyed as he explained the formalities. Too bad. I was the one paying his damn hourly fee, so he could just deal with the fact that I was a few minutes late.

I went to the restroom. On my way back out to the lobby, I saw Marcus. Crystal walked a few steps behind him. She looked to be about five months pregnant, and their daughter, Samantha, held his hand. I was taken aback. Sometimes it still felt like our divorce was just yesterday, but obviously it had been long enough for their first child to grow into a toddler.

Marcus approached me, and Crystal stayed back. "Hello, Rhea."

"Hello, Marcus." I watched his eyes travel to my swollen belly.

Crystal couldn't even look me in the eyes. I had no earthly clue why she still seemed to be so intimidated by me. After all, she had him now.

I wondered if that gutter trash bitch ever finished her degree. I doubted it. Once she had Marcus, she was probably glad to live the pampered life of a doctor's mistress.

"Daddy, who's that?"

I looked down. Samantha was the spitting image of Marcus. Her hair was a reddish-brown and styled with cute little pigtails. She had a caramel skin tone like Crystal, but Marcus' mysterious grey eyes. She didn't look like a gecko anymore.

"This is Ms. Rhea." His voice was shaking.

"Hi, Ms.Rhea," she said.

I tried to fight back the tears. "Pleased to meet you, Samantha." My ex-husband's three-year-old daughter and I shook hands.

Marcus had tears in his eyes. "Daddy, are you crying?"

"Daddy's fine. I've just got something in my eye. You go with your mommy and tell her I'll see you guys later on tonight, okay?"

"Okay, Daddy."

Marcus watched until Samantha made it safely over to her mother. "Have a seat." He pointed to a wooden bench.

Daniel walked over. "Are you okay, Rhea?"

"I'm fine. Just come get me when it's time to go in." He walked away, but not without giving Marcus a menacing stare.

"Rhea, this is a mistake. I don't want to go in there today."

"What?" I was baffled.

"I love you. I always have. I just didn't realize just how much until after we were apart. You are . . ." He seemed to be searching for the right words to say. "You were my wife and I fucked up."

"Marcus, where is this coming from? You already have one child, another one on the way, and I'm pregnant by someone else. Besides, I may be getting married again. What about our marriage vows you broke?"

"I'll do anything to have you back. I don't care what it takes. I don't love Crystal, and she knows it. Hell, I don't know why she came today, honestly. But we are not together. I want you back, Rhea. I'll do anything."

"It's too late, Marcus. I'm in love with someone else." I sighed.

"I know you still care. We were married."

"Yes, we were, and you destroyed that!" I raised my voice.

"Calm down, Rhea. The stress is not good for the babies."

" 'Babies'? How did you know it was twins?"

"Toussaint told me."

It figures!

"What else do you know?"

"Enough. I know you're practically supporting your babies' father and his entire family."

My suspicions about the phone taps were finally validated.

"All I'm saying is you need a man that can take care of you."

"Like you did?" I replied sarcastically. "It's not always about money and what you can buy someone, Marcus. It's about love and respect."

"Oh, is that what you get from Davis with his other two baby mamas? Is that love and respect that you got at Hooters?"

"No, it wasn't. My relationship is not perfect, but we're working on it. How dare you judge me? Maybe, just maybe, had you not done what you did, I wouldn't be in this mess."

"I think about that all the time, Rhea. Look, I'm not here to argue. I love you. I just want you to know that. Those should be my babies you're carrying, but

I know I made the biggest mistake in my life by cheating on you. Can you ever forgive me?"

"I already have."

He bent down and kissed me on the cheek then slipped something into my hand. "I will always love you, Rheonique. Please call me if you ever need anything." He walked away.

I opened my hand to discover a beautiful daffodil pendant. I read the engraving on the back—*To Rhea, the most beautiful daffodil that God ever created.*

Five minutes later, my attorney walked out and told me Marcus had just dropped the case.

I thought about Marcus. I'd lied to him today. I never forgave him. I was still deeply hurt by how he had shattered my self-esteem. Was it that pain that had pushed me into Davis's arms? Maybe I would never have ended up with Davis and his ghetto drama if I had felt better about myself. But maybe I had to blame that on more than just Marcus. After all, my mother had been making me feel unworthy my whole life.

No, it wasn't that my mother or Marcus had pushed me into Davis's arms. He had pulled me there himself by showing me the love and acceptance that I had been craving. I was in love with Davis. Despite his unemployment status, his age, or his baby mama drama, I loved him with all my heart.

But would love help me get through all of this? Could I marry Davis, or did I really deserve a man without so much baggage and financial issues? I went home and prayed for some direction in my life.

CHAPTER 29

Davis called me at 6:30 that night.

"Hello."

"Hey, boo, you won't believe this."

"What's wrong *now*, Davis?"

"Noel let her mother claim Little Davis on her income taxes."

I told you so. That girl can never be your friend.

Davis must have read my mind. "I know you told me so. She just played me again then blamed it on her mother."

"Davis, don't you think it's ironic that every time something happens with Noel she blames her mother?"

Is he naïve or just plain stupid?

"Look, I'm just sorry I never listened to you. You told me that she would probably do this. How did you know?"

"I know people, niggas especially. They will stab you in the back for a little bit of money, even earned income tax credit."

"I mean, I just don't know. She said her mom did it."

"Did what?"

"Her mom just put it on the tax form without telling Noel about it. When I spoke with Noel a few weeks ago, she said she knew I was taking care of the baby and she wouldn't have any problems with me claiming him. I suspected Terri was going to take the income tax money for Ashley, but I never suspected Noel."

"Oh really, Davis. You didn't think she'd do it? Was that before or after you told her you asked me to marry you?"

"How did you know I told her about that?"

"I didn't. You just told me." *Big mouth bastard!* "What do you want me to do about it?"

"I may need a loan."

"For what? And how much this time?"

"I told Noel to come get Little Davis. For the past couple of years, I've been busting my ass to take care of these kids. I can't even help you as much as I'd like to with buying all the stuff the twins need."

"Davis, you love your son. Don't make any hasty decisions right now. Don't send him back. I guarantee you'll regret it. You already said Noel's mom mistreats him."

"I'm just sick of all of this shit! Can you help me out, baby? Please? I wasn't going to ask you, but my dad said you were a good woman and would help."

See, that's the kind of shit that pissed me off. What the hell kind of people had I gotten mixed up with? The whole damn Hickman family, friends, associates, and comrades were losers. These people had no morals, no goals, and to top it off, they were broke. The whole lot of them.

Ernest was crazy if he thought I was going to take care of his grumpy ass. I was tired of apologizing for who I was and what I had because other people fucked up their lives. I didn't owe anybody anything. Whatever I did out of the goodness of my heart should have been taken as a token of appreciation because of my love for Davis, not an obligation.

Motherfucking lazy-ass Ernest better go to Super Wal-Mart and greet people at the door. He could pass out them fucking yellow smiley-face stickers like the rest of the broke-ass geriatrics in America who fucked up their money. Hell, he could sit down and prop that raggedy-ass cane in the corner over by the grocery entrance. I was tired of visiting Western Union for Davis and his family.

"Rhea, I want to come out there this weekend so we can finish the nurseries. Can you spot me the money for the ticket?"

"Sure, whatever."

I did need some help with the nurseries, since my father was still in Cuba, but Davis was not going to get any pussy at all. I was going to start charging him. I had a mason jar with a slit cut in the top of it next to my bed when he came that weekend. I taped a sign on it that read: *The Pussy Jar. Fifty dollars a stroke.*

Enough was enough. I made Davis work like a dog that weekend. He painted the nursery, shampooed the carpet, fixed my fence and mowed the lawn. I got my $150 plane ticket money back out of his monkey ass. I couldn't afford to take care of him and the twins.

CHAPTER 30

As soon as he got back home, Davis began working two jobs, one as a customer service rep during the day for the University of Colorado. He got a discount on tuition and was planning on taking classes in the summer. Then he found a job at night working at the Tyson chicken factory on the assembly line. I was proud of him for finally making an effort.

He called and asked me to marry him again. "I'm really ready to commit to you totally and settle down, Rhea. I won't ever talk to Noel again unless it's about the baby."

"No, I will not marry you right now. You wouldn't give Noel's alleged platonic friendship up when I asked, but as soon as her mom takes your income tax money you're willing to totally commit to me? What happened to 'no ultimatums'?"

"Rhea, if you don't want to get married, then I think maybe we need to start seeing other people."

Davis just wants some pussy. He thinks if he plays this little game he can justify going out to fuck somebody else.

"Do what you need to do, Davis. I'm not paying for any more weekend escapades. I will only pay for one more ticket for you, and that's for you to come for the babies' birth, which I really shouldn't have to do."

"You need to get it together, Rhea. Stop taking me for granted."

"I need to get it together? You live with your fucking mama with your two kids, and you've got two more on the way. You don't have a college degree and pluck chickens for a living. Your car is going to be repossessed because your other two baby mamas stole your income tax money. You couldn't pay your car payment which was four months behind and *I* need to get it together?"

"If she really loved you, she'd buy you a new car. All that money she got." Ernest was on the other line, eavesdropping. "Rhea, we were all talking today about how you need to just go ahead and get that house here. We can all stay together, and me and Willie Mae could help y'all with the kids."

I hung up the telephone, Davis insinuating that he was going to be with another woman. The thought killed me inside and got my hormones raging again. I'd been way too stupid for far too long. Why were he and his dad discussing me? Ernest was too nosy. Davis played into that shit and would sit with his parents around the kitchen table like a bunch of geriatrics at a convention.

One of his baby mamas would be the topic of discussion each day. They gossiped about Terri's gay sister and her lover. Ernest would come up with his personal opinion of how he felt about a subject. Even if Davis and his mom didn't agree, they'd still go along with him, like he was Reverend Ike or something.

Davis told intimate details of his sex life to his parents, like the fact that I preferred to have sex with the lights on, and how Noel made a tape of herself masturbating while he and his boys watched. He told them how Terri liked it in the butt while watching porn. Davis bragged about every piece of ass that he'd ever had. He was disgusting. What kind of shit is that to tell your mom and dad?

Oh, but I bet he conveniently left out the fact that he ate pussy like he was at the daily lunch buffet and licked assholes like lollipops. He probably didn't tell his mom how he liked to be spanked with a fucking paddle with a pacifier in his mouth.

He made me so sick sometimes. That's why his ass was starting to get fat anyway. I was starting to believe Terri, because he stopped washing his ass as much too, just like she said he would. And that nigga must have had a zinc deficiency or something, because his toenails were turning black.

Something was wrong with him and his two-faced mammy. He told me that after our first trip together he was in so much pain because my coochie was so tight. He said he showed his mama. Unbelieveable! This big, burly, baby-making, 24-year-old bastard was still showing his mama his dick. And that simple bitch poured green alcohol on it. I'd looked far and wide, and Willie Mae just may win the Simple Bitch Contest. Her ass could very well be the grand martial for the Simple Bitch Parade.

What the hell! This whole family was fucked up!

I should've tortured Davis until the day he died, or the day my family killed him, whichever came first. I was beginning to think that he was not the one for me after all.

CHAPTER 31

Pastor Lee's wife called that afternoon to invite me to the annual church revival.

I apologized for being out of church so long and told her that I would come. I hadn't been to church in months. Instead of hanging out with Davis, this was where I should have been. Only God could help me at this point. I came to the conclusion that something had to be fundamentally wrong with me to put up with his shit. A part of me loved him, but the other part hated him with a passion, and I needed some help.

I felt a little embarrassed, walking into the church pregnant. I looked like a stuffed turkey, waddling in and sitting down amidst the stares from the congregation. Why people took joy in other people's misery was totally beyond me.

Sister Lula came over and sat beside me. "You look so pretty, Rhea. You are glowing."

Whatever, heifer! My nose has spread across my face. My feet look like an elephant's, and my hair is out of control. So what you're saying is that I look like you? At that point, I was pissed at the world. "Thank you so much."

"What you having?"

"A boy and a girl."

"Twins?"

"Yes, ma'am." *Nosy ass!*

"I saw Marcus the other day when I went to see my doctor. Girl, he had an office full of patients," she whispered a little too loudly.

She wants to know if I'm pregnant by Marcus.

Someone behind us hushed us.

Thank God!

People kept staring and whispering about me, so I was glad when Sister Corrine came and took the attention away. She bolted through the double doors with a pair of army fatigues on.

"Testifying service ain't over yet, is it?" she yelled, almost falling down in army boots that were obviously too big for her.

"No, sistah! Come on, tell your story!" The whole congregation turned around as Deacon Brown yelled. They were the most hollering group of people on the planet!

Sister Corrine walked up to the front of the church, took the microphone, and gave her testimony. She said she had no money and couldn't pay her gas bill, but because she paid her tithes on time, she mysteriously got a check from one of her grandkids for fifty dollars.

"Ain't God good?" she yelled.

The crowd started clapping. People were yelling "Amen!" from all over the congregation.

She didn't stop there. She was on a roll. "I came to church tonight in this army uniform 'cause I want the world to know that I'm a soldier in the Lord's army."

Everyone snickered. The uniform was two sizes too big and had the name *Santiago* stitched on the nametag. Sister Corrine's last name was Cambridge. She ignored the snickering and proclaimed she was an officer and had earned the rank of captain in the Lord's army.

She walked over, whispered something to the piano player then went back to the microphone. "Sing with me, church," she blared out. "I'm a soooooooul-jah."

The crowd responded to her with, "In the army of the Lord."

"I'm a soooooooul-jah."

"In the aaaar-my."

There was a host of parents pinching little kids who were laughing. All of the teenagers were given the evil eye by their parents to keep them from losing control.

Sister Nay-Nay looked over at her son, Rob. "You too old to be laughing at people in church. I'm going to get you when I get home."

Even Sister Lula had to comment. She whispered to me, "Oh, Lord. I know Corrine didn't come up here in no Army uniform, talking about she a souljah in the Lord's army."

Sister Corrine was truly out of control. And I was trying not to laugh out loud, because I did not want any pee to seep out. I wasn't trying to smell like cod, and pregnant cod at that, on the way home.

All of my home training went out the window, though, when Sister Corrine took the microphone out of the holder and began prancing down the aisle, singing the second verse to the song. She was double-clapping at the same time.

"I got my war clothes on," she screamed and almost shook her wig off.

"In the army of the Lord," the crowd responded.

I followed about fifteen other parishioners, all waving their hands in the air, out in the hallway. We all marched out of the sanctuary to keep from laughing. The circus had truly come to Atlanta, and Sister Corrine had her clown shoes on.

After I collected myself, I came back in, and the church had finally settled down. A guest minister, a prophetess from Nigeria, conducted the service. The sermon was about generational demons and how to break generational curses. I started thinking about my own demons and problems.

Am I cursed? Did someone in my family do something that I'm being punished for? I wasn't a bad person, but I kept getting the short end of the stick. Did I try to please my family too much instead of doing what I wanted to do? What caused me to choose the men that I did? Was it my strained relationship with my mother? There were so many possibilities and scenarios for the things that I'd done in my life and the decisions that I'd made.

The sermon didn't last very long, which was good, because I started to get restless. There was an altar call, and as much as I needed prayer, I was too embarrassed to walk down the aisle. *How did I get here? How did I go from being this overconfident, independent woman to a miserable, pregnant woman with so little hope?*

I looked up, and my eyes locked with the minister's. I closed my eyes and put my head back down quickly.

Please! Please! Please don't call me out!

Davis was on my mind. I loved him with all my heart, but he was selfish. He never asked me about my feelings and constantly put his burdens on me. I was so tired of listening to him talk about how he hated Terri and how Noel wouldn't take care of her responsibilities. If he really loved me as much as he said he did, surely he should be able to see I needed support too. Didn't he know that I wasn't as strong as I seemed? I thought about running away.

"God is dealing with somebody out there. Stop running. You can't run forever," the minister said.

I knew she was talking about me. All my life, I'd run away when things weren't going like I wanted them too.

As a little girl, I'd run away whenever kids would make fun of me. "How come you got good hair and pretty eyes, but you so dark-skinned? Dark-skinned people ain't supposed to look like that."

"You think you something 'cause y'all speak Spanish and French."

"You trying to be white, with your black self."

"Come here. Let me see if your hair is real."

When all else failed, I'd simply run away.

After my first lover and I broke up, I ran away from Brown to UCLA for a semester to study theatre.

The choir sang softly in the background. "I sing because I'm free. His eye is on the sparrow."

I couldn't stop the tears from flowing.

After the minister dismissed the service, I gathered up my purse and Bible from the pew. I headed toward the door, ready to "run" home.

As I entered the foyer, I felt a tap on the shoulder. An usher told me the minister wanted to talk to me.

I nervously approached the minister.

"Hello, darling. My name is Sister Olgatu." She smiled.

"Hello, Sister. My name is Rhea." I extended my hand, but instead of shaking it, she rubbed it softly.

"Do you have a few minutes to talk, sweetheart?"

"Yes, ma'am," I said meekly.

"Come on, let's go in Pastor Lee's study."

I didn't mind talking to her, but I didn't feel comfortable talking in front of Pastor or Mrs. Lee. People's business had a way of leaking out of the pastor's study.

"They've already left for the evening." Sister Olgatu must have known what I was thinking. "Have a seat," she said.

Pastor Olgatu walked across the room and sat down at the pastor's desk. She quickly jumped back up and helped me sit down on the couch.

"Before you say anything, I want you to know God spoke to me about you. He wants me to tell you to name your son Solomon."

"'Solomon'?" I repeated while rubbing my belly. "What about my daughter?" I asked.

"I don't know about that baby. You're having twins?"

"Yes, ma'am."

"Well, Rhea, I'm a vessel. I only do and say what God tells me. Understand?"

"Yes, I understand."

"Well, King Solomon was a wise king, a peacemaker, and God is going to use your Solomon in a great and miraculous way." She took some oil from her bag and traced a cross on my forehead then put a little dab on my belly. "I want to pray with you, okay?"

I nodded.

She grabbed my hands, closed her eyes and meditated.

After a few seconds, she opened her eyes suddenly, almost like she had been in a trance. "I know you feel all alone right now, but you're not. Jesus is with you always."

"I'm glad that God still loves me."

"Of course he does, Rhea. You have a wonderful heart and spirit. That's why God has chosen you."

"Chosen me for what?" I asked, confused.

"Rhea, you are very special. God has chosen you to carry this special child, Solomon, just like Mary's purpose on earth was to give birth to Jesus. The Biblical King Solomon was a wise mediator who gave hope to warring peoples."

If I remember correctly, King Solomon had about one hundred wives. I wonder if my baby is not only going to be a wise man, but another generation of Hickman whores.

"So many bad things have happened to me."

I told her everything that had happened. I was so tired of carrying baggage.

She listened patiently, then came over and gave me a hug, when I was finally done.

"Rhea, you're getting ready to go through a great period of pain and suffering. I wish I had better news to give you, darling. You are going to feel even more alone in the near future than you are now. But always remember, God is going to be with you. You have to be reverent and stay in prayer constantly, okay?"

"I will," I whispered hoarsely. "You said something about loss and suffering. I don't understand."

"Rhea, through the midst of your trials, God is going to perform a supernatural miracle in your life. In fact, he already has."

"'Supernatural miracle'?"

"Yes. You see, God sometimes has to show Man that he is still God."

"What do you mean? I'm confused."

"Think about this, Rhea—People say they believe

Jesus walked on water and that He was dead for three days and rose again from the grave, right?"

"Yes, ma'am."

"But if someone were to tell you that it happened to someone now, you'd probably think that they were lying. Am I right?"

She had a point, because I'd probably think they were on crack.

"God is the same today, yesterday and forever. He is going to elevate you so that the whole world can see you and your talents, but not before you fight a great battle. God does not want you to give into evil thoughts and desires that are going to come to tempt you. Rhea, listen to me carefully. I want you to remember that God will devour all of your enemies. He will kill them where they stand, but you must remember to hold your peace and let the Lord fight your battles."

"Who are my enemies?"

"That's not for you to know right now. God sent me to warn you there is going to be major chaos, suffering, and pain in your life. You will eventually overcome and be exalted high for the whole world to see. Keep on praying, baby. God hears your prayers. I want you to dedicate your children to Christ. Remember the scripture says that the promise is given unto you and your seed."

Sister Olgatu stood up, and after a quick kiss on the cheek, she led me out of the study and walked me to my car. Not only was I even more confused than I'd ever been in my whole life, but even more suspicious of everyone I knew.

CHAPTER 32

As soon as I walked into my house, I sat down on the couch to ponder what happened at church. As usual, the ringing telephone interrupted my thoughts. It was Davis, calling and asking me to marry him again. Once again, my response was no. I didn't tell him what transpired at church, only that we needed to name our son Solomon. He came up with the name Sienna for our daughter.

"Davis, doesn't that sound a little country?—Sienna Hickman?"

"With a name like Hickman, I don't think we can avoid sounding country."

We both laughed.

I liked *this* Davis. The Davis that made me laugh. The Davis that brought out the schoolgirl youthfulness inside of me. He **was** overall a sweet guy, just so immature.

I rubbed my belly. "Solomon Edwinn Hickman, if I have to raise you all by myself, you will learn to be a man. And little Miss Sienna Hickman, Mommy is going to teach you to be self-sufficient."

"What are you talking about, Rhea? Solomon is going to be just like his daddy," he said.

"That's what I'm afraid of." I laughed.

"What you need to be saying to Sienna is that Mommy doesn't want you to grow up and be a super-freak like her."

"You like it."

"Oh, yes I do. In fact, I love it so much I want it every night."

"Is that so? So, are you saying the only reason why you want to marry me is for the sex?"

"The sex, the cooking, the fact that you are going to be the best mommy to all of these kids. Girl, I love you."

"Spare me that crap, boy. Davis, I have to go to bed. I'm so tired."

"Why? You got your boyfriend over there?" He laughed.

"Goodbye, Davis. You're silly."

"Bye, pretty lady. I love you."

"I love you too. Well, sometimes at least."

CHAPTER 33

I was so exhausted, I stayed in bed the next day. Dad called with some bad news. My mother's father needed to have open-heart surgery, and everyone in the family was en route to Haiti.

"Mom didn't tell me," I said.

"She didn't?" Dad sounded surprised. "She and your brother have been there for three or four days now."

I began to cry. Damn, I wished my hormones would stop working overtime. I was getting on my own nerves, crying all the time. "Daddy, if they want to keep me out of the family, that's fine, but someone could have called me."

"I'm leaving Havana for Haiti in a few hours. I'm not trying to cut you short, but we need to talk, princess. You didn't tell me everything about Davis, did you?"

"No, Daddy, I didn't."

What did they tell him?

"Daddy, how sick is grandfather?"

"Very sick, princess. He may not make it. His surgery is in four days. I tell you . . . first my mother, now your mom's dad."

"Daddy, how is grandmother?"

"She's fine, baby."

"I'll be there in a few days then."

"Is it safe for you to travel? You're eight months pregnant."

"I'm healthy, and besides, I'm just going to rest when I get there. I'm getting a hotel. It's not like anyone is going to talk to me anyway. They've ostracized me, remember?"

"No one's ostracizing you. We're just all very concerned about you."

We? So, they've sucked Daddy in with them.

I changed the subject quickly. "How's the family in Cuba?"

"Everyone's fine. Your Tia Amille made the twins blankets." He sounded relieved at the change of subject as well.

"Tell her thanks."

"I will. So, I'll see you in a few days, princess?"

"Yes, you will. And I love you."

"Love you too, daffodil. I got your email. Yes, Solomon and Sienna are both very regal names. I was thinking maybe we can do two different nurseries, one in Winnie the Pooh and the other in Peter Rabbit."

"Dad, you're a genius. Those are the exact nursery themes that Davis and I came up with."

"Great minds think alike. My grandkids are going to be smart." He chuckled.

"They will be. You'll like Davis, Dad."

"You really love him, don't you?"

"Yes, Daddy, I do." I sighed.

"Well, as long as he treats you well and takes care of my little grandbabies, everything will be fine. I'm actually looking forward to working on the nurseries with him, to get to know him."

"Okay. When we get back from Haiti, you and Davis can paint to your heart's content."

"Good. I might even let him marry my daffodil if he can mix the primer and paint correctly."

We laughed.

"Princess, I've got to run now. I need to get to the airport early to get through Customs."

"Okay, Daddy. I'll email you the hotel information so you can meet me when I get to Haiti. I'll pick up a rental car."

"You don't want anyone to pick you up?" he asked.

"No. I'm a little embarrassed to be around anyone. I'd like to get a hotel before I have to deal with the comments."

"Okay. Love you."

"Love you too, Daddy."

I called Davis and filled him in on everything that was going on. I was a little apprehensive about traveling at that stage in my pregnancy, but Davis convinced me it would be fine. He knew I would never forgive myself if my grandfather died without me saying goodbye.

"Rhea, why don't I go with you?" Davis said.

"Would you, Davis?" I was so happy. It was time for him to meet my family anyway. They would just have to get over their class prejudice.

"Yes, if you promise not to let your family kill me," he joked.

"Don't worry about them." I was too happy to even think seriously about the thought that there were still family members who would probably like to kill him. "Do you have a passport? And you need to get luggage. You can't go meet my family with your clothes in Little Davis's baby bag."

"Okay, I'll get some luggage, and I have a passport. Hey, maybe we can announce our engagement as well." He laughed.

"You're silly, Davis."

"Well, at least you didn't come right out and say no this time. Hey, I've got an even better one for you. How 'bout we just stay down there and you can have the twins in Haiti?"

"You're really tripping now. I'm not having my babies in Haiti. I can only imagine the kind of doctors they have. Totally gross. No, thank you. I'll stick to my lavish birthing center at ATL's finest. Let me go, Davis. I need to start packing. Tell your mom the blanket she gave me is so comfortable. I sleep on it every night."

"I sure will, Mrs. Davis Hickman. I'll be sure to tell mom that her next grandchild will be conceived on that blanket."

"I told you I'm not having any more babies."

"I know. Four is enough for me, but I do like conceiving them, though." I gave him my credit card information to book both of our flights.

He called back the next day with the itinerary.

I told Davis, "I'll marry you. Just don't make me change my name."

"Whatever, Rhea. You're going to drop that other shit. You foreigners have too many damn names as it is. Your name is just going to be Rheonique Hickman."

"Don't play, Davis."

"No, *you* don't play. Girl, I'll have you popping babies out every year like Christmas."

"I'm getting my tubes tied after these two. No more babies for me."

"Shit, I'm thinking about getting a vasectomy. Hey, Rhea, how about a Christmas Eve or New Year's Eve wedding ceremony? Maybe we can invite Jerry Springer to be the wedding host." He laughed. "Let's see, we'll have two infants, a toddler, a pre-schooler, my brother's son, my two baby mamas, your ex-husband and his baby mama and the daughter they had while he was still married to you. Then afterwards, your brother and uncles will be outside with surveillance cameras, ready to cap a hole in my black ass."

"I'm ignoring you, crackhead. We'll just elope because our guest list would be a little too wacky."

"Whatever you say, beautiful. We need to meet at the Delta departure counter. You can just meet my flight when it gets in from Denver, and we'll both be on the same flight to Miami."

"Did you get our seats together?"

"Sure did. Hopefully they'll keep the lights off so I can finger-fuck you."

"You're nasty, but that's the only kind of fuck you're going to get until after the twins are born. And after that you'll have to wait another six to eight weeks."

"As long as your mouth works, that's cool."

"Davis, you're disgusting. Your hand is your friend."

"But you love this disgusting man, don't you?"

"Yes, I do. I love you so much, Davis."

"Rhea, I love you too. No, that's wrong. Mrs. Hickman, I love you."

"Good night. I'll see you tomorrow at the airport."

"Give my babies kisses for me. Tell them that Daddy

will blow on Mommy's tummy tomorrow and make them jump."

"Sure will. Night, Davis." We both hung up.

Mrs. Davis Edwinn (with two *N*'s) Hickman didn't sound too bad after all!

I woke up early the next morning, finished packing my suitcase, took out my passport and got ready to go to the airport.

Cheryl dropped me off, but she kept reiterating what a dumb ass I was for marrying Davis.

CHAPTER 34

I waited on Davis' flight to come in from Denver to Atlanta. The flight was delayed, but after it finally landed forty-five minutes late, I discovered he wasn't even on the flight. I waited and waited, but still no Davis. I called his parents' house, and Noel answered the phone.

"Noel, where is Davis? And what are you doing answering my fiancé's phone?"

"Davis is unavailable at the moment. And if you were really his fiancée, you'd be here now that he needs you." She hung up.

I called back and got a busy signal.

What was Noel talking about? Davis needed me? Did something happen to him?

I tried to call up, until it was time to board the flight to Miami, but I kept getting a busy signal. I had no choice but to leave.

I tried to call again, once I got into Miami. After my sixth attempt, Noel picked up.

I was sick of her ass. "Look, bitch, where is Davis?"

"Bitch, you're the stupid bitch. Thanks for all the money you gave Davis. We use that for our hotels. And by the way, thanks for sucking his dick. That saves me a lot of trouble. He said you give good head." She hung up.

I tried to call back, but the line was busy again. That bitch probably took the phone off the hook. I was fucking infuriated. Did this motherfucker take money that I'd given him and spend it on Noel?

What is she doing there? Where is Davis? This nigga didn't even bother to leave me a voicemail to let me know he wasn't coming.

My phone rang.

" 'Davis'?"

"Davis? This is Michelle. Girl, I'm just getting into Haiti. What's wrong, Rhea?"

I told her what happened.

"Michelle, I don't think I'm going to make it. I'm going to catch a flight back to Denver to check on Davis."

"Rhea, if you want to be a good mom, you need to leave Davis alone. Raise your babies by yourself, and if he comes around and accepts his responsibilities, fine, but if not, kill him."

"What?"

"Kill him! Hell yes, I said it. He's not worth the air he breathes."

"Maybe something happened," I protested.

"Something like what happened? He slipped and fucked his other baby mama again after proposing to you? Rhea, I don't know who you are anymore. You're so fucking stupid and simple! Your mother would never forgive you. I would never forgive you if you didn't show up and Grandfather died. Don't even lie and use your pregnancy as an excuse. You can fly pregnant all over the country for this man, but you can't do it for your own family? I understand you feel mistreated by some people in our family, but our grandparents have never done anything but love you. That little boy will be waiting to keep on playing the same fucking games when you get back. So I'd advise you to hop your happy ass on that plane. And while on the flight, you need to think about all the mistakes that you are making in your life.

"I'm going to tell you like Toussaint did. All you have to do is say the word, and we will take care of his black ass once and for all." She hung up.

CHAPTER 35

*   *   *

Davis walked back into the house and collapsed on the couch after having spent all day at the hospital with his parents. He was startled to see Noel come out of the kitchen.

"What are you doing here, Noel?"

"I'm here because my son is here," Noel said.

"How did you get in?"

"Please. I copied your key months ago."

"Noel, you don't need to be here. You should've called first."

"Oh, Davis, don't look so concerned. Your fiancée called before. Let's just say that your little wifey wasn't too happy that I answered your phone."

"What the fuck? I love Rhea and we're getting married. I was supposed to meet her at the airport, but my dad's brakes gave out in the car. He and my mom had an accident. You know what? Why am I explaining this to you?—Get the fuck out!"

Davis dialed Rhea's cell phone number. "Rhea, baby, I'm still coming to Haiti. My parents were in a bad car accident. Mom has a broken leg, and Daddy had to have emergency surgery on his spleen. The surgery took forever. I found out about my parents' accident when I got to the airport. I kept calling, but your voice mail was full and your phone must have been turned off. I had to make so many decisions, Rhea. Where were you when I needed you? You aren't here for me when I need you, baby.

"My brother is coming in to take care of my parents and the kids, and I'll be flying there tomorrow. I had no idea Noel was here. She just came to pick up Little Davis. Please don't be upset. I love you, Rhea, and I can't wait to see you again. Please touch your belly and tell the babies that daddy loves them."

He hung up and turned around to see Noel glaring at him.

"What are you still doing here, Noel? I said, 'Get the fuck out'!"

"I was here to do what Rhea won't do for you. Where's your little rich bitch now that you need her? On second thought, fuck you, Davis. Marry her. I don't care. It's not like you're going to be faithful anyway. You can't commit to one woman. As soon as you have your first fight with your li'l wife, you'll be coming back to me to get some pussy."

Noel snatched the door open, just as a UPS delivery man was ringing the doorbell.

"Delivery for Noel."

"I'm Noel." She was suprised to be getting a package at the Hickman home. Davis looked equally surprised.

Noel opened the manila envelope. Inside were photos of her mother leaving a parking garage from work. There was another photo of her in her dorm room having sex with another girl. The third photo, of her brother getting off the little short bus that the handicapped kids ride, sent chills down her spine.

There was a letter inside that read: *Nobody fucks with my family. Watch your back, bitch, and tell your little boyfriend so sorry about his parents' accident. Next time, his mom and dad might not be so lucky!*

Davis snatched the photos out of Noel's hands. "You're a nasty, stank ho." He read the note, sat down on the couch and began to cry. He jumped up screaming and began to shake Noel.

"I told you not to fuck with Rhea. I told you her family was crazy."

"Me? Davis, you're the one that hurt her, not me. I'm getting my baby and getting the fuck out of here."

Noel went into the back room and, after tossing Little Davis's belongings in a blue Wal-Mart bag, she walked outside, just as her mother pulled up in the driveway. She was terrified and had every right to be. Was her family going to be targeted next? She was so mad at herself. Why did she lie on Rhea and tell Davis that she'd received a threatening letter from the LaDay family when she really didn't? Why did she lie and tell Davis that Rhea was calling her in her dorm room? Why did she go see that voodoo woman? She'd had a feeling that day like she was being followed.

That morning, her biggest worry was trying to figure out a way to get her learner's permit without all of the teenagers at the DMV making fun of her because she didn't know how to drive at the age of twenty-two. Now she had to hope and pray that Rhea or her family would not come after her.

Davis walked toward his closet to get his suitcase. He needed to be with Rhea. As he bent down to pick up his "church shoes," he was instantly reminded of that special time when he and Rhea had their spiritual sex union there. That, to him, was still unexplainable.

He called a taxi to take him to the airport then sat down on his bed to think. What were his son and daughter going to be like? Would Solomon look like him? Would Sienna have Rhea's eyes? He missed Rhea and knew he loved her more than he'd ever loved anyone.

The taxi arrived to take him to the airport within ten minutes of his call. He got into the back seat and smiled at the other passenger, a very pretty woman with long, jet-black hair, and rich, dark skin. Something about her reminded him of Rhea. She didn't smile back, though.

Davis was used to foreigners snubbing their noses on black men, but he knew after being with Rhea that all those island girls secretly wanted some chocolate dick or *Kunta,* as Rhea would yell out as she rode him.

Damn, Rhea was perfect. Davis swore to himself that he would never fuck up again. She had the four B's: beauty, brains, bucks and a badunkadunk! As he fantasized about Rhea, he didn't notice the white van following the taxi.

Ten minutes later, they were approaching the airport, but the cabbie took the exit right before the airport entrance. So did the white van.

"The airport is this way. You're going the wrong way, sir," Davis said, frustrated as he looked down at his watch. He only had an hour to catch the next flight to Miami and was anxious to see Rhea.

The big, burly cab driver ignored Davis and began humming.

"Sir, I need to get to the airport quickly. This is a life or death situation!"

The driver put on the brakes abruptly, turned around with a sinister smile, and said, "It's not life that you should be concerned with." The man had a heavy accent.

The pretty young woman reached inside her bag then turned to Davis. "We warned you."

Davis reached for the car door to try to jump out, but discovered the handle was missing.

CHAPTER 36

I boarded the flight in Miami, wondering where Davis was. *He'd better have a damn good excuse this time. I will declare war on his black ass if he made up some lame-ass lie.*

Two hours later, I landed in Port-au-Prince. Though I had told him I didn't need anyone to pick me up, my father and cousin, Gabrielle, were waiting on me.

"Hi, Daddy. Hi, Gabby." I ran toward them.

"Don't run, girl," my cousin Gabby said as she gave me a hug. "You look beautiful."

She feels sorry for me.

Gabby was a Haitian citizen but lived in Miami ten months out of the year. Her mom and my mom were sisters. My Auntie Novella was the complete opposite of my mom. She was sweet and humble.

Haiti, my beautiful Haiti. I was proud of my Cuban and Gullah heritage, but there was something so mysterious about Mother Haiti that I wanted to celebrate her culture, her customs. I screamed, "I love Haiti!"

My dad and Gabby both laughed.

The hotel I'd booked was thirty-five miles away from the airport. I was going to get a rental car and go out to my grandparents' home the next day.

Gabby stopped me as I was going toward the Hertz counter. "No, Rhea. I'll take you to your hotel."

"Thanks, Gabby, but I want my own transportation."

"Rhea, you want me to ride with you?" my father asked.

"No, because I'm not going out to the house tonight. I'm going to my room to get some rest."

Dad looked concerned. "I don't know if your mom will like that. Everyone is going to be upset we didn't bring you to the house straight from the airport."

"Dad, please! They'll get over it."

He took my luggage and put it in the trunk. I had my overnight bag, and put the blanket that Willie Mae had given me in the back seat of the car.

They left, and so did I.

I turned on the radio in the car to some local station. It was becoming dark very quickly, and the chorus of the song on the radio sounded like a tribal chant.

This was such beautiful countryside. The stars, the sun cresting over the water was breathtaking. I started to miss Davis so much that it hurt. This would have been a wonderful trip for him. Something must have happened in Colorado to prevent him from making his flight, because I knew he loved me.

I closed my eyes just for a second to think. I was torn. A part of me wanted to marry him and live happily ever after, but the other part of me wanted to strangle him. I tried to concentrate on happy things, like our house, our babies' birth, our wedding, our honeymoon.

What was Noel doing at his house? I couldn't figure that one out.

I opened my eyes, just as the left side of the wheel hit the side of a hill. All I saw was rocks coming toward me. The last thing I remembered was the car being tossed to and fro in the Haitian wind. I screamed.

The car landed with a thud, and for a moment, everything went black. The car tumbled over an embankment. With every bump and turn, I was passing in and out of consciousness.

I woke up to excruciating pain. I had no idea how long I'd been out of it. My insides felt as if they were going to explode. Everything was pitch-black, and there was an eerie silence all around me. I wanted to scream for help but felt too weak. The smell of fresh blood along with my screams was sure to conjure up some type of wild animal anyway. I would be defenseless against any type of predator in the open terrain.

I began to pray. "Jesus, please help me. Please let my children be okay."

I got an immediate answer to my prayer, when I felt their kicks inside my womb. They were both alive.

Oh God, what was that smell? Something reeked. It smelled like a combination of a burning tire, fresh blood, and feces. I puked then I peed on myself. I had chills, and when I touched my arms, I felt the gritty feeling of glass. My arms were both cut open so badly, like a toy racetrack. I needed to climb out of the overturned car quickly.

I managed to kick some debris aside. I didn't have to worry about any wild animals, I tried to tell myself. My dad was coming to rescue me.

"Help . . ." I said with almost no sound.

The pain was overwhelming.

"Dear God, please, please don't let this car blow up or catch on fire." I was so weak, I didn't have the energy to crawl out of the wrecked convertible on my own.

My arms and face were stinging. I tasted blood and felt large shards of glass in my hair and scalp. I tried to kick what looked like some type of metal plating out in front of my face, and I fell back hard. My world went black.

I know I probably dozed in and out of consciousness at least three or four times. What time was it anyway? What day was it? *Okay, Rhea, calm down. Try to take your time and think.*

I felt a sudden rush, like a damn had crested inside of my body and started to overflow. I lost all bodily functions as the realization hit me like a ton of bricks. The day that Davis and I had planned for was unfortunately going to take place where my ancestors had been brought to the new world of Hispaniola as slaves. I lay back in pain. Surely I couldn't die. What about all of the things that Sister Olgatu had said? She said I'd be exalted.

I prayed again. "Lord, please cover me with Your blood. Let Your angels of mercy encamp around me and my children."

Finally, I mustered up enough strength to reach the dashboard and turn on the emergency lights in the vehicle.

After what seemed like hours, I heard a male and female's voice.

"Do you speak English?" I yelled.

There were so many French dialects in Haiti. I needed whoever it was out there to understand everything that I said completely.

"Yes, my wife and I are English," the man said.

"Are you okay?" the woman asked.

"No, I'm pregnant and I think that I may be delivering soon." I was trying to hold back the tears, but I couldn't.

"Don't cry. Let's pray. We're going to climb over the ravine and try to get you out." The woman began crying.

We recited the Lord's Prayer, and when the couple were finally close enough, they reached inside the car to get me. That's when I heard a new voice.

"No! No, don't touch her! I'm a priest at the local convent hospital. She may be in shock or have broken bones. Let's ease her out slowly," he said.

"My water just broke. My babies are coming. Daddy, where are you?" I was in so much pain.

Davis, you bastard. You should be here with me!

"Solomon, Sienna, stop pushing up against my pelvis. You're hurting Mommy. Jesus, help me. It hurts, it hurts."

I heard so many voices. The priest said, "She's becoming delirious. She's screaming uncontrollably. Calm down, young lady!"

There were a million voices. I felt like I was losing my mind. It was like I'd left my body and was looking at myself dying. So many unfamiliar hands were touching me. The glass was cutting deeply into my back as I was being pulled out of the broken window.

"We need something to lay her on," the English woman said.

I remembered the blanket Willie Mae had given me. "Look in the back seat. I have a multi-colored blanket."

The man came back with the blanket a few moments later. "It's amazing. That car turned over a few times, and the blanket doesn't have an ounce of dirt or blood on it. It was still up under the seat in the car."

They laid me on the ground. The priest asked, "Have you ever had a baby before?" I felt his cold hands between my legs.

"No, this is my first time," I said between clenched teeth.

"Okay, I hate to disappoint you, young lady. You may not be able to make it to the hospital in time. Don't worry. This will be a first for me too. But women have been having babies since biblical times."

I began crying. It wasn't supposed to be like this. Davis wasn't with me, neither were my parents. The nursery was supposed to be ready back in Atlanta with the Winnie the Pooh and the Peter Rabbit themes all waiting on Solomon and Sienna.

"Where's my daddy?" I asked.

"Who?" they all said.

I had a contraction. "It hurts. It hurts."

The English woman held my hand. I heard someone else say, "I'll go ahead to the convent and let them know that you're coming, Father."

"Please do," he said. "And ask for Sister Mary Catherine. She's my assistant. Tell her that Father Brinson sent you." He turned back to me. "Young lady, the hospital is about an hour and a half away. We're going to make you as comfortable as possible, but you are going to deliver here."

Everything suddenly became quiet and still.

"Move over. I'll take care of her," a woman said in broken English.

I knew, when I looked up and saw her face, what

she was. She had the traditional white paint around her eyelids, and her long, black hair was wrapped in a turban. This was the local midwife, who, in Haiti, was also called the mambo or witch doctor. It was the woman I'd dreamed of right after my divorce!

She burned a hole in my soul with her piercing, catlike eyes. Her presence was so commanding, I knew she possessed supernatural powers.

The priest moved out of the way to play second chair. The English couple immediately backed away.

The contractions were coming full force. I screamed.

She snatched off my skirt and panties, cleaning me with some rags that she had in her big straw bag.

I pushed and pushed for what seemed like an eternity.

Father Brinson was above my head, holding my hands, praying. The mambo motioned for the English woman to come and help hold my legs.

"It hurts, it hurts!" I screamed.

The Mambo never made a sound. She diligently put oil all over my thighs and vagina. Although the oil numbed me somewhat, I could still feel the scraping of her elephant tusk bracelets. As she touched my insides, her matching necklace mesmerized me to a semi-hypnotic state.

The priest recited the 23rd Psalm. As soon as he said the passage, "I will dwell in the house of the Lord forever," the first child began coming. I pushed really hard.

After a few minutes, I heard him cry for the first time. I looked down and fell in love instantly with Solomon Edwinn Hickman.

The witch doctor looked down as well. She cut the umbilical cord with a knife. I could barely feel it, but the thought of a knife on my skin gave me goose bumps.

She whispered to me in French, "Solomon, the world has been waiting on you. I am your servant."

How did she know his name? I never said it!

She kissed his forehead then began chanting in a language that I didn't understand. I could only make out a few words. They were something about "spirit of creation," and "old spirits of the ones who have already passed."

I didn't understand a lot about voodoo, but when she produced a black pole out of her bag and stuck it down in the ground, I knew what it was. My great-grandmother had taught me that a pole was sometimes used in lieu of an altar in ceremonies.

She stood in front of the pole and held my son up to the moonlight. Afterwards, she wiped the blood off of him with a rag that had been dipped in rosewater.

"Where's my baby?" I reached out to get Solomon from her.

"Not yet!" The witch doctor screamed at me. "He has to be dedicated to the heavens properly!"

Before I could protest, the excruciating pain started again.

Soon, Sienna Hickman was born. Everyone cried when Sienna took her first breath and screamed to announce her arrival. She was stunning.

"My little girl. Davis, you motherfucker, I will never forgive you for this," I whispered.

Meanwhile, the old witch doctor was anointing Solomon with oils and a grassy mixture, whispering in his ear. She finally brought him back over to me. "Take care of him, and I will await our next visit."

The old woman cut Sienna's umbilical cord and

wiped her off carefully, but not as meticulously as she had Solomon. The villagers loaded me into an older model sport utility vehicle. As I turned around to thank the midwife and question her about the things she uttered to my son, she had disappeared. She simply vanished into thin air!

I held both of my babies in my arms, while resting in the back seat.

My mind was reeling. I kept thinking about the prophetess, Sister Olgatu, at my church. I tried to ignore the tiny fragments of glass that were embedded inside my arms. The whole supernatural thing, the pain, the loss, the suffering. Things didn't add up.

I looked down at my beautiful babies and thanked God they were fine. The English woman had cut the blanket in half, and Solomon and Sienna were wrapped in their grandmother's blanket.

Sienna was very small and had beautiful, pecan-toned skin. I'd never heard of a newborn smiling, but she did. She had big, dark eyes like my dad, but when she smiled, she looked just like Davis. She had that same goofy grin that he'd given me when he picked me up at the airport our first time together.

Davis, you son of a bitch! You should have been here. I hate you for this!

Solomon started to cry. I kissed him. Solomon Edwinn Hickman was the larger of the two. He appeared to be all of eight pounds, with very white skin and green eyes. I was laughing to myself, trying to figure out how Davis and I, as dark as we both were, could produce a white baby with green eyes. But my mom was a yellow, green-eyed heifer. That's one thing about being from the islands—we had all colors in my family.

I looked behind his ears and at his fingers to see if

there was any brown coloring. Grandma always said, "You can tell if they're going to get darker or not." Not a drop of brown anywhere. So much for me having two pretty little chocolate babies. I was going to have one yellow baby and one brown one.

Solomon looked like both Dad and Davis. He had my father's curly hair, and a deep dimple on the left side of his cheek, like Davis. That was the only thing the he and his twin sister had alike, their father's dimple. I tried to wipe off the concoction the mambo had put on my son.

I kissed them and prayed as Sister Olgatu had instructed. "Lord, I dedicate my children's lives to you." Just as I completed the prayer, I felt something like nerves or gas moving inside of my stomach.

What was the witch doctor doing with that oil, and how did she know Solomon's name? What was she talking about, until we meet the next time?

When I got to the hospital, I gave the nun at the desk my grandparents' information. I kissed my babies and saw them off to the nursery. The English couple promised to come by the next day to check on me.

The pain started to kick in. Maybe the adrenaline flow with all of the excitement had blocked it out earlier. It came back full force, and the shards of glass implanted in my scalp were sending waves of unbearable pain up and down my spine. I'd pushed out two babies without an epidural, and every bone from my head to my toes was aching. I would have thought the hospital would have cleaned me up like they did Sienna and Solomon. I didn't question it, even though I was bloody from the placenta and delivery, and I had glass everywhere.

I welcomed the needle when the man in the

priest attire came toward me. They cleaned me up
eventually.

I felt like I slept for days. When I woke up, the
blinds had been opened and I saw daylight. I looked
around to observe my surroundings. The glass
seemed to be gone. I'd been washed, and my hair
smelled of lye soap. I had on a clean hospital gown as
well. The sun was bright, and I could see a group of
nuns congregated by a statue of the Virgin Mary
praying.

I felt so weak. It took me a few minutes to remember everything that had happened. How long had I
been asleep?

I forced myself to stay awake and look around the
room. On the table by the bed, I saw a bouquet of
daffodils. I sat up in bed and stretched my arms to
reach for the note, but there wasn't one. Instead, there
was a manila envelope. Hopefully, somehow Davis
found out what happened and he was in Haiti. My
family was probably all congregated out in the hallway waiting on me to wake up. They were just allowing me time to rest. My mom and my aunts would
surely be in the nursery doting over Solomon and
Sienna.

I opened up the envelope to find photos of Davis
and Terri making love. I looked closely at the photo.
I couldn't tell where the picture was taken. It wasn't
Davis' bedroom, but it didn't look like a hotel either.
Could it have been Terri's dorm room? In the picture, she seemed to be enjoying herself, but Davis
had a strange look on his face, almost like he was
scared or something. Then my eyes wandered to the
date on the bottom of the picture. It was taken only a
few days earlier. Now I didn't care where the fuck it
had been taken. And now I knew why he hadn't been

there for the birth of our children. Davis was a lying, diabolical, nasty bastard. I had been such a fool all along.

As I cried and looked at the pictures, Michelle and Toussaint rolled the twins in to my room.

"How are you, sweetie?" Michelle sat down at the edge of the bed and handed Sienna to me.

I could barely find my voice as I looked down at my beautiful daughter.

Where did the photos come from?

"Don't worry, even after your accident, you have two healthy babies, little sister." Toussaint sat down next to me.

I looked down at the photos of Davis and Terri, then at my two beautiful babies. This nigga was fucking another bitch while I was giving birth.

"Are you ready for the rest of the family to come in now?" Michelle asked.

I shook my head.

"Well, we'll leave you alone with your babies now. Do you need anything else?" Michelle had tears in her eyes, when she saw the pain that I was in.

I smiled at my babies, but I was heartbroken. I handed Sienna to Michelle to be put back in her carrier.

I had honestly tried to not make the same mistakes with Davis that I'd made with Marcus. I had tried to be kind and understanding, even after Davis continually fucked up. I thought I was doing the right thing by being more docile, since Marcus had accused me of being too strong. Apparently, the docile Rhea didn't work either. It was time for me to be me, for better or worse.

I took one last glance at the photo of Davis and Terri, then over at my beautiful babies lying there innocently. They didn't deserve this, and I was not going to let Davis ever hurt them the way he had hurt me.

I took a deep breath. "Yes, one more thing," I said between tears. "Please do what you need to do with Davis Edwinn Hickman."

You Wrong for That is Toschia's debut novel, and she is currently working on her next book, *See, What Had Happened Was* . . . Please check Toschia out online at *www.toschia.com*